ONE DEATH TOO FEW

ONE DEATH TOO FEW

VALENTINA WINTERS™ BOOK THREE

MICHAEL ANDERLE

L M B P N

DISRUPTIVE IMAGINATION

Copyright © 2021 by LMBPN Publishing
Cover Art by Jake @ J Caleb Design
http://jcalebdesign.com / jcalebdesign@gmail.com
Cover copyright © LMBPN Publishing
A Michael Anderle Production

LMBPN Publishing
PMB 196, 2540 South Maryland Pkwy
Las Vegas, NV 89109

Version 1.00, June 2021
ebook ISBN: 978-1-64971-853-2
Print ISBN: 978-1-64971-854-9

THE TEAM

Thanks to the Beta Team
Kelly O'Donnell, Rachel Beckford

Thanks to the JIT Readers
Dave Hicks
Zacc Pelter
Diane L. Smith
Deb Mader
Peter Manis
Wendy L Bonell
Dorothy Lloyd
Veronica Stephan-Miller
Jeff Goode
Debi Sateren

If I've missed anyone, please let me know!

Editor
The Skyhunter Editing Team

DEDICATION

.

To Family, Friends and
Those Who Love
to Read.
May We All Enjoy Grace
to Live the Life We Are
Called.

— Michael

PROLOGUE

Before

Rain lashed against the tiled rooftops, bouncing in angry sprays and catching the soft white of the moonlight as it poked its eye through the thick veil of clouds. The air was thick and charged with electricity. The sky gurgled and growled.

The courtyard was square, as large as a football field. Pagoda towers rose in tiers, trapping the young girl in its clutches. Silhouettes of enemies surrounded her, silent as the grave, some with arms limp by their sides, others with arms raised in defensive stances.

All eyes on Valentina.

While the enemies were silent, Valentina was not. Her fists and shins and feet pummeled their bodies, feeling the satisfying cave of the cushion around their stomachs, watching their heads roll off their necks, their arms twisting to their sides, their knees buckling as they folded to the ground.

She tightened her grip on her bōjutsu—an item she had come to label her "bō"—before swinging it around her body and attacking those closest to her. One, then two, then three broke and fell to the floor, as silent in death as they were in life.

Rain slicked from her head, her hair now saturated with moisture. Salt sweat combined with the drops and stung her eyes, but she merely blinked it away, savoring the pain, using the anger it brought to spur her on. No obstacle would block her. Nothing would come close to defeating Valentina, no matter the weather or the location, or her emotional state. This was what she had come for, to destroy and to conquer.

To become invincible.

A rock stood to her left. Despite its slick surface, she pressed measured feet delicately against the side, springing off and into the air. The bō rose above her. She brought it down in a heavy swing, one fell swoop smashing the enemy's head open and revealing the brittle stuffing beneath.

She rolled on the landing, balancing the bō in her hands before rising and swinging a fast figure eight. Two more went down with that swing, another nearby. When she was a child, she had drawn along the dot-to-dot books her parents had given her. Now this felt the same, strategically plotting her path to victory, reducing the number of the enemy until none remained and she emerged the victor.

Who would dare take me on, now?

Thunder crashed. Lighting tore the sky open. In the strobing flash of light, Valentina worked her peripheral vision, counting the remaining twenty. The terrain was uneven, and the grass slick beneath her. Only once did she slip. Even then the enemy's swing missed, its body spinning a three-sixty-degree turn as she ducked under its blow and kicked it in the stomach.

Valentina's breath caught in her throat. Her chest heaved with exertion. On a summer's day, this onslaught would be a breeze to neutralize, but the elements were against her. Even though she was incredibly tired, a grin found her lips all the same.

A downpour on a stormy night. Kit on the doorstep. It's times like these that test your mettle, push your boundaries, show you your weak spots...

The enemy ran at her, appearing from out of nowhere as she crashed into it. While nearly all of them wore shades of brown and faded yellow, in the moment of memory, she had forgotten about the black ones. She groaned and used her momentum to twist behind the figure and lock its arms. She dug her heels into its groin, twisted the body, and helped it to the ground.

The figure was silent.

With a deep breath in and a quick swipe across her stinging eyes, she continued. A dozen more fell. Soon only a handful remained, standing in formation around the three-tier fountain and the golden koi swimming in the lower basin.

The nearest one held their gun, trained too far left of Valentina. She sprinted, then ducked into a skid, shooting between the enemy's legs. She dropped her bō, then grabbed its thighs and used the muscles to propel her up. She chopped into the elbow. The gun clattered to the ground.

Placing a foot behind the enemy's legs, she threw it off-balance before hurling it at the next nearest. The two collided. Both went down. She picked up the bō, swinging around before releasing the weapon and sending it spinning into the next enemy. The stick caught the figure in the neck although it didn't fall. She dove to her hands, then sprang back onto her feet. When she was upright once more, she struck with a twin-jab, followed by an uppercut to the gut. The figure lifted off the ground and flew back.

Valentina's throat was dry despite the rain. She blinked, vision growing fuzzy on the final two, which she despatched without another thought. The last one found its bed among the koi.

She stood for a moment, head downcast and sucking in breaths as though there were none left in the world. Rain streamed off her, and her hair clung to her sodden skin.

"I appreciate the effort, but the koi have no quarrel with you."

Valentina spun, her hair whipping her face. The rain was painful, needles against her exposed skin. A man stood a short distance away with his fingers laced behind his back. He wore a black *gi*, tied about the waist with a black belt. He was slender, the same height as Valentina, though the lines of his face told of many more stories than she had to tell.

He cast a look about him at the dozens of training dummies lying in pieces on the ground. "You seem to have some anger to vent."

Valentina gritted her teeth as the cold seeped into her bones. Her eyes narrowed, and her chest heaved.

"Or perhaps some measure to prove?" He asked the question but already knew the answer. There was no need for her to say a word. "It's one thing to attack those who cannot fight back, but it is another to attack a soldier who trained for such a purpose. One man with honor in his veins will survive an army of a thousand hay-stuffed corpses."

"I was embracing the elements, sensei," Valentina replied. "I did not seek to fight the living."

The man cocked his head a little to the left. "Then perhaps that is your problem. For what will happen when the two join hand in hand?"

She didn't need to guess his intention. He made it clear by revealing the bō behind his back. He brought it in front and leaned on it with both hands like a man with a cane, but Valentina knew better than to let her guard down.

Valentina swiped the rain from her eyes, her fists doing nothing to staunch the flow of water. She grimaced as she drew on her focus, knowing that this wouldn't be easy.

They stood apart, still for a moment that stretched endlessly as the night roared around them. While Valentina's eyes began to twitch, the older man showed no sign that the weather affected him. When it became clear that her sensei wasn't going to make the first move, Valentina rushed at him.

He remained motionless, a statue caught in the beating downpour. For all he cared, Valentina could have been a fly. She brought her bō up to strike, and as she swung it down at the man's neck, he reacted so suddenly that it would have shocked any other man or woman.

Valentina had seen this before.

Using his bō, he parried Valentina's and jarred her movement. She jerked right, and he twisted to her left. She spun, intending to catch him, but he was too fast. By the time she found him again, he was standing where she had been moments before, the soaking rag of the practice doll lying at his feet.

Valentina smirked. "The fish can't thank you."

"They don't need to. I do not need thanks to understand my place in this world, Englishwoman."

Valentina's smile slipped, and she frowned. The air stank of electricity and the damp dew that filtered through the moss. "Enough chatter."

"You started it." The man once again held his bō like a cane.

This time, Valentina kicked a dummy that lay by her feet. The arm was loose, and her kick brought it in front of her. She caught the weighty package and flung it toward her sensei.

He swept the missile aside with a sweep of his forearm, and as it cleared his vision, Valentina appeared before him.

"Boo," she announced, managing to catch him in the side with her bō.

He grunted as his eyes darkened. He blocked the second attack, then grabbed Valentina's bō. She held it with both hands while he held it in one, but still, his grip was strong. He jumped back onto the lip of the stone basin, gaining height on her, and kicked at her face. Valentina leaned back, avoiding it, but it soon became clear what his motive was as he used her backbend to flip over the top of her, never letting go of his staff or hers.

Valentina jerked, twisting with the bō until she faced him. As he landed, a punch sprang out and caught her on the cheek. A second caught her shoulder, jarring a nerve somewhere near the bone.

Her grip on the staff slackened.

A third punch caught Valentina in the throat.

Valentina stumbled backward, hands clutching her neck as she struggled to catch her breath. The man was quick—of course, he was, it had been he who trained her, after all—but there had to be a way she could bring him to his knees. She glanced down at the cardboard cut-out of the gun and wished it was real.

The man followed her gaze. "Thinking of quitting?"

"Never," Valentina growled.

"Only the weak bring a gun to a knife fight." He advanced on her, closing the distance with surprising speed. Valentina had seen men his age who struggled to push themselves out of a La-Z-Boy, but her sensei had all the mobility of a man with a quarter of his years.

"This isn't a knife fight." Valentina blocked a blow from one of the bōs. Another strike caught her in the leg and forced her down onto one knee.

He snorted in derision. "Not much of a fight, either."

Valentina cast her gaze down at the wet ground. His shadow loomed over her as another bolt of lightning struck and lit up the training area. She could smell the grass, could taste the water-logged earth. There was a scuff where she had jumped, the grass torn to reveal the mud beneath, the path of the track leading straight to her master...

To her *superior.*

"Alas," the old man uttered, soft and gentle to her ears. "I had rather hoped that you'd use some of that fervor you showed the static dolls on me. Seems you've got a long way to go. Now, remain still, Valentina. If you move, I may miss, and you wouldn't want that now, would you."

She glanced up at him, towering above her. The whites of his eyes were all she could see among that mask of contempt. "You're going to do this?"

"How else do we learn?" There was no compassion in his tone.

"The world is harsh. You must see things through. You began this tonight. I will end it."

Flashes of beatings ran before her eyes, moments of her training where sensei had demonstrated his commitment to the craft. The bruises had healed, but the welts took longer. Scars and bone chips and torn muscles as she progressed up the ladder and honed her skills. The other recruits were leagues behind, but Valentina still couldn't finish the one contest she knew she must master before she left into the wider world: the gatekeeper of it all.

Then, as the bō whistled down toward her, and Valentina braced against the blow that would undoubtedly strike the back of her skull and send her from this world for another three days at least, it came to her...

Your surrender is your weakness. Your disbelief in yourself is your obstacle. Perhaps it comes from where you were born, not where you say you were born?

Had she ever truly believed she could beat him? Hadn't she submitted the moment he showed his face in the square?

"Greatness accepts no competition. Limits are the bars of your prison." He'd uttered those words to her. They'd broken like waves against the shore, unabsorbed. Yet they came to her now in an angry cascade of irony. The whistle reached a fever pitch as the sky called to her, and she knew what she had to do.

Valentina twisted to the side, her whole body spiraling, gaze meeting the bō as it cracked down on the side of her cheek. Her cheekbone exploded with heat, but her movement caused the staff to slide past the rest of her body as it struck the ground.

Using her hand to push off the ground, she rose before her mentor and struck out with her leg. The flat of her bare foot pressed into his ribcage and drove him back, the older man still recovering from missing his mark.

A laugh escaped his lips. The bō stuck in the ground. Valentina's rested in the chasm between them. They glanced down, and both ran for it. The man grabbed the stick first, but Valentina snatched a grip on the end before it left her reach.

They wrestled, spinning around, connected by the bō staff. Valentina jabbed the stick forward, catching her sensei in the throat with the blunt end. He coughed, then laughed again, delight in his eyes. "At last, you find the dragon within you."

Before Valentina could praise herself, he jabbed the stick back. The end missed by millimeters, but it distracted her enough for him to close the gap. He threw a jab. She blocked it. He followed with three strikes which she also blocked, not following his limbs but watching his eyes. The deep green of those orbs monitored her every move, attentive and keen. Valentina blocked blow after blow, after blow, using the bō staff to catch his fingers.

The man grunted in pain and shook his hand. "See how you free yourself…"

Valentina didn't want to give him the knowledge of being right. Instead, she raised the bō staff behind her, appearing as if she was going for another strike. He seized his moment, punching her in the stomach, but Valentina knew what she was doing.

She javelin-tossed the bō away from them both. When a kick came for her kneecap, she strafed right. Her return kick twisted his leg away, catching him behind the knee.

He folded onto one knee, and his laughter grew. "A challenge. Yes, Valentina. Finally, I see what you can do."

Valentina kicked the back of his head. The man flopped onto his front in the mud. The sky darkened as clouds covered the moon. It was impossible to tell if it was blood or muck caking the back of his bald head, but she thought she knew which it was.

The man chuckled, though the sound was wet and pained. Valentina froze, looking down at the man in pity—a far cry from how she had come to see him.

He pushed himself to his knees, the effort lasting a lifetime.

When he was upright, he wobbled slightly, the rain pelting him relentlessly as the smile creased his face.

"You have come a long way, young apprentice," he managed, his voice barely there. "A long way indeed…"

Valentina knelt in front of him. Her eyes were blazing now, red, raw, and irritated. The crack on her cheek scalded, and she wondered if he'd fractured the bone with the staff. She panted, placing her hands on her knees as if about to offer a bow.

"I've learned from the best," Valentina replied stoically. "Never would I have wished for another mentor. You have crafted the woman I wished to be."

The man shook his head, eyes dark with pain. "No. I haven't." He glanced up at her. She wasn't sure if his eyes were tearing or if it was an effect of the rain. "If I had taught you correctly…"

Valentina reached out behind her, hand blindly finding the end of the bō staff he'd knocked out of her hands. Without hesitation, she brought it over her head and cracked it down on the older man's skull. The hollow sound of a wooden egg beaten against a wall resonated. The man let out a pained grunt before flopping forward, his forehead hitting the mud with a dull *thud*.

"You *have* taught me correctly." No pity remained in Valentina's eyes anymore. "You taught me to follow through on the kill, no matter who the target or what the cost."

She sat there in the rain with him for what felt like hours. Thunder rumbled, the clouds roiled, and lightning *cracked* in a steady rhythm of flashes. Eventually, she bowed, hands finding the slick mud. She shifted forward until she loomed over him, then planted a soft kiss on the back of his skull, tasting the coppery tang of blood on her lips.

She pressed her cheek to his. His back gently rose and fell as his labored breath dragged cloying air into his lungs.

"Let's get you to Akari," she mumbled and scooped the older man in her arms. She dragged him to his feet, his body frail and light now that his ego wasn't nearby to support him. She picked him up, then threw him over her shoulder.

As she headed toward the medicine room, Valentina wiped her tired eyes with the cloth of his *gi*. It wasn't dry by any measure, but it wasn't as wet as hers, which counted for something.

Neither one of them paid attention to the dark figure watching from the safety of the shadows on the balcony.

CHAPTER ONE

Present day

Atlantica was dark, a faint rumble of thunder in the distance.

Car headlights lit the streets, a feverish excitement in the air as Atlanticans made their way home from their day jobs, ready to dress to the nines and find their way inside the local bars and clubs. It was a Friday, which meant the same here for half of Atlantica as it did with the rest of the world: spend your hard-earned coin on booze, drugs, and sex, sleep off the hangover, then return to work Monday morning with the stale scent of beer on your breath and pockets that were considerably lighter.

The rest of the Atlanticans—the bar owners, the investors, the manufacturers—raked in dollars from the self-serving ecosystem.

Isabella walked along the sidewalk, an ant among the giant buildings beside her. She'd pulled her hair back into a lazy pony-tail with small tendrils escaping the band and had a sour expression on her face. She had to work today, but that was the last thing she wanted to do since Valentina had informed her that there was no sign of Bradley after her raid on Harper's building the night previous.

The day had passed in a miserable cloud of dismay. She could hardly remember what the work entailed, only that Naomi had been less than pleased with her performance. She was on her last chance, and a battle raged inside her, debating whether she should quit the damned place before her manager fired her. Things were fine before the heat from Sauron's gaze found its way onto her, but now her safe, boring day job had become a chore.

She stopped once on the way home for a bottle of wine. Ordinarily, she didn't drink, but she felt like tonight would change that. When she arrived at her apartment, she paused with her key in the door. Crime scene tape still cordoned off Bradley's apartment, but only one officer was on duty tonight. He offered her a brief wave, then she entered her apartment, silent and clutching her wine.

She kicked off her heels and sat on the couch, foregoing the glass and drinking straight from the bottle. The sour mash of grapes burned her throat, but she relished the sensation. She closed her eyes, listening to the soft music playing on the radio. It seemed impossible that her world today could be so far from what it was yesterday. She wondered when it would all end. When the nightmare would be over, and she would have her brother back.

Valentina had waited for her in the early hours of dawn. It was an occasion that only happened once in a blue moon, but it was there. As Isabella roused from sleep, she found herself at odds with the other in her body.

Valentina's voice was heavy, laden with a burden. "You might want to sit for this."

"I'm lying down," Isabella replied. "*We're* lying down. We're in bed."

"Smartass," Valentina retorted before drawing a deep breath.

She told Isabella the bare basics—how Bradley was missing

from the building and that Deng had shown up to deliver the news that Archie was now missing, too.

"Archie?" Isabella searched her mind. "The man who's looking after Kit? What do you mean he's gone?"

"That he's no longer there," Valentina replied. "There's too much to go into right now, but he might not be playing on the right side of Valentina Winters anymore. He's earned his enemies."

Isabella pushed herself upright, wincing as a splash of light leaked through her curtains and pained her eyes. "What do you mean the right side of Valentina Winters? Val, he's got my *brother*. He's got Kit. You need to play nice to ensure that he gets better. You fucking promised he'd get better—"

"I know!" Valentina snapped, her voice coming from Isabella's mouth instead of her head. Her arm jerked forward as if trying to punch an imaginary manifestation of herself. "It's not my fault, okay. I'm working on it. *We're* working on it."

"Who's we?" Isabella replied? "I can't do anything with you. We're not compatible, remember? You tag in. I tag out. That's how this works." Her voice lowered to a mere mumble. "Not that it ever worked for me."

"You know I can hear you when you mumble," Valentina commented. "I'm in your head."

"Yeah, well…I wish you weren't." Isabella folded her arms and glowered.

Valentina sighed internally now. She spoke in a soothing tone. "Me too. But, you know what? We're stuck like this until one of us can learn to control the other, so here's what you need to know." She told Isabella about Deng's discovery, how Deng knew Valentina's true identity, and how Archie had wronged her by stealing the AI and disappearing underground.

Isabella's breath caught. She had no idea how to process all of this. Her world, the world she and Valentina had knit together, had been compromised, and now all that they were, all that *she* was, risked public exposure.

Plus, her brother was gone.

Isabella's brow wrinkled. She gritted her teeth to stop herself from screaming in frustration. "You've fucked it, Val. You've fucked it all up. How the hell are we supposed to make it through this? I'd suggest leaving the goddamn country, but that's not going to happen until my baby brother is back in our sight…" Hot tears flooded her eyes. "We have to get him back, Val."

Valentina soothed her, whispered reassurance in her ears, but Isabella wasn't listening. She could only make out the odd snatches of phrase as her mind tried to comprehend the truth. Kit was gone. Archie was gone. A tech tycoon with the ability to monitor them and to hack into their systems had the most sacred information she treasured: her identity.

"We can get through this," Valentina insisted, her voice fading as sunlight blazed and Isabella wrestled control of their consciousness. "Leave it to me. I'll make everything right. I'll make everything better. Give me a couple of days, and Kit will be back in our possession."

But our privacy won't.

"I heard that," Valentina replied, falling quiet shortly after.

Now the wine slipped down her throat like a crimson fish. She knew that soon she would black out and it would be up to Valentina to take the reins again, but for now, Isabella was in control, and wine was good.

Marvin Gaye came on the radio, sweet notes crooning and filling the room. "Let's get it on," he exclaimed to a chorus of soft, sensual music. Isabella smirked, her eyes glazed and out of focus. When was the last time she'd "gotten it on?" When was the last time she'd been in control enough of her body that she'd allowed herself to enjoy a man's company?

Her mind flashed to the man she had met on the beach. Myles, that was his name. His body rippled with muscle and caught the sun, gleaming from some form of sunscreen. She thought of Bradley, how soft his lips were despite his rugged appearance and the way her body had tingled from his touch.

She closed her eyes, breath coming in deeper waves. She knew she should head to the closet. She knew that she should trigger the process and get into character. Soon the room slipped away, and Isabella fell into slumber.

Rousing herself from Isabella's body was like surfacing through a pool full of molasses. Valentina's head rolled on her neck, her eyelids heavy and thick. The room was dark, filled only with the gentle music of some jazz station that Valentina didn't care to remember.

"Okay, so that's how you want to play it," she muttered after spotting the nearly empty wine bottle on the table. The words came out, "Orky, sur thatzhahya wannplayheet."

She pushed off the chair, each movement a Herculean effort. She wobbled unsteadily on her feet, toppled forward, and had to grab the nearest wall to balance herself. She frowned as her arms shook and discovered she couldn't tell whether it was the effect of the alcohol or the subsidence of Myers Briggan's serum.

"Fuck. Fuck. Fuck. What have you done, Izzy?" she complained as she grabbed the wall and worked her way toward the closet.

The room spun. Valentina felt as if she were navigating the apartment underwater. She found comfort in holding onto the closet handle. She scanned her way inside, struggling to align her fingerprints and retinas with the scanner, unable to stop swaying long enough for them to register until finally, she could.

The closet slid open. Valentina closed the doors behind her, more loudly than she hoped she would.

"Dammit," she protested as the white of the room burned her

eyes. She raised an arm to shield herself, but it did little. She needed to fix this. This was a real problem.

Her legs were shaking now. Her thighs spasmed as though she had run a marathon and they were punishing her for it. She glanced over at the seemingly smooth wall, knowing what she must do. She still believed it too early to top up, but if there was one sure-fire way to get rid of the effects of alcohol and tiredness and to stop her muscles from twitching as though she were hooked up to electric nodes, then…

Needs must.

The needles were painful. The serum was freezing as it coursed around her body, but although it caused her to gasp at its sudden chill, the effects were immediate. A strange sensation that had grown in her throat and almost caused her to vomit faded. Her vision cleared in a moment. By the time she stepped back out and into the room, it was over. It had countered the alcohol, and Valentina could finally breathe—could finally *think*.

She glanced at herself in the mirror, at the unremarkable girl that was Isabella Carter. She stepped closer until she was only a foot or so away. Ordinarily, Izzy would have done the hard work of painting her face and transforming herself into Valentina, but it seemed that wasn't in the cards tonight.

Valentina cocked her head. The mousy-haired woman in front of her copied the move. *Unremarkable but remarkable all the same.*

She studied herself for a long moment as Beethoven played his *Moonlight Sonata* from the hidden speakers. She hadn't had a chance to see Isabella—really *see*—in years. It was a strange sensation to see the woman who was you but wasn't you at the same time. To be able to see what you could have been if you weren't who you'd become.

She raised a hand to the mirror. Isabella copied. Their palms touched, separated only by the millimeters of cool, silvered glass. Her breath fogged up the image, and Isabella's face faded.

Valentina lowered her eyes.

"We're the same, you and I. But not the same..." she commented, barely a whisper.

A moment later, she was climbing into her fatigues.

She had a dragon to find.

CHAPTER TWO

Valentina hesitated a short distance from the compound.

Night had taken root above her, yet the building was visible from miles away. The last time she had looked upon the pagoda roofs and viewed the single-track road that led to the Tynamo compound, she had been running reconnaissance with a view to infiltrate and recover the AI for her employer.

This time was very different.

She strode through the darkened fields, remembering the barking dogs and the prickle of her skin as she had escaped the compound. The driverless taxi had deliberately dropped her off a safe distance from the place, but even now, as the building drew closer, she wondered whether she was doing the right thing.

It could be a trap.

What was there to lose? Deng already had her identity. Archie already had Kit *and* Bradley. What could be worse for her?

The guards halted her at the gate. Valentina informed them that she had been personally invited by Deng Zenim herself. The guards glanced at each other with skepticism, then patched through to the big boss. Their faces fell serious at the reply, and soon Valentina was ushered inside.

Security led her through the labyrinth of hallways and levels of the compound, accompanied by a sight she had come to expect whenever in the presence of the great Deng Zenim: the Cyclops strip.

The black line traced around the walls wherever she went, a constant eye monitoring and tracking their progress as a muscled woman led her onward. She walked down halls she'd never trodden before and through rooms that all seemed a lot more above board than she had viewed on her last visit. Her stomach gurgled at the injustice of it, her knowledge that there were people below deck being experimented on, but that wasn't why she'd come. Today she had a vendetta to overcome.

Besides, if Valentina were to clean up every injustice in Atlantica, she'd be exhausted. Sometimes you had to learn to turn a blind eye. That didn't mean to forget...Valentina added the injustices to her mental memory bank, knowing that if the turn served her, she'd know exactly how to tear the fuckers down.

She passed through a series of aviaries and gardens filled with tropical plants, flowers, and birds. She even spotted a sugar glider soaring overhead, eventually gripping the trunk of a thick and ancient tree that looked like it belonged in a fantasy film.

Soon they reached the central pagoda—the only place that Valentina recognized. They passed the storage cupboard where she and Dick had once hidden as they infiltrated Deng's private quarters and stole the AI. Her stomach flipped as she thought of her last interaction with Dick Chambers. She had left him her number, yet again another sign of her vulnerability, but he hadn't called. That shouldn't upset her.

But it did.

She climbed the stairs, this time turning right instead of left, finding yet more stairs that snaked around in a large loop to the top of the tower. Painted murals covered the walls in Eastern calligraphy, golden dragons shining down upon her, cherry blossoms, fires, and fury.

"Haven't got anything by Van Gogh?" Valentina asked. "Sunflowers? Lilies?"

The guard ignored her and continued treading upward.

"I'm just saying," Valentina continued, undeterred, "anyone would think your boss set herself on a path of destruction. Look at this." She stopped by a tapestry showcasing an image painted in reds and golds, a giant dragon snaking around the top of a large tower, fire pouring from its mouth as the shadows of villages watched from beneath. Valentina raised an eyebrow. "Hold on, a Japanese artist didn't create this, did they?" She turned back. "These are Chinese-inspired."

The guard lost her patience and whirled. She spoke softly through gritted teeth. "We do not question our Madame's decorative fancies, nor her choices. Madame Zenim is a woman of the world, and as such her inspirations are taken from many sources. She appreciates all walks of Eastern culture and frowns upon the cheap, processed bullshit from the West. Americans and Europeans have pissed on their forebears and formed a culture around plastic, convenience, and artificiality. Madame Zenim preserves honor, loyalty, family, and all who follow such cultures."

Valentina gave a thoughtful nod. "Still, seems a bit egregious, doesn't it?"

The woman glared, her mouth silently opening and closing. Valentina wasn't sure if it was questioning her boss' artistic tastes or the fact that she'd used a word that sailed over the other's head, but a moment later she snapped, "Enough dawdling. The Madame awaits."

The climb up the stairs seemed endless, with more and more violent artistry decorating the walls. Eventually, they arrived at the top. An open landing with a floor of clean white marble unfolded before them. Four guards holding ancient pikes stood sentinel at the door.

They bristled upon the pair's approach.

The guard leading Valentina stopped before the vanguard and lowered to both knees. She pressed her palms to the floor and bent low. "I bring a guest for Madame Zenim. By her orders."

One of the guards approached. The others remained as still as statues. He stopped with the base of the pike next to the woman's head. "Rise."

"Not one for small talk, eh?" Valentina muttered. The guard flashed her a look.

The woman arose and handed the guard a piece of paper. The guard examined it, then glanced again at Valentina. She wondered if there was a knowing in his eye. She contemplated whether he remembered her the same way that she recalled him, one of the many faces that had flashed her way as the chaos broke out in the server room. Valentina rarely forgot a face. Maybe he didn't either.

The guard grunted, then nodded. He stepped back into formation, then called an order in a language that Valentina assumed was Japanese. The guards simultaneously stepped to the side, allowing access to the golden door behind.

Valentina swallowed, then followed the woman to the door.

Light flooded her from the room's bright and ornate interior. A multitude of aromatic candles and a gentle breeze met her as she stepped to the entrance. There was a bed pushed against the far wall, at least double the size of a king. Cushions and lounge chairs littered the space. A small pond formed a centerpiece, teeming with fish that occasionally broke the water's surface in excitement before rejoining their brethren.

The guard waited at the door for Valentina to pass inside. She announced her name, then disappeared. The doors closed.

Valentina was left alone. There was no sign of Deng.

She stood for a moment, waiting for Deng to make herself known. When it became clear that wasn't going to happen, she walked around the space and breathed in the decor—the glam, the art, and the insane display of wealth. The bed had golden dragon heads carved into it. A small kitchenette lit up in colors of crimson and gold.

Get rid of the gold, and I'm here for it.

She scanned the apartment, her attention drawn to the heavy red curtains at the far side of the room, leading out through folding doors onto a balcony that Valentina hadn't noticed before. She scanned her memories but couldn't remember seeing the balcony during her previous reconnaissance.

Nothing is ever as it seems.

She strode to the balcony, feeling the cool touch of the wind on her face. Her muscles were corded, boosted by Briggan's serum, and she felt powerful stepping out into the open. From here, the view was incredible. She could see the surrounding fields and farmhouses for miles around—until the fog claimed them, that was. A smattering of headlights dotted the country roads, straight lines into the city proper. It was no wonder Deng had claimed her place here. It was like looking out over a kingdom.

Every lord and lady in this place has worked hard to have their ego stroked. Why would Deng be any different?

The air changed around her. Valentina sensed the woman before she arrived. "I wondered where you were hiding."

Deng smiled as Valentina turned. Again, that unconvincing grin, powered only by the lips and not by the eyes. "I don't hide. I sneak."

"As if there's a difference."

Deng nodded. "You would know."

They stood for a moment in quiet, each woman sizing up the other. Valentina had a good few inches on Deng, but there was no way of telling what she'd be like in a scrap. *Not without experiencing it first.*

Valentina was the first to break the silence. "Shall we get to it?"

"Let's." Deng returned to the room. Valentina followed close.

"Unfortunately, there's not much to tell you in the way of progress. However, we've taken measures to ensure that we can find Archie once more and hold him to account. I know that he has your treasure as well as mine, so have you considered the proffered allegiance discussed last night?"

Valentina's instinct told her to say "no" and turn her back on Deng. Ordinarily, she would prefer going rogue in these situations, but what choice did she have now? "I suppose, when the argument is so compelling."

"You mean when I have your metaphorical balls in the palm of my hand?" Deng fell into the plush arms of a nearby couch.

Valentina's eyes narrowed. "How do I know you two haven't set this whole thing up to test me? How can I trust you? For all I know, you could have me on a string, working between you both to manipulate the truth and get exactly what you want."

Deng's eyebrows raised ever so slightly. "You're smart, Valentina."

"Thank you."

Deng continued. "Smart doesn't make you wise." She unfolded a hidden pocket from the arm of the couch, revealing a compartment filled with mist. She spoke a command that Valentina couldn't hear, and a tall glass of something bubbly and golden presented itself. She took a sip and gasped appreciatively. "Can I offer you one?"

Valentina shook her head, remembering the grogginess of Isabella's bingeing. "You said progress. What did you mean?"

Deng sipped, then placed the drink beside her. "We are in the process of unifying the AI with a tracking agent—something that can detect any frequencies or signals emitted by the intelligence that we can latch onto and use to home in on its location."

"Shouldn't that be easy?" Valentina asked. "Surely you had a tracker built in when you created the damn thing? Seems a certain oversight that you'd not put in a failsafe."

"We did." Deng's stoic grin appeared. It highlighted the harsh cuts of her cheeks and the ruby red of her lips. "The only oversight we have to confess is that we never imagined someone would take the technology into the bowels of the island. While we have made incredible advancements in the technological space over the years, we've yet to create a technology that can penetrate meters and meters of rock. How deep Archie built his tomb determines how small the traces might be. There may be nothing there at all."

"Then how the hell are you supposed to track him?"

Deng's cheeks hollowed as she sucked her tongue. "That is the question we're trying to address. We have some methods, but each one is as questionable as the last." She sipped her drink, eyes darkening with thought. "A man can only hide so long, Valentina. If Archie has taken all of his equipment with him, he'll need a source of power. Now, there can be many ways to address this: direct lines from the power stations, fueled by the Atlanticores. They could have some other means lost in the folds of the mountains to draw power underground. At least if he's using these, we can trace him."

"And if he's not?"

Deng met her gaze, an intensity sparking between them. "If he's not, Archie has somehow found his own Atlanticore that will allow him to sustain his self-sufficiency below ground."

Valentina nodded. "The chances of that are…"

"Next to none," Deng finished. "It has been years since anyone mined fresh Atlanticores. The existing mines are drained bare, used and utilized among the power grids to fuel the city, and stolen by some of the moguls to run their compounds." A slight slip in her façade told Valentina all she needed to know. Deng was one of them. "Our best bet is that Archie has provided a power source, which would expose a part of his operation to the elements."

"So you're scanning the island?"

"You catch on fast. I currently have teams and cameras

sweeping the island for any trace of power not currently registered on the grid. We've detected two dozen of these, but that doesn't mean they're all Archie. Many of them will be lone organizations trying to detach themselves from the government's ecosystem. I have operatives investigating and reporting to me daily."

"So, what can I do?" Valentina looked down at the tiny woman in the oversized, cozy chair. "How can I help?"

Deng's smirk returned. "There's that can-do attitude I've come to know about you. Still, there is nothing you can do for now. Until my team acquires intel that will benefit our cause, we're in limbo."

Valentina clenched her jaw. "You lured me into your nest to tell me that I'm useless in this fight?"

"For now." Grim satisfaction covered Deng's face.

Valentina hated the power she currently held and wondered if it would slow progress to cave in that pretty white face with a dose of lead and gunpowder.

"Don't be alarmed, little dove," Deng continued.

Little dove? Nicknames? Are you fucking kidding me?

"Your allegiance is noted and appreciated. It is comforting to know there's a powerful ally in this race."

Valentina's face curdled. "Ally is a strong word. Hostage might suit it better."

Deng chuckled. "You'd offer yourself as a hostage?"

Valentina reconsidered. "Probably not. A hostage couldn't kill her captor in the wink of an eye."

"Very well," Deng replied. "Just know that our partnership will be one to be envied, and I feel confident that we can conclude this matter swiftly if we remain on each other's side." She rose to her feet and offered a cold, thin hand. "Are we in agreement?"

Valentina hesitated, then gripped her hand. They shook. "We agree."

As Deng was about to withdraw, Valentina increased her grip

and drew her closer. Deng looked displeased, which gave Valentina a turn at satisfaction. "But if you fuck with me—if you take one step out of line and I catch you—there's nothing I won't do to burn this entire place to the ground, hold open your eyelids, and make you watch as your empire crumbles. Do you understand me?"

Deng remained silent. The answer showed in her eyes, but her pride stopped her from speaking. Valentina released her hand and swept from the room, feeling Deng's eyes burning a hole in the back of her head the entire way out.

CHAPTER THREE

Valentina sat on the rooftop of the Atlantica Opera House and looked down on the sights around her.

The building was a dome, set into the stone like the gods had hurled a shot-put, and the mortals turned its half-buried contents into a theater dedicated to music and the arts.

Climbing the building was a challenge, but it was one that Valentina was up for. She appreciated the effort since it kept her mind off things. The building's external layer was made entirely of metal, and Valentina found a use for the magnetic handholds she had developed some time ago. When she had first tried them, she laughed, finding it absurd how the inspiration came from a children's cartoon—a black and white illustrated cat using suction cups to scale to the upper floors of a terraced townhouse to catch a bright yellow canary. Still, most absurd ideas were grounded in some kind of truth, and the workout eased her active mind.

The top was a little less comfortable, but she didn't mind. Watching the people around her allowed her mind time to process and work on the problem. In her hand were three silver orbs that looked like ball bearings. These she juggled around each other with the flexing of her fingers, not the least bit concerned about their contents. One sharp movement would break their shells and fill the air with a potent toxin that would send her straight to sleep, but Valentina was nothing if not careful.

She could make out the Atlantican jungle in the distance from her vantage point, the edge of the forest as the trees thickened and rose on the hillside. In this part of town, spotlights lit the border. The nearby businesses used the forest's edge as an attraction to draw people to their beer gardens and outdoor eating areas. "The best views in Atlantica," many promised, and none delivered.

There's more beneath this island. Much, much more.

She glanced down and imagined Kit encased in glass, surrounded by precarious stalactites that could fall at any moment and pierce his heart. She thought of Bradley, terrified and confused, drawn into this fight for no reason, another innocent bystander in this game of chess.

Valentina pocketed the orbs and crossed her arms over her legs. Citizens strode confidently beneath her, unafraid and unaware of the larger games at play. Could she ever become one of them? Would she ever be able to set this life aside—

Sparks flew beside her. The heat of something fast tore past her knee. Screams rose from below.

Valentina reacted on instinct, rolling sideways barely in time to miss another glow of something hot as sparks flew in the place where she had been only a second ago.

She crouched with one hand touching the cool metal of the Opera House roof. She glanced around for the source of the disturbance as a bullet ricocheted between her legs, narrowly missing her flesh.

A muzzle flash flared from a nearby roof. Valentina dodged again, rolling back the way she had come. There was no cover up here, only more smooth metal that curved toward the ground. A glance showed a miniscule dark figure on the building across the road—one with a curved sandstone front and influenced by the Egyptians, it seemed. The whole place was built out of large stone blocks yet flattened at the peak.

Another strike. Valentina now recognized it as bullets meeting metal and creating the small burst of sparks. She shoved herself backward, moving swiftly down the descending curve of the large dome. At first, there was no pull from gravity. Then as the third bullet nicked the flesh of her forearm, she felt its powerful grasp drag her down.

She fell faster and faster, slipping as the curve edged toward the ground. The metal stroked her flesh, drew her top up, and threatened to burn her stomach. Soon she was near free-falling. The rooftop of the building across the way was out of sight but not out of mind. Valentina dug her hands into her pockets and found the handles of the magnetic grips. As she reached the outermost edge of the curve and started to slip off, she slapped them onto the metal.

The stop was sudden and jarring and strained every joint in her arms. She gasped as men and women ran around below her, alerted by the sudden gunfire. She hung there, still at least forty feet off the ground, legs dangling in the open as she caught her breath.

When she finally made her way to the ground, she dropped into a thick cluster of hedges and waited a moment for the foot traffic to clear. Already the AJS sirens blared their approach. She needed to find a way out of there before law enforcement bombarded her.

She eased along the edge of the Opera House and craned her neck until she could see the sandstone building where the figure had shot at her. Red and blue lights pulsed against the nearby buildings, and AJS cruisers rumbled nearby but out of sight.

Valentina slipped out of the bushes and broke toward the sandstone building. She ran until she hit the sidewalk, then slowed, her hands in her pockets as she half-jogged to match the pace of the civilians around her, trying her best to blend in.

She crossed the road, narrowly avoiding several cars trying to speed through the area, alerted by the AJS interference. A glance up at the roof revealed nothing of note from this level. She knew she'd have to get higher and fast.

Should always remember to bring my grappling gun.

She melted into the alley beside the building and broke into a sprint. Dumpsters made makeshift steps, giving her enough spring to leap up and grab a pipe secured to the side of the building. She scaled it fist over fist, never doubting herself as the pipe wobbled precariously in her grasp.

Something *pinged* off the wall above. Dust sprayed in her face as a screw fell loose. The pipe lurched away from the surface. Valentina kept her composure and glanced at a window ledge beside her. She swung, breaking free from the wall as the pipe fell away. Her fingers braced against the stone while her body dangled freely above the growing drop below.

They don't build anything to last these days. She pulled herself up and used the ledge as a step before jumping for the next. The pipe had only broken away in its center section, but she wasn't going to risk the rest of the shoddy work.

After leap-frogging up the windows, she spotted a balcony that snaked around the side of the building. With a hefty swing, she passed over the gap and grabbed the rail. She vaulted over it and glanced up once more.

She still couldn't see the top of the building. The angles were strange and experimental, and a large jut of rock overhung where she stood. She glanced around, now able to view over the lower rooftops.

Something caught her eye.

Three buildings away, a glint of metal winked between the break in the vent housings.

Fuck. Valentina threw herself to the floor. The bullet shattered the glass doors behind her, sprinkling sharp fragments all around. The metal railing had many openings for the projectiles to penetrate, so this was no place to hide.

The figure made no show of hiding this time. They stood, aiming the sniper rifle at her. Valentina pushed to her feet and sprinted, skirting the balcony until she reached the end railing. She vaulted, springing with two hands on the rail, soaring over a five-foot gap until she landed on the neighboring balcony. She tucked herself into a roll, absorbing the impact and keeping momentum as more glass shattered behind her.

Sniper rifles are great for static targets, but can they track a zigzag-ging rabbit?

Valentina paused, feet skidding across the slick floor. Shouts of disturbance came from the balcony behind as heads appeared, tentatively investigating the disruption. Valentina held her breath as the bullet passed a foot in front of her, embedding in the sandstone wall.

Think fast, Val. He's coming for you.

She drew her pistol and lined up the shot. It happened in a heartbeat. She pulled the trigger, and the bullet whistled through the air. It missed its mark by a clear mile, but she had never expected it to land. She was good, but she wasn't *that* good. The figure ducked out of sight, and in that brief pause, Valentina bought herself some time.

She held the railing's edge and looked down. She weighed the possibility of mortal death versus a badass survival attempt and opted for the latter. She had tried riskier, hadn't she? Plus, remaining there was adjacent to suicide.

She took a step back, making a show of raising her hands and preparing for the swan dive into the city below. A nest of electrical wires snaked between the buildings, and if she timed it right, they could save her. Oh, lord, let it save her.

She removed her jacket, discarding additional weight. On the count of one, she jumped, body flying down into the city below.

The sniper found her and tracked her with measured accuracy. Three bullets tore through her leather jacket, which sailed toward the ground.

Or so it seemed.

Something was wrong.

Valentina listened to the bullets as she raced into the dark building, away from the bait and switch. The jacket had fanned widely enough to mask her retreat into the room where the glass had shattered, and now she ran.

She sprinted through the room—an office of some kind, complete with potted ferns, charts, and motivational posters—then slammed her shoulder into the door. It didn't budge, but a persuasive kick at the handle broke it open.

That triggered an alarm. She tore through the hallway, hunting for the stairs. They weren't too far away, and she leaped them three at a time, skidding around corners until she was a couple of floors below.

Flashes of blue and red appeared through the windows, and Valentina knew the AJS would be having a field day tracking this bullshit. She shot the handle of another door and entered a break room. Couches and video game consoles blurred by as she found the far window. She fired at the glass, then finally executed her dive into the outside world.

She had located it perfectly. Her body sailed across the gap toward the top of the pole, which carried electrical cables through the city. She grabbed the small metal handhold, then sprang off to catch the brickwork of the building across from her. A short trip upward allowed her to stand atop the roof, her pistol drawn and ready to fire at the sniper.

They were gone.

Valentina cautiously eased ahead. She didn't lower her guard, and she used whatever she could to hide and cover her body while making her way to where the mysterious figure had shot at her.

When she arrived at the vent housings atop the building, the sniper was nowhere in sight. She crouched in the shadows and sniffed, checking for a lingering scent of perfume or aftershave, but the wind had stolen it. She looked across to the building where she had escaped from, imagining the sight from their eyes.

Someone was after her. They had made that clear tonight. The mistake they had made was trying to fuck with Valentina Winters.

She rose, and her foot crunched on something hard. She moved her foot. The metal winked at her, catching the stray fragments of moonlight. It was a brooch in the shape of a spread eagle's wing, painted white.

Valentina's face hardened. Her jaw clenched. She glanced out into the night, wondering what the hell *he* could be doing in Atlantica.

CHAPTER FOUR

Dick Chambers sat in his brand-new La-Z-Boy recliner and grimaced.

It wasn't as comfortable as he thought it would be. Although he'd heard rave reviews about the recliners and thought he'd splurge on something nice for himself, there was something wrong with the chair.

Or maybe it's not the chair.

He raised the mouth of the chilled bottle to his lips—Blue Moon beer, a favorite on the nights when bourbon wasn't necessary—and sipped.

"Maybe it's me," he announced.

Doug Nevill appeared from the kitchen with a bottle of Blue Moon in his hand. "It's always you, Dick. When are you going to learn that?"

"What do you mean?" Dick adjusted his ass to try and get comfy.

Doug chuckled. "You're the problem. The weird one. The outlier. You're the man who can't settle down. You think it's any wonder you're not comfortable in that chair?"

Dick gave him a dirty look.

Doug rolled his eyes. "Don't you get it? You can't even commit to a woman, let alone a chair." He stood over Dick and stroked the thick leather arms. "She's a keeper. The La-Z-Boy is an investment in comfort, in rooting yourself in one place, in staying there long enough to call it your home." He gave Dick a knowing look.

Dick shook his head. "This coming from the man who hasn't spent more than a couple of years in one place?"

Doug shrugged, then sat on the couch. "Different circumstances."

Dick tapped a button on the side of the chair and the legs extended, offering him a solid footrest. He gave a small grunt of alarm, then lowered the footrest again, careful not to spill his beer in surprise. "*You* told me to get this damn thing. 'Best money can buy,' you said."

"I did." Doug helped himself to a chip from the open bag on the table. The TV continued flashing its images of Bruce Willis trying to outsmart Alan Rickman. "Thought you could use a little comfort in your life. Might take something away from the bottomless pit of booze and nicotine you throw yourself into."

"I'm cutting down on cigarettes." Dick's gaze went to a half-empty carton on the table and an ashtray thick with soot.

Doug chuckled.

"I am!" Dick protested.

Doug smirked and turned to the TV. "Well, return it, then. If you want to sit with sticks of fire up your ass and call that comfortable, fine. I've started learning the meaning of 'creature comforts,' and I'm good with that." He sipped his beer. "Speaking of, when are you going to come over and see the new place?"

Dick tried once more to shift into a comfortable position. When that failed, he glowered at the chair, then rose and crossed to the couch beside Doug. "When time allows."

"We have time now," Doug informed him.

Dick raised an eyebrow. "It's 2:30 in the morning."

"I'm not tired."

Dick remained silent.

Doug laughed. "You haven't changed, have you, Dick?"

Dick fixed his gaze on the TV.

Doug continued. "Unless there's a chance at some lady parts, you just ain't interested."

"Tuesday," Dick announced. "Tuesday evening. Me and you. Beers and pizza. Can try out that new pool table you keep going on about."

Doug looked satisfied but doubtful.

"But…" Dick declared.

"There it is!" Doug laughed and threw his hands up, beer threatening to spill.

"What?" Dick replied.

Doug looked at him. "Always a catch, isn't there?"

"You know what my work is like," Dick replied. "If a case comes in…"

"You're on the clock," Doug finished. "I get it. No, seriously, I do." He rested his head on the back of the couch. "Once my business finally gets up and running, I'll be in that situation, too."

"How's that going?" Dick asked.

"Slow." Doug's humor left his face. "I don't quite have the rep that you do anymore. Not since… Well…"

Dick nodded, remembering how the pair had reunited over a person who soon became a mutual enemy. It must be tricky getting work once you'd betrayed one of your clients and turned over a new leaf in Atlantica. Word spread fast among the rats of the city. One black mark could scar your reputation for life.

"Hey," Dick encouraged, "if there's any way I can help…"

Dick stopped speaking as his hand slipped into his pocket, and his fingers brushed against the note he hadn't removed since he'd found it on his nightstand. He thought of red hair, porcelain skin, and the heady stink of perfume.

"…been trying for weeks." Doug's voice came into sharp focus.

"One or two jobs, sure. That's not enough to sustain me. Honestly, if Turnberry hadn't paid so well, I'd be struggling to get by. As it is, I've had to sink a bunch into investments and stocks, and—Dick, are you listening to me?"

Dick broke from his reverie and realized his beer was torturously close to spilling from the neck of the bottle. He recovered and turned his attention to Doug. "'Course. Bonds, stocks, all that shit." He drank deeply, letting the carbonated bubbles soothe his throat. It was rare he had a night free like tonight. Ever since Valentina had left, work had been crazy. In the last few days, Dick had been traveling around the city non-stop, the smell of scum and injustice embedded under his fingernails. He put a hand to his head. "I'm sorry, Doug, it's just that—"

Doug waved a hand. He finished the dregs of his Blue Moon and set the bottle next to the coaster on the table, much to Dick's chagrin. "No need. Sleepy Dick. I get it." He stood and grinned. "First time I've ever used that excuse in the presence of a man."

"Sure that won't be the last." Dick's reply sent them both into raucous laughter. He guided Doug to the doorway and saw him out with a wave. When he was gone, he turned his attention to the La-Z-Boy. It was larger than he thought it would be, a looming presence in the center of his modest living room. He brought the bottle to his lips and sipped, then shook his head. "Maybe he's right. Maybe you are everything I long for but will never have." He let out a derisive snort. "Fucking metaphors."

Dick couldn't sleep that night.

He lay in the dark, listening to the sounds of the city. AJS sirens, shouting matches, and the thrum of engines formed the bass line in the town. The dark was soothing, but his mind raced. The covers slipped to his waist, revealing a matt of thick, dark hair on his chest. In the center of the forest was a note.

Dick twirled it around his fingers, the ink from Valentina's scrawl occasionally flipping into view. He was still trying to work out what it all meant. Why would she have left him her number after all they'd been through? Valentina was as secretive with her identity as politicians were with the truth.

So why…

And should he?

The urge to drop a message had played on his mind ever since he found the note, the room still stinking of her perfume. She was gone come morning, of course. Should he expect anything less? Ordinarily, there was little left of Valentina. This, though… after all they'd discussed.

Dick eased himself into a seated position, held the note before his eyes, and frowned. He didn't want romance. He didn't have time for it. He didn't *need* it. Still, there was something about Valentina that drew him closer. There was a kinship, an unspoken bond between them. Their motives were the same, but their actions were different. They both fought for justice on opposite ends of the scale. Dick considered himself righteous, moral to the end. Valentina…

Valentina killed for coin.

Yet he could see in her eyes that there was more to it than that. He supposed he would never know what that was exactly.

His phone flashed beside him. A notification lit the screen: a job. Always a job.

He picked up his phone and thumbed through the information. It was nothing that he couldn't answer come morning. Now the phone was in his hand, and his thumb typed the number. Before he knew it, a message was on the screen, words written in his voice. "You left something at mine."

He grinned, imagining Valentina's face as she read the message. Would she know it was Dick messaging? Of course, she would. He was texting the Red Countess for God's sake.

No sooner had he hit "Send" than something raised his hackles. The curtains fluttered, though that should be impossible. The window was closed.

Not only closed but locked from the inside.

A head with bright red hair and dark, hypnotic eyes poked through. A pale face with a shining crimson grin looked his way. "You took your time."

She stepped into his apartment, and his heart quickened. She was graceful in every move, finding her footing on his hardwood floor as she stood there in all her glory. For once, her leather jacket wasn't fastened around her body but hooked over the crook of her arm. His eyebrow raised. She offered a grin in response.

"Always one step ahead, aren't you, Val?" Dick nodded at her jacket.

"Down, boy." Valentina held up the leather, the sight of the three holes in it weighing her down. Through the largest, she made out Dick looking back at her. "Hazards of the job."

"Rough night?" He rose from the bed wearing only thin cotton pajama pants and made his way to a side table where a glass container of amber liquid awaited. It looked golden in the lamplight. He poured himself a tumbler and offered one to Valentina.

"Sure." She accepted without thinking about it. "Though not the worst night I've ever had."

Dick nodded. "Want to tell me about it?"

Valentina considered this before neatly folding the jacket and placing it over a nearby chair. Why Dick had a chair in his bedroom, she'd never understood. It wasn't like he often invited company over. The most action that chair would have ever seen would be…

Well, it involved Valentina.

"It involves some form of a sniper rifle and a man with a grudge," Valentina finally answered.

Dick glanced at an imaginary watch.

Valentina smirked. "What?"

"Well, it makes sense. A typical Tuesday for you, huh?"

"I suppose." Valentina sipped the whiskey, enjoying the fiery channel it carved down her throat. They stood a moment in lingering silence, the initial niceties exchanged, yet the hangover from their last conversation still an ever-present obstacle between them. Valentina glanced at her toes, pissed off at how bashful Dick could make her. "So you finally decided to contact me?"

Dick chuckled as color flushed his cheeks. "I mean...I guess." His eyes were dark and held level at her eye line. "Though, I'm now wondering if I was the one to break first, or if it was you?"

Valentina gave him a strange look.

"Well," Dick continued, "considering that you appeared the moment I hit "Send," it seems a little suspicious. Would you have found your way here without my encouragement? Is Valentina perhaps the weaker of the two when it comes to carnal desires?"

Valentina laughed, a rich, warm sound. "Mr. Chambers, I'm offended—"

"I'm just saying," Dick interrupted, "that perhaps there's more to it than you previously claimed. I mean, I've had stray cats come into my abode less frequently than you appear, Ms. Winters."

Valentina held a quip on the end of her tongue, the mention of cats and the connotations with sex. She swallowed it. *Way too easy.*

She studied Dick, absorbing the deliberately cheeky and evocative tone he threw her way. It was part of the reason he was so alluring. That charm was honed to an edge so fine that it could slice through her steely exterior with ease. She was glad clothing covered most of her skin because the goosebumps would have been a clear giveaway about how his words affected her.

"For your information, I needed a safe place to hide out. Seems someone has put a target on my back, and I needed a place to lie low."

"I feel so used." Dick grinned. He sipped his drink, dark eyes and rash of stubble catching the lamplight and highlighting the cut of his cheeks. "If I'm not mistaken, your back is fine. It's your arms and hips your attacker seems to want to destroy."

Valentina glanced at the jacket. Two large tears in the right seam, one in the bicep. Had she been leaping to the ground, she'd be dead. No question about it. Sadness clouded her face.

Dick stepped closer, sensing the sudden change. He laid a hand on her arm, and she tingled at his touch. "Val...it's okay."

Valentina steeled herself with a determined expression. "No." Her smirk appeared; the same one she knew brought Dick to his knees every damn time. "No, it's not. Life's too short, and we're wearing far too many clothes for my liking."

Before Dick could reply, her lips were on his.

CHAPTER FIVE

The air was heavy and warm. Valentina lay beside Dick as thin plumes of smoke curled into the room. Their chests rose and fell, and a gleam of sweat oiled their skin.

Valentina grinned, then leaned across Dick to take her glass. "We have to stop meeting like this."

"No. That's not how this works."

"Oh?" Valentina chuckled. "How does this work then, detective?"

Dick raised an eyebrow. "Detective?" He scoffed. "No, thank you. Investigator will do just fine." He adjusted his position, sitting up and taking another drag of his cigarette. "I don't know how this works. I try not to question the good things in my life. Most of those are few and far between."

"You have Doug. He's a good thing, is he not?"

Dick nodded. "Another thing I don't question. After the way things ended, the time we hadn't seen each other, it doesn't make sense. I don't question it. It just is."

Valentina thought about her first encounter with Doug, a man hired to eliminate Dick. An old friend, wires crossed, anger corrupting his heart until he was able to see the light. Valentina and Dick had brought him into her style of witness protection, and in abandoning his employer, Dick and Doug had reunited and rebound their kinship, which they believed lost all those years ago.

"How very Zen of you," Valentina commented. "Didn't have you pegged for one of those meditation, karma, bullshit gurus."

"You don't believe in that stuff?"

"You do?" Valentina chuckled. She thought about it, falling into a heavy silence before replying, "I don't know what to believe anymore."

Her gaze flickered to her jacket, the tears looking almost like bear claw scratches. From there her mind flashed to her assailant, then to Deng, making the bridge of connections across to Kit and Bradley and the fucker formerly known as Archie.

When she turned back to Dick, he was watching her closely. "What's going on, Val? You're troubled."

Valentina drained her glass. "It's nothing."

Dick watched her a few moments longer. "You know you can talk to me."

Valentina glanced at her bare stomach. "No. You know I can't."

Dick nodded. "Yeah, I know."

They were silent a moment longer before Valentina rose and stalked around the bed. Dick's eyes followed her the entire time, admiring her curves, the smoothness of her skin. Valentina had a few imperfections on her body—mostly scars and bruises—but otherwise, she knew she could hold most men's gazes. She poured herself another whiskey, this time filling it. She drained half in one go, then grimaced against the fire raging through her.

"Val?"

Valentina met his eyes.

"It's going to be okay." Dick's smile was disarming. "Whatever it is, it's going to be fine."

"Oh, I know. Because there's no other option."

Dick grinned. "There never is."

Valentina set her glass down. She strode over to Dick and straddled him, pinning his waist to the bed below the duvet covers. She planted a kiss on his lips, her breath catching as he kissed her, his rough stubble scratching her face.

When they broke apart, she picked up the scrap piece of paper on the side table and held it in front of his face. "Yours to use. I'm not always going to make the first move."

"So you admit you moved first?"

Valentina rolled her eyes. She kissed his lips before rolling off the bed and onto her feet. She started getting dressed, "In this case, maybe. I'm used to having to encourage men to make their move."

Dick pinched the note between his fingers. "Understood. So, this new arrangement. Whenever I want, wherever I want?"

Valentina frowned. "Let's not get carried away, Dick. I'm not your little plaything."

Dick laughed. "Fine. Understood."

Valentina finished getting dressed, then crossed to the window. They'd left it open all night, and now the sun was beginning to crest the horizon as a gentle breeze rolled through. She wondered how many people nearby had heard their furious love-making. She realized she didn't care.

Dick extinguished his cigarette and placed a lazy arm behind his head. "You know that you can use the door?"

Valentina looked from the door to the window. "Where's the fun in that?" She stepped one leg through.

"Wait," Dick announced.

Valentina froze.

"Before you go," he continued, "how the hell did you open that window? It's supposed to be break-in proof."

Valentina scoffed. "Oh, Dick. Haven't you learned yet? If Valentina wants something badly enough, she's going to get it."

She climbed out into the street and left Dick with a grin that lasted a long time after.

———

Valentina made her way through the city, torn between two minds. On the one hand, her thoughts drifted to the stasis that hung between her current situation and her goal. On the other, her mind was sharpened and honed for anyone who might be following her.

Even the distraction from Dick didn't last that long. The longer she left things, the less chance there was of claiming back Bradley and Kit for herself. Every passing minute was a chance for Archie to dispose of two innocents, and the wait was killing her. She drew her cell out of her pocket and checked her messages. There was nothing from Deng, so Valentina shot her a quick text to urge her onward. They needed answers, and they needed them now.

Then there was her attacker. A man who she hadn't thought about in years. A person who, for some reason, had reappeared in her life and was now gunning to take it. A man who might be the only one to...

No. Valentina wouldn't let herself go there. She was the alpha. She was the true graduate.

Valentina approached her apartment block as the sun rose. She could feel Isabella beginning to wake, and she made a note to herself to return earlier if she could in the future. It wasn't fair for Isabella to keep waking up mid-transition. Their worlds needed to have definitive boundaries.

Like yours and Dick's? a voice in her head noted.

Valentina stepped inside the white room and disrobed. She stood there naked, only her red wig still in place. In her hand was the torn jacket. She studied the rips, wondering if she'd be able to repair it, then thought better of it. She opened the hidden closet and tossed the jacket to the floor. Hanging from the rail were six identical copies.

Rule number seven: always be prepared.

Not a rule she'd learned from the Scouts.

No…a rule that she'd learned from somewhere far more fundamental and cut-throat.

Valentina closed her eyes as her mind took her years back to the place that birthed the Countess.

CHAPTER SIX

Before

Smoke erupted in a cloud the size of a football. There was a purple hue to the vapor, and a hand waved at the smoke, attempting to dispel it into the darkened room.

"Shit." Marcus Collins grimaced, one arm folded over his face to protect himself from the noxious gas. It muffled his words, and as he took a step back from the wooden desk, laughter reached his ear. "Piss off, Val. It was a minor miscalculation."

"Enough to get you killed," Valentina replied without turning. She bent over her table of gizmos and gadgets, pots filled with various items and components to piece together and concoct devices of her creation. She pinched a soldering iron between her fingers, deftly applying a touch of solder to seal the circuits within. Inside the tiny orb of metal was a vial, as small as her thumbnail, with a deep purple liquid inside—the same agent now filling the air around Marcus. "You can't make mistakes here. Not one at this level."

Marcus frowned at Valentina, and his face turned a strange shade of red. He put distance between himself and the gas as he made his way to a large desk at the end of the room where an oxygen mask and tank stood. He applied the mask to his face and drew deep lungfuls of clean air.

Valentina shook her head and fiddled with the final component of her device. The orb was smooth, the size of a golf ball. Outside of the circular entrance, there were no distinguishable markings. She clicked the component into place, then closed the cap. Once in place, she admired her handiwork.

Marcus returned to his desk waving a sheet of paper. The gas had mostly dissipated now. "Show-off."

Valentina grinned. She was proud of her work. Eleven spherical devices lined her desk, all perfectly identical. She placed the final one in the line and sat back with a sense of satisfaction. "It's easy once you know how," she explained. "You just have to appreciate the fine art. The subtlety in the lines. You have to breathe in the mechanisms," her voice morphed into a theatric display of their teacher, "you have to feel the vibrations, the intricacies, you have to *become…*"

"…become the device." A deep voice finished the sentence for her.

Valentina and Marcus spun. Framed in shadow in the doorway, a man stood with hands folded behind his back. Light reflected off his bald head, the egregious folds of his robes too large for his slight body. "Winters, ten laps."

Valentina frowned. "My apologies, sensei. It's just that I…"

"Fifteen." His words were declarative. There was no room to argue, and Valentina knew better than that.

She nodded. Her eyes strayed to Marcus and found the smile on his face. Shouldn't it be him getting the punishment, not Valentina? Even after months, Marcus struggled with any activity that required finesse. His clobbering hands were of no use to the finer arts of mercenary work. He might make a great berserker, but spiders killed in silence. Rhinos killed with force.

Her laps were swift, running around the outskirts of the dojo in near silence. A thin veil of mist covered the surrounding fields, blocking the view of the distant city. It cloaked Valentina in a world where no one else existed, running in a sort of limbo since the only marker to count her laps were the stone steps that she passed fifteen times on her rounds.

When she made her way back to the crafting quarters, the room was empty. She wandered over to her desk and found her dozen smoke bombs, perfectly balanced, perfectly crafted in accordance with the recipes and ingenuity of greater mercenaries than her. Well, *almost* all perfect.

One orb stood out to her. The fourth from the right, not placed back with Valentina's careful precision. She picked up the bomb and turned it over in her fingers. A faint purple smudge from a fingerprint covered the cap. She shook her head and made to return it to Marcus' desk when a voice spoke to her.

"Quite the astute observation," Sensei Reyner commented. "You have a real eye for detail, Winters."

"Thank you, sensei." Valentina placed the orb on Marcus' desk and looked for her missing item.

"You will not find it. Your enemy is a shrewd man of great pain. Your talents bring great stormy weather to his vision of a flawless voyage."

Valentina shrugged. "He should try harder. Be better. Though he'll hardly excel at intricacy with fists the size of anvils."

Sensei Reyner nodded thoughtfully. "Perhaps it is this that you want to be cautious of." He turned to leave. "Come."

Valentina did so.

They walked through the quiet halls of the dojo, the decor deliberately minimal. They passed dividers where other recruits slept, none of them concerned about utilizing the night to their advantage and gaining a lead in their classes. Why would they? They didn't have to fight the fight that Valentina did. Valentina had to fight with her other, only able to attend the classes at night. To the other recruits, Valentina Winters was nothing more than a whisper in the wind, a bat that flew in the darkness and fueled itself from the smoke of their dreams.

Sensei Reyner led Valentina into his office, a modest affair with walls lined with bamboo. An oil painting took the center of the right wall, with swirls and patterns of gold, red, and black. Valentina sat across from her sensei, waiting until he had seated himself first.

He bowed.

She bowed.

"You underestimate your opponent," her sensei declared at last. He poured himself a green tea from a nearby pot. "Marcus is a warrior with a lion's heart. You must approach with caution. Do not provoke that which you cannot stop."

Valentina let out an involuntary laugh, stopping when Reyner caught her eye. "You're serious?"

It didn't make sense. Valentina excelled in all classes with Marcus. One of the only other night time recruits, Marcus had fallen at every hurdle he had met. His craftwork was questionable, his weapon handling was subpar, and his thievery skills were laughable. On more than one occasion, Valentina had caught Marcus trying to steal items from her person. Each time she had replied with a swift blow to the head and a curse under her breath.

Sensei Reyner looked pained as if merely speaking to Valentina about this hurt deep down. "I have trained a lot of recruits, Valentina. More than I care to admit. Many have passed through our regime and flown the nest to achieve great things, but few have shown the skills you now possess. You have grown quickly, excelling in the areas that ordinarily take months, if not years, and with that, you have grown overconfident."

"Confidence breeds success. One must believe in themselves to truly master the path." They weren't her words. They were her sensei's.

Sensei Reyner nodded. "True. Though, as with all wisdom, the blade has two edges. You must learn to tread between them both. One who underestimates their opponent will surely provide a blindside for them to attack from. Marcus is deceptive. He is cunning. I have seen his type before, clouded in a dark aura, and it would behoove you to think twice before you place your final assessment."

"What do you mean? What aren't you telling me?"

Sensei Reyner sipped his tea, little finger raised. He poured another, then handed it to Valentina. "Some things you must figure out for yourself. A teacher does not do for their students. A teacher merely lights the paths and lets their students choose."

Valentina accepted the drink, eyes deep in thought. Marcus was a buffoon. A man who, while capable, was vastly overshadowed by Valentina. She'd watched him slice himself with his sword, trip over a plant pot as he tried to pick Valentina's pockets, explode his detonation devices in the classroom. What threat would a man such as he pose to her?

"You are close to graduation. With all the colors of the phoenix, I wish for your success. Never have I had the privilege to train a person so capable in the ways of our dojo. Heed our lessons, and tread into the world with wisdom, for arrogance is folly, and the devil hides in many guises."

Valentina drank deeply, the small cup only yielding so much tea. She stared thoughtfully at her sensei, then set her cup down. Before she could ask another question, he added, "You are dismissed."

Valentina bowed low, then rose. She hesitated only briefly at the door before making her way back to the craft room.

Sensei Reyner watched her leave, then finished his drink. Without looking up, he addressed the man peering through the shadows of the rafters in the roof. There was no fear or quake in his voice. "Students are reminded not to harm other students under our roof."

The man in the shadows blinked, then slipped away into the darkness.

Three weeks later, Valentina was alone in the crafting room.

It had quickly become one of her favorite places. From the moment she first set sights on the space, she had fallen in love. Pockets and shelves filled the walls, each dedicated to intricate items that did nothing alone but together created something beautiful. Under the careful tutelage of sensei Reyner, she had discovered the art of the jigsaw, formed a kinship with the tools and paraphernalia needed to create minute trinkets of destruction, disruption, and distraction. There was beauty in the craft, a need to plan and prepare for every eventuality. Lessons consisted of creating items she'd use to complete a hypothetical brief, and from these scenarios, her mind went into overdrive.

She couldn't count the hours she'd poured into her craft. She couldn't put a value to the number of items she had bent, broken, and eventually learned to mold into the tools that would later earn her the title of one of the world's greatest mercenaries. Valentina was a weapon in herself, but that didn't mean that additional items didn't help.

She hunched over her desk, the surface illuminated by the bright lamp strapped to her forehead. Over the months she had been at the dojo, she had yet to master the forces of electromagnetic energy. On the table in front of her were two shackles, open at the clasp. Their curved edges showed the serrated teeth that would hold the prisoner in the handcuffs, but there was no chain to bind them together.

She fiddled with a delicate wiring network, careful not to damage the copper coils that would form the electromagnetic connection. After a satisfied *click* of her tongue, she sat back. She moved the two restraints to either side of the table.

Drawing a deep breath, she thumbed a small trigger placed in front of her.

A sudden *zap* of electrical energy ignited. The shackles glowed a violent blue, shaking on the surface only for a second before clashing with such violence that the metal created a spark.

Valentina jumped back, letting out a surprised laugh. She looked upon the handcuffs now touching each other, seemingly inseparable. She tried to pull them apart but couldn't. She gave a satisfied grin and turned off the trigger.

The shackles fell apart with no more energy to connect them.

Valentina picked up each piece and held them in front of her face. Without the need for the adjoining connector, she could store the handcuffs in small storage units. Not only that, but her design allowed for them to fold along a series of intricate yet reinforced joins. What used to hang off an officer's waistband could now be condensed into a single fist.

Valentina grinned until something moved behind her.

She turned, looking over her shoulder at the darkened room. She waited a few moments, but nothing showed. She held her gaze, eyes narrowing toward the door where a sudden movement caught her attention. Something whizzed through the air. She ducked in time to miss the knife, which embedded itself in the chalkboard's rigid surface.

Valentina jumped out of her chair as the shape ran, darting to the left of the hallway.

She was at the doorway in seconds and glimpsed the figure off to her left. She pushed off from the doorframe and sprinted after them, unsure who would dare attack her on sacred ground. Sensei had told the other recruits the rules. They knew better than that. The punishment for breaking them to such severity was simple: death.

An eye for an eye.

Their chase was near silent, the assailant betraying little in the way of footsteps or motion. This gave her the first indication that she was dealing with one of her own. No one else would know the soft spots on the floor, the places where the flooring creaked, and be able to avoid it other than one of their own.

She ran past sleeping recruits, nothing more than a shadow in the night. She gained ground on the assailant as they made the mistake of glancing back over their shoulder and launching another missile. Valentina ducked sharply to the right, dropping a shoulder as the blade spun through the air and landed with a clatter on the floor.

She followed through a series of short corridors and out into the open grounds. Moonlight lit up the sky, a blaze of silver from the full moon. Valentina saw the assailant running across the waist-length grass, down toward a creek that skirted the bound-aries of the dojo. They sped up, determined to outrun her, but Valentina was having none of that. Adrenaline coursed through her, and now she had a taste for revenge.

Shame that you're running outside of the boundaries now, buddy. In the open world, there are no rules.

The assailant dove into the creek, swimming the breadth of the water and emerging on the far bank. Valentina took another approach and ran up the trunk of a crooked willow, using the branches to propel her into the air and over the water. Her feet landed softly on the bank.

A knife soared toward her.

She dove out of the way and pushed herself to her feet swiftly after, her hand grabbing a fallen branch that was whip-thin and snapped when she waved it.

The assailant was close, clad in black robes, their eyes the only feature visible as they caught the moonlight. Her attacker stood there in a ready position, a blade in each hand.

Valentina felt exposed and vulnerable. Two knives against a slender piece of wood.

The assailant sensed her hesitation and sprang.

Their jump was impressive as they cleared several feet and

came down with both blades. Valentina stepped back and lashed out with the makeshift whip. It whistled through the air and caught their cheek. The force of it shifted some of the material and revealed skin with a carpet of stubble.

Before she could analyze, the blades came at her. Valentina blocked with her forearms, the knives dangerously close to her flesh. She kicked and spun and wrestled until one of the weapons fell free of the assailant's hands.

Anger rose in those eyes. The assailant was strong and easily had fifty pounds on Valentina. He advanced, throwing his weight toward her. They toppled onto the bank, the soft, damp grass enough to cushion the blow. Valentina's head rocked back. The knife caught her shoulder and sliced through her top.

Warm blood flowed onto the soil. A gleeful expression reached the man's eyes. He grunted, then reared back with the knife.

Valentina rocked her body sideways, the gentle decline along the bank into the creek enough to give them momentum. They log-rolled toward the water, which caught the man off-guard. He dug the blade into the bank to stop their descent, the metal dragging through the soil until it pulled from his grip.

Then they were underwater.

Rocks and debris poked into their backs. The gentle current wasn't enough to carry them, but it was enough to slow the attack. Valentina rose to her knees and buried her fist in the man's stomach. Her clothes clung to her skin, and so did his. Her wound stung with a white-hot heat, but she knew at that moment that this wasn't a game. This was life and death, and she knew which side she wanted to be on.

The man spat into the water. His eyes flashed before he clocked Valentina with a meaty fist to the jaw. Valentina sprang back, the water softening her fall. The man was instantly on top of her with his hands clasped around her throat. Water rushed up her nose and poured into her throat.

The world was a blur of silver, black, and blue. The bubbles rising, she knew, were her final breaths. The man's fingers dug into her windpipe. He was determined—had drawn her out of the dojo, she now realized—and all that awaited her in the outside world was her demise.

Her hands scrabbled at his face. Fingernails clawed the material and pulled it down, but she couldn't see his features beneath the water. Stars bloomed in her vision. Her hands fell, fingers reaching for anything that could help. Something round and smooth fitted snugly in her palm, and she swung it at her attacker with sudden urgency.

The rock crashed into the man's jaw. The feel of bone shattering vibrated through her arm. His fingers released. She tried to draw breath, realized she was still underwater, then pushed herself quickly up.

She gasped for oxygen, eyes stinging, throat raw. Water still lined her throat, and she coughed and spluttered until her airway was clear. The fog that clouded the edges of her vision started to dissipate as the man doubled over nearby. One hand held his jaw, and the liquid dribbling from his mouth stained the river's surface around him.

Valentina gasped, light-headed. She glanced at the knife on the bank, but even that short distance felt a mile away. Instead, with the rock in her hand, she rose unsteadily to her feet and waded over to her assailant. A wet, dark crop of hair crowned his head, and as her shadow loomed over him, he started laughing.

The choking splutter of blood and saliva was an awful sound. Valentina held the rock high, intending to cave in the bastard's skull.

Something stopped her.

The man turned, and a familiar face greeted her—though some of the familiarity was gone in the places where his jaw was crooked, and bone poked out where it shouldn't have.

"You bitch," Marcus spat, the words muffled as though he

were drunk. Red dribbled from his chin, and a glazed look set in his eyes. "You fucking bitch…"

Valentina watched in horror. Where they stood represented the dojo's boundary line. Sensei Reyner had made it clear on the day she had first arrived that the creek was the divider. Anything beyond it was open territory, but safety was secure within the boundary line.

Marcus stood knee-deep in water, tucked in the safety of the boundaries. Valentina frowned, her breath coming in short, sharp bursts. Her shoulder was on fire, and she still fought the urge to cough out the last splutters of creek water from her throat and lungs.

"Why?"

It was all she could manage. None of this made any sense. Marcus was subpar to Valentina on every level. How could he lure her out here and nearly match her in combat skills? He had almost drowned her.

"Why not?" He laughed that strange choking sound once more. His arms wheeled around him erratically, as if someone else was controlling them. He stepped toward her, foot splashing loudly in the creek. Beyond him, Valentina could see the dojo's silhouette, its outline glowing in the light of the moon. A place of safety. A few steps backward and anything would be fair game.

"Why the fuck not?" Marcus continued, voice rising. He stumbled and wobbled to maintain balance. "Why wouldn't I come for the bitch that holds the sensei's favor? Why wouldn't I remove the competition? Why wouldn't I make things easier for me? You know who likes someone overshadowing them?"

Valentina took a step back.

"No one!" Marcus exclaimed. "So I waited. Bided my time. Learned all I needed to know and hid it from you. Caught you off-guard."

Valentina took another step back. Marcus moved forward, back hunched and stalking like the Hunchback of Notre Dame.

The words Sensei Reyner had uttered made sense to her now, not to underestimate Marcus. He had taken her by surprise and employed skills she didn't know he had. Still, she had the upper hand now, surely? He was weaponless, dazed, and blabbing about his intentions like a fiction book crook. All she needed him to do was…

He took another step forward. Valentina's heels nudged the bank. The knife was nearby, glinting in her peripheral vision.

"We're mercenaries, Val," Marcus exclaimed. "Killers, born and bred. We don't get to kill shit in that place. How are we supposed to prove our worth if we can't choose worthy opponents to destroy?"

Valentina climbed onto the bank. "So that's your plan? Kill the greatest mercenary to grace those four walls to prove that you're better? To continue your legacy and take some kind of metaphorical throne?"

Marcus grimaced. He wiped his chin. "It worked for Sensei Reyner, didn't it?"

Valentina paused. "What are you talking about?"

"You didn't know!" Marcus laughed, clutching his stomach, mouth hanging at a crooked angle. "How do you think Reyner took the mantle? He killed his competition. Took the throne by force. I can't believe he never told you."

Valentina wasn't sure whether to be sickened or impressed. It would make sense that the head of one of the most fabled schools for mercenaries was a stone-cold killer at heart.

Valentina took another step back, eyes darting to the knife now by her foot. Marcus caught the look.

"Don't even think about it." His hand darted into his robe, then drew out another throwing knife. Without warning, he hurled it at Valentina.

Valentina ducked, hand wrapping around the hilt of the weapon. Pain exploded in her thigh as she rose to her feet, the heat overwhelming her until she fell back onto her ass. The blade stayed buried deep in her muscle as she tried to retreat backward.

Marcus moved surprisingly quick, looming over her. The moon crowned his head but left his face shadowed as thick, metallic blood dripped onto Valentina. "Outside the boundary lines. Very good girl." He wiped a hand over his mouth and groaned in pain. "A perfect spot for killing."

Valentina gritted her teeth. "I agree."

Before Marcus could react, Valentina withdrew a small orb from her pocket. Smoke erupted, clouding the space between Marcus and herself. He cried out in anger and fell onto the ground to straddle her, but she was gone, rolling to the side, holding in her pain by biting her tongue.

She moved behind him, one leg more functional than the other, each step a burden. She drew out her cuffs and slapped one on each wrist. For a moment, Marcus protested, shimmying his shoulders to free himself until he realized that no coil attached the shackles.

He stood, coughing as the gas entered his lungs. They each stepped back, unable to see the other.

"Fucking idiot," Marcus announced, words still slurred. "What good is a pretty piece of jewelry going to do to stop me?"

The gas dissipated, swept away by the breeze. Marcus leered at her, hands raised to his head to feel his jaw. He put one hand to the back of his neck, the other to his chin, looking as though he was about to force the bones to crack.

Valentina smirked.

"What?" Marcus asked.

In answer, she thumbed the trigger.

The cuffs activated, the insides lighting in a violent blue light. A buzzing sounded as the magnets drew Marcus' hands together. The only thing standing in the way of the shackles connecting was the meat of Marcus' neck.

He gasped and spluttered as his hands drove together,

restricting his airway. Valentina watched with cold, dead eyes as he dropped to his knees. She fell on her ass and turned her attention from the man before her to the blade buried in her thigh. His gasps formed the background music to her mission as she gripped the handle in both hands and pulled it free with a sharp tug.

She cried out, unable to hold it in anymore. Then she tore her sleeve off and tied the length of fabric over the gash to staunch the bleeding. She fell sideways, her thigh bashing against the ground.

When she finished, Marcus lay still before her, eyes closed. The cuffs had pinched the skin of his neck, and now the metal hoops were touching. Valentina remained there a few more minutes, waiting for any sign of life from Marcus, but none came.

Her trip back to the dojo was long, each step a throb of agony. Sensei Reyner met her at the doorway. Although they exchanged no words, Valentina knew that he had watched stoically from a distance. Valentina had proven her worth. She killed a man along the way but held her own.

Her first kill.

A dead recruit.

Or so it had seemed at the time.

CHAPTER SEVEN

Present day

Three days passed, and still there was no word from Deng.

Valentina applied pressure with constant reminders and questions up until the point that Deng fell silent. By the fourth night, Valentina was an angry shade of pissed.

"Twenty-four hours and *nothing*?" she muttered to herself, looking out across the stretch of farmland that led to Deng's compound. She couldn't see the building through the wall of mist, but she still imagined Deng sitting in her throne, laughing at the messages Valentina had sent and relishing the power her situation wrought. "I'm no one's fucking plaything. If she's not going to talk, I'll find ways to make her."

At ground level, she strolled up to a nearby Kawasaki motorcycle and straddled the seat. Her leathers made her seem to any prying eyes as though she belonged, and with a deft hand at the wires, the cycle kicked into action, vibrations thrumming against her ass. She twisted the throttle and pulled away before anyone could bat an eyelid.

The wind tore past, and her hair streamed behind her like ribbons on a kite. The city faded, and the country took over, her view restricted to greenery, crops, and the single-lane track that broke the squares of agriculture around her. When the Tynamo compound came into view, she twisted the accelerator even more. The engine screamed as she zeroed in on the front gates.

Two guards stepped out, one hand in front of them, the other resting on their holsters. When they saw that Valentina wasn't slowing down, they drew their pistols and lined them up with the redhead careening straight at them.

One of them shouted an instruction. Valentina cut the engine, the cycle still heading straight. She flashed the headlight, momentarily blinding them and forcing their hands to their eyes. By the time their arms lowered, Valentina had twisted the bike sideways and slammed the brake. The motorcycle skidded the final stretch and came to a perfect stop inches away from the one she assumed was the main guard.

His face screwed up in anger as he shouted, his pistol touching Valentina's temple. "Get your fucking hands behind your head and step off your vehicle!"

His shouts drew the attention of nearby workers, who all leaned around to see what the commotion was. Valentina didn't budge an inch. "Call your boss right now and tell her that Valentina wants to see her. Otherwise, things are about to get real ugly around here."

The guard pressed the pistol into her head. "I said get *down*."

Valentina glanced at the other guard's uncertain expression. She recognized him as one who had allowed her entry before. This new captain had no idea who the fuck he was dealing with.

"Last chance," Valentina warned.

The captain thumbed off the safety.

Valentina sighed. "Fine." She lowered the kickstand with her foot, climbed off the bike, and raised her hands. A look of triumph crossed the captain's face.

He didn't blink. "On your knees."

Valentina stayed where she was.

"On. Your. *Knees*." The guard grimaced.

Valentina's jaw clenched. "You're making a mistake—"

"I will not tell you again," the guard interjected.

Valentina nodded. "Neither will I."

The guard took a single step toward Valentina. Valentina moved rapidly, grabbing his wrist and twisting it sharply. The captain groaned but maintained his grip on his weapon as his face contorted into a mask of pain.

The second guard hesitated before raising his pistol again. That was his mistake. Still holding the captain's wrist, Valentina stepped onto the bike seat and launched herself into the air. The sole of her boot hit the guard square in the face, and his nose exploded with red. As she came down, she landed behind the captain and brought his wrist across his throat. The gun aimed precariously to the side, and as Valentina dug her knee into the captain's back, a shot fired. The bullet hit the wall lining the compound and ricocheted impotently into the fields.

Valentina twisted again, this time enough for the gun to slip from his grasp. He was almost twice her girth, but she was stronger. His face turned the shade of beetroot as his arm cut off his circulation.

"Do I need to ask again?" Valentina whispered in his ear.

The captain sputtered. Valentina dug her spare hand into her pocket and sprinkled something around his feet.

She chuckled. "I'll take that as a no."

The captain's eyes rolled back as he bordered on the edge of unconsciousness. The second guard remained on the ground, a hand moving to his nose. His gun laid a few feet away. She knew he wouldn't be stupid enough to try to stop her, so she released the captain and shoved him back.

The captain's hands moved to massage his throat. He turned to find Valentina strolling up the road leading to the first building inside the compound. His face melted from pain to rage as he tensed to run after her. Valentina held up a hand and clicked something in her palm.

Light exploded from the ground.

The man glanced down to find what appeared to be over two dozen ball bearings, all sparking with electricity. They zapped lines toward each other, forming a web of static that locked his feet together and caused him to spasm.

He fell in a lump. Valentina powered the devices down after a few seconds, a grin on her face as she looked up at Deng's tower.

Valentina met no resistance on her journey through the Tynamo compound. Instead, the green light within the Cyclops strip monitored her every move. It was a constant companion, always in her peripheral vision as she strode through the halls and past the guards who merely watched with indifferent expressions.

Valentina wasn't sure how to take the journey. Always prepared, she kept her senses on high alert, ready to fight if needed, but by the time she arrived at the bottom of the central pagoda, she knew there was no need to attack.

"This way," the guard announced and guided Valentina upstairs. The four guards outside Deng's door parted without a word, and when the doors opened, Valentina found Deng standing and waiting for her.

Deng grinned. "I had a feeling you'd be heading this way."

"A feeling?" Valentina asked. "Or invasive technology that tracks my every move and warns you of my approach."

Deng considered this. "That. Also your showdown with my front guard. Impressive moves."

"You expect anything less?" Valentina replied.

Deng didn't answer. Instead, she swept by Valentina and started down the stairs. "Come."

Valentina followed, her blood still simmering with anger. Her voice echoed around the stairwell. "You went quiet on me."

Deng laced her fingers behind her back, her silk gown flowing like water behind her. "You were a nuisance," she replied matter-of-factly, as though Valentina had asked her what color the sky was. "I don't deal well with nuisances."

"Then you partnered with the wrong lady," Valentina growled.

Deng stopped her descent at the next floor and passed through a set of double doors. "Apparently so. Did I not tell you that I'd contact you when I had information?"

"You didn't say you wouldn't if you didn't," Valentina retorted.

Deng snorted, amusement on her face. "Touché. Still, you were bothersome, and I had work to do. How am I supposed to track Archibald if you constantly bombard me with interruptions?"

Valentina grew tired of chasing Deng. She reached out and grabbed her wrist. Deng responded instantly, twisting and slipping out of her grasp. She raised her hands defensively, taking a stance. Valentina copied her, and for a moment the two were deadlocked in the hallway.

They held each other's gaze.

Valentina was the first to break the silence. "You move fast."

"Never lay a hand on me again."

Valentina smirked. "Then give me answers."

Deng lowered her arms, regaining her composure. She brushed a stray lock of hair from her face. "Very well. You shall have them."

She turned and strode off once again. Valentina frowned, annoyed that once again Deng had walked off without a word.

Valentina called, "Answers."

Deng shot back, "Follow."

Valentina considered her options, but as Deng entered a door on her right, Valentina submitted, moving swiftly.

The room was dark, lit only by the glow of a multitude of

monitors. A small walkway bridged the gap over a drop of around thirty feet, and a central pod allowed a single user to scan the many screens arranged in a neat circle. "Welcome to Mission Control." Deng's arms spread wide.

Mission Control? Valentina's heart beat a notch faster, unsure if Deng was deliberately evocative or if it was merely a coincidence. *How could she know about Isabella's central workstation?*

Valentina glanced around, feeling more like she was on a spaceship than in the middle of a classic piece of Eastern architecture. The screens held assorted information, the footage generated from the Cyclops system. It appeared to cover the entire city. Several displays contained charts and numbers and codes, and one showed a full-screen image of a section of forest with a strange glowing green pulse in the center of it.

"Where am I?" Valentina asked.

"Mission Control," Deng responded, turning to face her. Valentina looked out for the knowing eye, but Deng's poker face was impeccable. "The place where all the magic happens. The central feed of it all. Anything I want, I get. A world at my fingertips, controlled by the touch of a button. You want to watch the Smiths having sex on Fifteenth? Then you can do it from here. Want to monitor the activity of a group of hell riders known as the Dead Devils?" She tapped a button and footage of supercars careening through the streets rolled on. "It's all here. The world's most comprehensive CCTV system." She shook her head. "Wait until I roll this out upon the rest of the world. It won't only be Atlantica that fits in the palm of my hand."

Valentina's eyes strayed to a feed that displayed a large hotel that towered into the sky. The adjacent windows were all black. From afar, it appeared as though snipers were monitoring the balconies. Occasionally, red dots flashed at the camera. "What's that?"

"A work in progress," Deng replied. "Nothing to worry your pretty little head about."

She tapped a few keys, and the image of the forest filled all the screens, each monitor showcasing the next piece of the puzzle. "What you want to see is *here*."

Deng sat in a chair that could have belonged in the *Enterprise*. Its size swallowed her tiny frame as she played with the keys and brought information onto the monitors. Valentina stood behind her and leaned toward one.

"That is Merchant's Grove," she explained, the feed zooming out as if controlled by a camera drone or some kind of satellite. "And here…"

"Hold on," Valentina interrupted. "Merchant's Grove?"

Deng raised an eyebrow. "And here I thought you were a woman of knowledge."

Valentina held her gaze.

Deng returned to the screen. "Merchant's Grove is thirty clicks from the center of Atlantica, in a quadrant first discovered by Amanda Merchant, one of the founding pioneers of the island. The forest itself was originally drawn and quartered by the founders, but their original boundary lines were lost over the years as the forest continued to claim the lives of innocents. I assume you've heard *those* stories?"

Valentina confirmed she had. Everyone had heard the tales of strange goings-on in the jungle. While the outer edges of the woodland were habitable, and many Atlanticans often wandered beneath the foliage, more and more cases of people disappearing cropped up in the papers through the decades. Most of these were explorers who she assumed were either lost in caves or killed by wild animals. Still, enough people had vanished to have earned the wilderness a reputation beyond the normal.

"Merchant's Grove," Deng continued, flustered at the interruption, "lies in the heart of it all. People discovered a handful of ruins around that area, but no one has visited that particular quadrant since a cave-in occurred around a decade ago, taking out all the explorers in its path. There was no explanation as to what caused the cave-in or what became of the explorers."

Valentina gave a derisive laugh. "This concerns us how?"

"I'll show you." Deng sounded smug. She tapped a key, and the color faded from the image, replaced with that pulsing green glow among the trees.

"What's that?" Valentina's voice came out breathy.

"That is an electrical frequency pulse."

The pulsing light was small, looking more like a radioactive piece of fruit hanging from a tree than anything substantial. As Deng zoomed in on the image, the camera panned through leaves and trees until it pointed at the soil below. A small fissure split the dirt, with darkness below. On the screen, the gloom filled with the green light.

Valentina's jaw dropped. "He's there?"

Deng shrugged. "We don't know for certain."

"What else could it be?"

"Power source. Although that would be highly unlikely. No one has found any new Atlanticores for years. The current resource is all claimed and taken, and the more people try to export the cores from the island, the more cases of detonations we witness."

Valentina nodded. The Atlanticores, while one of the greatest sources of energy and power ever discovered by man, were also one of the most volatile compounds when taken away from the island. Every year stories cropped up of smugglers trying to sneak away to their homelands with an Atlanticore, and every time, a few miles out from the island in international waters, the Atlanticore broke down and exploded.

Scientists and researchers had yet to figure out the reason for this strange phenomenon.

"We have to investigate," Valentina stated. "We have to see if they're down there." She turned to leave.

"Wait," Deng called, voice echoing around the dark chamber.

Valentina rolled her eyes and spun.

"One must approach with caution," Deng informed her. "My team has yet to return."

Valentina's eyebrow raised. "Your team...Wait." Her hands balled into fists. "You knew about this for *days*, didn't you?"

Deng spun to face her, no fear in her at all. She offered a half-shrug. "I had to be certain."

"You wasted precious hours," Valentina spat back. She stormed closer to Deng, arms animatedly flying around. "You had me sit back and do nothing when I could have been there, finding that asshole and bringing him to justice."

Deng glanced down, not out of sadness but out of resignation. "Then what, Miss Winters? I send our greatest asset to an unconfirmed location and allow you to march through the jungle to a place where wild animals and savages roam? No. I will not do that. I will work in a professional manner, not led by my emotions." Her expression changed, then. She became studious, concerned. "Which is how I believed Atlantica's greatest mercenary might operate."

That took Valentina aback. As much as she wanted to lash out some more, Deng was right. What was happening to her? All these years she'd kept her composure and put business ahead of her personal feelings. Now...

Now Archie had taken a piece of her heart and was manipulating it. Deng was right. If she wanted to get Kit and Bradley back, she needed to keep her cool. Deng was trying to help her, after all.

Wasn't she?

Valentina closed her eyes and drew a long breath. "Your team?"

Deng took this as a cue to continue. "Four of them. Disposable units sent on reconnaissance. They went radio silent in the early hours of this morning."

Where were you in the early hours of the morning? Dick's grin flashed in her mind.

"No contact whatsoever? When were they supposed to report?"

"Every hour on the hour."

"Dropped signal?"

Deng shook her head. "Impossible. We sent signal booster drones to track them."

"No cameras?"

Deng sighed. "We did. Here's the last shot we have of them."

Valentina turned her attention to the screen. The camera watched from a bird's eye view as four intrepid adventurers with rifles stalked through the trees. It was difficult to track them, the canopy growing dense then sparse at irregular intervals. As they disappeared into another thick ceiling of foliage, the camera followed where their trajectory should have headed. In the next open space, they were gone.

"We have no sight of them after that," Deng explained. "Only this."

An audio recording began to play, slightly muffled as voices called over each other. They reached fever pitch, words distorted through hurried breaths. What sounded like gunfire mixed with an animal's growl erupted. Then all fell to silence.

"Shit," Valentina muttered.

"You still wish you went alone?" Deng asked.

Valentina considered this. "Whatever is out there, I need to know the truth. Maybe it's not Archie, but at least it's progress."

"You can't do this," Deng protested. "Wait a little longer. Give me some time to deploy my units and find out for sure. Be smart about this."

"Every second lost is another chance for Archie to fuck it all up." Valentina tried desperately to keep her emotions in check. "Time is not our friend. I can be in and out of there in a day or two—tops."

Deng remained unconvinced. "You can't go in there alone. You're best suited for the city. What hope have you of surviving a place that half a century later explorers still haven't completely charted? There are animals in there, plants that poison and kill, insects, caves..."

"And ghosts?" Valentina finished. "I don't care what's in there. I'm going. You want a job done right? You do it yourself."

Deng rose to her feet, fists clenched. "Valentina. Don't do this. Not alone."

Valentina grinned with a mischievous glint in her eye. "Who the fuck says I'm going alone?"

CHAPTER EIGHT

Dick Chambers stood in the shadows, lost in the darkness. Anyone passing on the nearby street might glimpse the brief flare of the cherry on his cigarette, but soon that too was extinguished, leaving only the glint of his eyes.

He leaned against the brickwork, listening to the homeless shuffle around in the alley behind as they struggled to get comfortable among the bags of trash. In a nearby apartment, two eager lovers explored each other's bodies, lost in the whirlwind of their lovemaking, blissfully unaware that their song leaked out into the night. As ever, far off in the city, the AJS sirens rang their raucous tune.

Dick's gaze remained fixed to the window of the apartment block across the road. Five stories up, third from the left, that was where his informant had said he'd find him. He waited with the patience of a statue, keeping an eye out for any movement behind the glass.

So far, not a thing had budged. All was still inside.

"Only a matter of time..." Dick grumbled as the homeless pair broke into a fight. Their voices raised as glass shattered. Dick ignored them, one hand resting assuredly on the butt of his gun in case things turned sour.

The homeless fight died as they reached an agreement. Dick checked his watch and waited for the hour to turn two. On the stroke of the minute hand, he broke from the shadows and stalked across the road. His eyes remained on the window, certain that he had seen something twitch. If he were waiting inside, he'd likely have spotted Dick, but that didn't matter. No one ever truly believed that Dick could break in.

Even though it's so damn easy.

Dick skirted the building, then climbed the steps. He stopped at the door, which had a metal intercom panel on his right with a series of apartment numbers. On the bottom of it was an icon of a key with a space to scan a card.

Dick brought the plain white card from his pocket and held it to the panel. A light flashed green. The door unlocked. Dick grinned. *Ringo, you bastard. You've done it again.*

His climb up the stairs was quiet but not silent. Although Dick moved with a grace not usually found in a man of his stature, he still couldn't help the soft pad of his shoes echoing up the zigzagging staircase. He reached the doorway of apartment 3B, paused, and pressed an ear pressed against the wood. A slow stream of air whispered around him. Otherwise, all was silent.

Dick's face hardened. He gave a soft grunt, then put his back to the wall beside the door. He lit a cigarette and took a long drag before bringing his gun to his chest. He closed his eyes and counted to five.

At the five-count, a crash exploded through the door. Splintered wood now framed a hole as large as a dinner plate. "You lying son of a bitch!" a gruff voice called.

"He was there! I saw him! Fucker was right there!" a woman replied.

Dick counted to five again. Footsteps came through the apartment hallway. At the second count of five, Dick faced the hole, aimed his gun lower, and pulled the trigger as a second hole appeared.

A howl of pain filled his ears, and he glimpsed a bloodied foot leaking its juices onto a dusty old carpet. "Fuck!"

Dick fired again, this time at the lock. The mechanism broke, and the door swung open at the kick of his boot.

A skinny excuse of a man sprawled on the floor. Black veins stained his arms, and his blond mullet was unkempt. Dick only took a second to kick the man's gun from reach before turning his aim on the woman standing in a doorway behind. She was three times his girth, with thick red lips. The top of her chest was flushed and peppered with a layer of sweat.

"One sudden move and you both become chowder," Dick warned, closing the door behind him—not that there was much point, given there was no mechanism to hold it. With his gun fixed on the woman, he leaned down and grabbed the man by the collar. "On your feet, asshole."

The man erupted into howls of pain as he hobbled under Dick's grip. Dick dragged him to the living room and threw him at a threadbare couch with stuffing exposed like strange fungi. "He din't do nuffin'," the woman protested. "Whatever you thaynk you've got, ain't nuffin'. He's innocent."

"I'll be the judge of that," Dick growled. He gestured at the woman with his gun, indicating she should sit beside him. The man whimpered and clutched his wounded foot. Blood now soaked his questionably grey socks, but Dick knew that it would heal with medical attention. Medicine had advanced considerably in Atlantica. "Tell me what you know," he commanded.

The man's eyes grew wide in fear, and his lips trembled.

"I'm telling you, he don't know shit," the woman announced. "Go badger some other—"

Dick pointed the gun at the woman's face, and she silenced. He narrowed his eyes, crouched, and fixed his gaze on the pathetic excuse for a man. "That's all well said, darling, but I've been in the business long enough to know that those who have no information to contribute to my cause tend not to hide in the dark in the hopes that I won't see them. If you've got nothing to hide, why the fuck were you hiding?"

The woman put a hand across the man's chest. "It's night time, asshole. We was sleeping, not hiding."

Dick grinned and returned the gun to her face. Her stare hardened.

The man seemed to find some of the courage that had drained from his pale face. "Don't aim that thing at her."

Dick lifted an eyebrow. "No? Should I use your shotgun instead? You were eager enough to come at me with that beast, who says I shouldn't use this measly thing on your lover."

The woman scoffed. "Lover? Excuse me, honey, ain't no love going on here..."

Dick fired at the ceiling. He hit a pipe and water sprinkled down on the pair. The woman complained but stayed still as Dick waved the gun between them. "Make this easy for me, Stevenson. Tell me what I need to know, and we can call it a night. If you don't give willingly, I will find...alternate methods to make you squawk."

The man named Stevenson held Dick's stare for a moment. He glanced uncertainly at the large woman, then down at his knees. "Fine."

"Honey, no!" the woman contested.

Dick smirked. "Not a lover, huh?"

Her eyes flashed. A moment later, Stevenson started talking.

Dick stepped out of the apartment building a short while later. He left through the back door, knowing that if he used the front, he'd open himself up to potential attack from Stevenson and his not-girlfriend.

He clung to the side of the building, ensuring he remained out of sight from Stevenson's windows. Although he held Stevenson's shotgun in his hands—he wasn't stupid enough not to confiscate it—he would never know if the man had other weapons hidden.

The back entrance led to a parking lot lit only by a single streetlight. Dick aimed his pistol at the bulb and shot it out, the silencer reducing the sound to a simple puff of air. A smattering of cars occupied the space, and as Dick snaked between them, satisfied with the information he'd received, he couldn't shake off the feeling that someone was watching him.

Pay attention, Dickie-boy. Your Spidey senses are tingling.

The watcher was somewhere behind him. Dick didn't know how he knew, only that he did. He'd always had a sixth sense that pulled him out of many jams in his time. He reached the other side of the lot and stalked down a narrow alleyway.

His watcher followed, and as Dick emerged onto a well-lit street, he glanced into the darkness. Two dark eyes glinted from a short distance away. Dick turned back to the road and continued.

If they wanted me dead, they'd have surely shot me in the dark.

Hands deep in the pockets of his jacket, collar turned up, Dick strode down the sidewalk and made his way toward his apartment. He lit a cigarette, ignoring the dark glances he accrued from passersby. Sure, he stood out in the glow of the streetlights, looking like a dodgy drug peddler from an Italian 60s film, but he disappeared in the shadows, melting like ice into a puddle.

He stopped briefly at a nearby bistro and grabbed a cup of hot joe. He ordered it to go and warmed his hand with the paper cup as the night chill surrounded him. He scanned for his pursuer and found no evidence of them still tracking him, but he didn't lower his guard.

A shortcut through a park decorated in marble statues and fountains brought him closer to home. Halfway through the area, he heard a commotion in the bushes. A glance confirmed a homeless pair deep in the throes of love on the ground. He rolled his eyes and tossed his empty cup into a nearby trashcan. Only one area of the park was dark, thanks to a broken light. As Dick passed through this pocket of shadow, footsteps approached from behind.

Dick paused and glanced over his shoulder. A woman stood there, her arms extended and hands shaking as she held a pistol aimed at him.

"I'd be careful with that, darling." Dick slowly turned to face her. "An action like that is permanent. You can't undo murder. Believe me. I've tried."

The woman grimaced. She was thin, and her arms showed the familiar dark lines indicative of an ink-head. Though her face was in shadow, Dick smelled her desperation.

"Money," she grunted through cracked lips. "Now."

Dick remained still, his hands in his pockets. "Who's to say I have any?"

She jabbed the gun forward. "Money."

Dick gave an understanding nod and brought his hand out of his pocket. The woman's eyes flicked to his palm, expecting notes, but Dick brought a cigarette to his lips instead. He cupped the end and lit it, providing a tiny sliver of light on his hardened face. He took a long drag, then expelled the smoke in a thick plume. "I understand your desperation. Only problem is, in a mostly cashless society, how do you expect to mug a man for cash?" He held out his cell phone. "You got the Satiata Cash app?"

The woman raised an eyebrow, teeth audibly chattering. It was no wonder. She wore a thin V-neck shirt with tears at the seams, in the middle of the night. "You think I have a cell phone, chum?"

Dick shrugged and pocketed his phone. "Shame, then. It's all contactless now. A tap of the screen on the screen and *boop*, the cash goes right into your account."

"Bullshit," the woman cried, urgency spat through her teeth. "If I have to kill you and search your body, I'll do it."

Dick's hand clenched against the small wad of notes in his pocket. Truth was, he always carried around *some* cash. If he ever needed to get off the grid for a short time, at least he could pay without leaving a digital trail as to where he'd been. That kind of thinking had helped him out a lot in recent weeks and months.

She came closer, no more than an arm's length between the pair. The gun shook, and even though Dick knew the shot wouldn't be accurate, it would certainly hurt.

"Fine," he announced at last. He took the bundle from his pocket and held it in the air.

The woman's eyes lit up. The gun lowered a fraction.

Dick licked the tip of his finger, the cigarette wobbling precariously when he spoke. "How much?" He slid out one note, then two, then three. His eyes locked onto hers. "Tell me when to stop."

The woman's mouth slowly fell open, as if a hook was in her bottom lip and someone was reeling. The gun lowered a touch, then a touch more. As Dick got halfway through his count, his eyes moved from his money to the woman. The greedy look she gave the notes was clear as crystal. A spaceship could have hovered overhead, and it wouldn't draw her attention away.

He took the opportunity presented to him. With a chop of his hand, he forced the gun out of hers. Before she could exclaim, he grabbed her wrist and brought her closer to his face. "Charity doesn't require force."

Before she could react, he kicked the gun away and slapped a stack of notes in her hand. He closed her hand for her, then turned and left.

She stood there, frozen. By the time she looked up, he was gone.

Dick reached the final stretch of the park and exited onto the street. As he rounded the corner, clapping sounded from overhead.

Valentina smirked down at him from the top of the wall. From where she sat, a typical passerby wouldn't detect the woman watching them. "You're a good guy. You know that, Dick?"

Dick continued walking.

CHAPTER NINE

Valentina hopped down and matched Dick's stride. "I would have blown that bitch's head off."

"No, you wouldn't," Dick replied calmly. He fixed his gaze ahead, neither one of them wanting to meet the other's eye out in public.

"Sure I would," Valentina continued. "Someone aims a gun in my face, and I aim one back. Only difference between the other person with a gun and me is that I'm faster and don't hesitate to kill. It's a luxury I can't afford."

"You have morals," Dick reminded her. "Ethics. It has to fit in with some kind of code."

Valentina grinned. "I'm fueled by two things and two things only. Money and revenge."

"Revenge with positive moral implications," Dick argued. "Also known as 'justice.'"

Valentina theatrically shivered. "Gross."

Dick chuckled.

At Dick's apartment building, he scanned his card and the door unlocked. He held the door open for Valentina, but she was gone. He shook his head, then made his way to his apartment.

When he opened the door, Valentina sat on his couch with a glass of wine in hand and a whiskey on the table.

"You're incorrigible."

Valentina laughed. "Save the fancy words for someone who needs them." The moment Dick closed the door, she rushed at him, threw her arms around his neck, and kissed him deeply.

He responded to her touch, and their bodies pulled together as if by magnets. Her tongue darted into the cavern of his mouth, and his tongue was there to greet it. They barely surfaced for air as he removed her jacket and she removed his. Next, their shirts were gone. Their pants fell in front of the bedroom door.

All went dark from there.

"You don't waste time." Dick chuckled and sat on the side of the bed. He pulled on his underpants, then reached for his whiskey and took a long drink.

"Life is short," Valentina mused, an arm behind her head. "Why fuck around when every second is precious and every moment fragile?"

Dick glanced at her over his shoulder. "Since when did you become a soppy poet?"

Valentina sighed. Now that the fun part was over, her thoughts turned to the job at hand. "I'm not."

Dick narrowed his eyes, then decided to let it go. "Fine." He stood and stretched, turning to find Valentina's eyes on his rear. "Enjoying the view?"

"Always." She rolled onto her side, giving Dick a full view of her body. "You?"

Dick's breath caught. Valentina smiled.

"And what is the price this time, m'lady?" Dick crossed to a chest of drawers and grabbed a pair of pajama pants. "Got a target to kill? Intel to impart? A new contact to source?"

Valentina frowned. "Kind of…"

Dick raised an eyebrow, genuine surprise on his face. "Hold on…you actually need my help? I was kidding."

Valentina rolled her eyes. "Don't get cocky, kid. Everyone can prove themselves useful once in a blue moon."

Dick laughed, his chest swelling with pride. "Hit me with it. What do you need?"

Valentina considered how best to say it. "I'm heading into the jungle, and I need backup."

The humor left Dick's face. "You? The jungle? I know you're a confident woman, Val, but it's dangerous out there. Deadly, even. That place holds nothing but trouble. If it's not the animals or the toxic plants, it's the—"

"Savages, bandits, rogue explorers," Valentina interjected, "ruins, earthquakes, and, oh yeah, the ghosts of Nazis past." She raised her eyebrows. "I know the stories. I know what I'm in for."

Dick rubbed the back of his neck. "Honestly, Val, I'm flattered you'd ask me to accompany you, but let's be honest. We're city folk. Our clients and expertise lie in politics, lies, deceit, money, greed, and power. I don't speak Tarzan, I'm afraid."

Valentina sat up and drew her knees to her chest. "Suck it up, Dick. I'm not talking about you."

Dick frowned.

Valentina got up and crossed to the window, standing in front of the glass in all her glory. She felt Dick's eyes on her, but it was toward the edges of the city where she aimed her gaze.

"I need someone with expertise. Someone who can guide me through the jungle and protect me from the things I don't under-stand. Before you say anything, I know that it's unlike me to pair up with anyone, but the situation is…delicate. Time is limited. I can't wait around and learn all I need to know. I need someone prepped, learned, skilled, and ready to show me the way to where I need to go."

She turned to face Dick. His eyes quickly moved from her body to her face. "I don't follow."

"I'm not surprised." Valentina rolled her eyes, then started putting on her clothes. "I need a guide, and if I'm not mistaken, you know the perfect person."

Dick's eyes narrowed. She could see his brain turning over, trying to connect the pieces. For one of the city's greatest investigators, he struggled when faced with a near-naked woman. She hoped it was only her who had this effect on him.

"Have you forgotten your little pendant friend?" Valentina nudged. "The woman who you came to me to help on your mysterious little adventure?" She skirted the bed, then straddled his lap, now fully dressed. "You owe me, Dick Chambers."

Dick shifted uncomfortably beneath her. "Sokolov?"

"That's the one." Valentina kissed his lips. "Can you put in a good word for me and pass me her number? I'm not sure she'll appreciate my typical methods of dropping in on people unannounced."

Dick looked troubled. "She's gone through enough. She doesn't need to get dragged into whatever shit you're in."

Valentina leaned back, eyebrows high. "Growing protective, are we? If you're not careful, I might find myself growing jealous." She paused. "Nothing happened between you two, did it?"

Dick shook his head and scoffed. "Please. Me and Santana? No. No, it didn't."

Not that you didn't try, eh?

Valentina kissed Dick again. "Don't you worry. I'm not going to draw her in. I simply need a guide. Plain and simple. Once she's taken me to my required destination, she's free to carry on her merry little way."

"I'm not sure she gives guided tours for fun."

Valentina laughed. "I expected nothing less. I'm sure my offer will be enough to spur her sweet little hiney into action."

Dick hesitated, clearly on the fence. Valentina took his face in her hands. "Dick. Trust me."

Their eyes connected. The magnetism that drew them both together flared and asked for satiation. Valentina resisted, but she could tell Dick was struggling. After a moment, he conceded. "Fine. I'll make the call."

Valentina folded her arms.

"Wait. Now?"

Valentina rolled her eyes. "I guess not. Not everyone is a night owl like us. I suppose Little Miss Sunshine will need her beauty sleep."

Dick shook his head and chuckled. "I'd rein that kind of speak back in if I were you."

"Why? Am I going to hurt her feelings?"

Dick's chuckle evolved into a laugh. "You don't know what you're getting yourself into, do you?"

CHAPTER TEN

Santana Sokolov listened to the faint buzzing above her.

It had been coming in regular rhythms now. One minute the buzzing reached a fever pitch. The next it faded away to a near indistinguishable volume. If her ears weren't as attuned to the faint frequencies in the jungle as they were, she would have missed them entirely.

She slapped her neck, destroying a mosquito beneath her palm. They were out in droves, buzzing around in thick clouds, but that wasn't what she was hunting.

What are you looking for?

The tree stood sturdy beneath her. She crawled along the branch, thicker than her waist, a good distance above the ground. Below was filled with darkness, a sudden fall enough to snap a neck and feed you to the jaguars. Above was fog and sky…

…and small black silhouettes looping in wide circles, scanning for something that Santana couldn't determine.

At first, she had thought they were bats until she noticed the four propellers driving the drones over the roof of the jungle. The green LED light on the front of their panels was also something of a giveaway.

Curiouser and curiouser.

She glanced around her, eyes fixing on the spot where a branch cracked. She knew she was in big cat territory, but that didn't sound like a predator. It would likely be a howler monkey or a marmoset poking a curious eye her way. She ducked as the drone performed another flyover.

When it had cleared from sight, Santana brought out the long bullwhip coiled at her side and flicked it in front of her. The lash wrapped around a nearby branch, and she swung across the chasm toward the ancient tree on the other side. She landed deftly on her feet, then pulled out a pair of binoculars.

They lit up the jungle in greens and reds and oranges, the thermal lenses creating a picture beyond what her human eyes could see. She tracked the drones, wondering what they were looking for. In all of her years of exploration, robotics in the jungle meant a limited number of likelihoods.

The first eventuality was the easiest one. A group of explorers believed that they would be able to use technology to penetrate the jungle's depths and discover the hidden relics within. Ruins, bunkers, and caverns littered the island, remnants from the brief Nazi occupation during the Second World War, before all life on the island ceased under a fog of mystery. It was years after that when people discovered Atlantica again.

The second possibility was that the drone had broken, or an intrepid explorer was wandering the jungle and using the drone to draw attention to themselves. They could have been out of flares, and they hoped that the concentric circling would draw in someone to help.

The third, and most likely reason, was that someone believed they had *actually* found something. Though much of the jungle remained unexplored, occasionally a wanderer would stumble upon what they believed to be the discovery of a lifetime. That had led to the discovery of Atlanticores, along with much of the island's gold. Historical weapons, armor, and paraphernalia sometimes surfaced that way, and the drones and technology would act as video cameras and scanners to further evidence their claims.

Santana had stumbled across many drones on the jungle's floor.

Santana stalked along the branch, working her way toward the trunk of the tree. The drone circled back, the buzz growing louder once more.

She took out her cell phone—a battered piece of machinery she'd picked up at a local thrift store—and lined up the camera to take a picture. As her thumb moved to the "capture" button, the screen lit up, flashing light into her face.

She grimaced against the sudden assault. She couldn't see for certain, but she was sure the drone flashed an additional light her way. She shoved the phone in her pocket and fought for balance, jumping down to the lower branches to get out of the drone's sight.

She hugged the trunk, disturbing a bird that took flight and burst into the air. The drone flashed at the bird, revealing a snippet of golden wings. Santana waited, holding her breath. The drone lingered for a few minutes but didn't pursue her. After a moment, it continued on its way.

Santana growled and unlocked her phone. She saw a missed call in her notification tray with a name attached to it that made her want to laugh and shout at the same time.

She tapped the name, then held the phone to her ear. "This better be good."

CHAPTER ELEVEN

Valentina stood on the corner of the casino, staring down into the street.

She wondered what people would think if they looked skyward now. Would they even see her, shaded out against the black backdrop of the night? Would they see a Batman-like figure and expect the Scarecrow or Killer Croc to appear and cause a disturbance in the city?

More than likely, they'd figure the figure was yet another suicidal Atlantican, at their end with life, looking for the only escape they could control.

No one batted an eyelid. No one looked up. Valentina slid her hands into her pockets and tracked the woman arriving from around the corner. The night was young, and the streets were busy, but Valentina could have picked the woman from a lineup without ever having met her.

Santana stalked along the streets with unbridled confidence. Her khaki shorts revealed toned, muscular legs ending in sturdy boots. She wore a short-sleeved top, muddied and covered with stains that Valentina could only guess at. Her hair was in a severe ponytail, and a coiled whip hung from her waist. She'd slung a modest backpack over her shoulders.

"Talk about being prepared for the jungle," Valentina muttered.

She had seen the woman once before, if only briefly, while Dick and Santana sat on the roof of an apartment building. Valentina had stared up at them, both blissfully unaware of her presence. She had also tapped into a few conversations on Dick's phone a few weeks back after installing her software onto his device and caught snippets of their chatter.

Not that Santana should know that, of course. To Santana, she was merely meeting a wealthy stranger.

Santana paused outside the dessert house. The front was violent neon pink, and a set of animated lights plucked and returned a cherry to the top of an enormous cupcake. Desserts lined the window, and 40s swing music escaped through the doors every time patrons entered or exited.

Valentina waited. Santana checked her watch and tapped her toe. People stared as they passed, which gave Valentina a strange sense of power.

Five minutes past their meeting time, Valentina turned and made her way down to street level.

"Miss Sokolov." Valentina turned up her collar then offered a hand.

"Miss Winters."

Valentina's smiling face faltered.

Santana waved a hand. "Don't worry. I'm not going to hand you over to the police. John told me you'd want your identity hidden, but he said it would be funnier this way."

Valentina tried to regain composure. "He did, did he?"

"He was right, too." Santana grinned.

There was no malice in her expression, but Valentina couldn't help but feel she was on the back foot now, and that wasn't a position she enjoyed.

Valentina brought her smile back. She waved a hand at the door. "Can I get you something?"

"I'd never say no to dessert."

The air was warm inside, a stark contrast to the city. As a server took them to their table, Valentina studied the room, taking stock of who was present and where the exits were. Eyes followed them around the room, but she predicted that this was because of the two beautiful women side by side and not because one of them might be Valentina Winters.

The server handed them menus.

"Thank you for meeting with me," Valentina commented. "I have to admit that I'm not overly familiar with people from your profession. I bet someone like you has a lot of stories to—"

Santana raised a finger. "Hold on. *Six* types of cheesecake? That can't be right."

Valentina bit her tongue, growing warmer beneath her collar.

Santana continued, reaching over to Valentina's menu and pointing. "Knickerbocker glories...*with* marshmallow and cream? Jesus. That sounds amazing. A dozen kinds of sweet pie. Holy... half of these flavors I haven't seen in years. Have you ever had kiwi ice cream? *Kiwi!*"

She looked up at Valentina with wide eyes. She was a few years younger than Valentina but acted like a kid, which grated on her dramatically.

"Miss Sokolov, I..." Valentina tried.

"Santana," she replied. "Please, let's forego the formalities." Santana placed a hand on her stomach. "God, I'm starving."

Valentina clenched her fist but bit her tongue. Who was this woman who could conquer a jungle but had problems focusing around desserts? She held back on questions, waiting for Santana to make her order—blackberry cheesecake, tiramisu with kiwi ice cream, and wild fruit strudel.

Valentina settled for a coffee and a biscuit.

Once the server was gone, Valentina studied Santana closely. Santana beamed around the store, then, at last, rested her head on her hands and gazed at Valentina. "So, tell me about your quest. John wasn't specific with the details."

Valentina raised an eyebrow. "John? Oh, you mean Dick?"

Santana scoffed. "Please. You don't give in to a man labeling himself after his genitalia, do you?"

Valentina cocked her head to the side.

"You do!" Santana laughed. "Honestly, he's tried a thousand times to have me call him...well...you know. Do I do it? No. I don't. Know why? Because it builds a man's ego. Any self-righteous woman who can look a guy in the eye and call him Dick has some problems to work out with their counselor if you get my drift."

Valentina's lips thinned. She drew a steadying breath. "Miss Sokolov..."

"Santana." Santana beamed.

"*Miss* Sokolov," Valentina insisted, "or at least you will be until I'm able to get a word in edgeways. You are aware that *I'm* paying you to help me, correct?"

"I am." Santana nodded. "Considerably more than most clients pay, too."

"How much would a client usually pay you?" Valentina asked.

Santana laughed. "Come on. You're playing with me now, aren't you? Don't you do your research before you hire a guide?"

Valentina held her gaze as the server placed their first dishes in front of them. That stole Santana's attention, and as she picked up her spoon, Valentina grabbed her wrist.

Santana frowned. "I suggest you take your hands off me, Miss Winters."

"I suggest you start respecting your client. I'm seriously reconsidering my price."

Santana nodded, then placed her hands in her lap. Her juvenile demeanor faded and intensity grew as she leaned closer to Valentina. "John was right."

It took Valentina a minute to remember who John was. "How so?"

Santana's stern expression broke into a smile, this time not of a little girl, but a mature woman. "You are very easy to play with."

Valentina's nostrils flared.

"See," Santana continued. "Even then. You can't deal with not being the one in the driver's seat, can you?"

Valentina remained silent.

Santana sat back, composing herself. "John told me to test you. Have a little bit of fun. If you can't handle not having some kind of control of the situation, how are you going to handle me leading you through the jungle?"

Valentina's face hardened. "I can learn to release the reins...slightly."

"Completely," Santana returned. "The jungle's a deadly place, Valentina. It's nothing like the city you inhabit. The world out there is dark. Every step is treacherous. Either you trust me fully with your life, or we call off this deal right now. You need to learn to become a passenger, and I'll be your driver. Can you handle that?"

Valentina hesitated.

Santana grinned. "I'm not screwing around. I mean it when I say I'm not a tour guide. I'm making an exception here for you and you alone."

"Why?"

"Two reasons."

Valentina nodded. "Cash."

"Yep." Santana chuckled. "Your offer tells me that you're not screwing around, and…" she placed a battered old cell phone on the table, "I could do with a lump sum injection of dollars."

"And the second?" Valentina asked.

Santana shrugged and relaxed in her chair. There was an air of calm around her that Valentina trusted, now that she had simmered down and stopped screwing with Valentina's patience. "I owe Dick a lot." Her fingers absently strayed to a gold chain around her neck that disappeared beneath the collar of her t-shirt. "Dick says you're good people. I'll trust him with that."

Valentina wasn't sure how to reply to that. As a lone wolf, it wasn't often you got personal references on your character. Most of her clients hired her off the basis of "This girl shoots to kill. Five stars. Would recommend."

"Thanks," Valentina replied curtly.

"Besides," Santana continued, taking her spoon and digging into her cheesecake. "I should probably heed my mama's advice and try to make more friends in this place." She scooped the spoon into her mouth, speaking between mouthfuls. "You keep supplying me with desserts, and we're going to be best friends for life."

Valentina raised an eyebrow. Nearby two middle-aged men at a table for two stared their way. "How about we start with a client-employer relationship and see how we go from there?"

Santana laughed. "Dick has you down to a "T," doesn't he?"

Valentina sipped her coffee and fell silent.

CHAPTER TWELVE

Although Santana led the conversation in the restaurant, Valentina learned surprisingly little about her.

She was impressed. It was a technique she had employed herself on many occasions. The art of communication was a learned one and something that many people failed to harness and utilize. You could talk for hours and tell someone nothing about yourself, or you could get someone to speak for five minutes and learn about their deepest and darkest secrets.

Valentina analyzed Santana, nudging her with questions and allowing her to run her mouth. The most she got from Santana was that she wasn't native to Atlantica—then again, few people were—and that she'd grown up with her parents in the motherland of Russia.

Santana told Valentina of the wilds and her passion for nature. She painted descriptions of glowing green auras in the sky, a canvas exploding with color and dotted with a thousand stars. From this, Valentina drew her conclusion that Santana's internal thermometer must have broken many years ago. For a woman to come from the snow-capped mountains of Russia, all the way to the humid tropic of Atlantica, it was no wonder that shorts and a top were her attire, even when the night chills took over.

Santana briefly mentioned her parents, highlighting that they brought her over to Atlantica when she was young. She didn't talk about them again after that, and soon she was trying to interrogate Valentina and asking her questions about her background.

"Oh, I get it," Santana replied. "Mercenary's code. You're good. You know that?"

Valentina told her she did.

When they emerged from the restaurant, it was almost midnight. A blurry moon shone behind the veil, and as they stood out on the street, Santana drew a long breath. "I suppose we should look at getting you to your destination."

Valentina put her hands in her pockets, fingers blindly tapping on her phone screen. "That would be perfect."

"Come." Santana started up the street.

Valentina didn't follow.

Santana stopped, turned over her shoulder. "This isn't going to work if you're going to trip at the first hurdle. It's a nice evening for a stroll. Let's get going."

Valentina pointed with her thumb as a sleek taxi pulled up curbside. "No offense, I'd rather cut out some dawdle time."

Santana laughed, then climbed into the cab. Valentina closed the doors behind them and announced their destination. A digitized voice confirmed the instruction before the car smoothly pulled out into traffic.

"Smooth," Santana commented. "I don't often use public transport."

"Scared of technology?" Valentina nodded at Santana's pocket where the cell phone pressed against the material.

"No. I prefer fresh air to the stink of cigarettes, booze, and body odor."

Valentina glanced out the tinted windows at the civilians

strolling past. To an outsider, it might seem like any other city, but Valentina spotted the sour expressions and the bravado of clusters of thugs out on the prowl. "You best stay away from my bedroom then," she quipped.

The taxi journey was smooth, and for the most part, they remained quiet. Twenty minutes later the cab pulled up outside a large factory house promising clothing and shoe repairs. A group of men and women loitered on the corner, out of range of the street light, and Valentina paused a moment before exiting.

The cab asked for its fare. Valentina touched her phone to the pay pad. A chime confirmed the transfer.

"Funny," Santana muttered.

Valentina glanced at her.

"Well," Santana continued. "I'd have thought a mercenary who wanted to be a ghost in the system wouldn't use her cell phone to pay. Wouldn't cash make more sense for you?"

Valentina fixed her with a look. Truth was, she'd hidden her bank account behind a wall of fog and misdirection. The bank's servers were surprisingly easy to modify. As long as you weren't transferring huge chunks of change from one account to another, it was simple to change your name and a few basic details—if you knew how. "If I'm to trust you without question, you're going to have to refrain from questioning my practices. I'll admit that I have no clue how you operate and I don't care to know. The less you know about what I do, the better."

Santana shrugged. "Fair enough."

They stepped out into the street. The cab drove silently away, performing a U-turn and heading back in the direction they'd come. The road ahead continued for a short distance before meeting a metal fence surrounded by several caution signs. Valentina couldn't read them from here, but she knew the gist. They were all warnings about the dangers that lay ahead.

Santana adjusted the paraphernalia around her waist and resettled the straps on her backpack. "Are you ready, princess?"

Valentina shot her a look. "Be *very* careful how you proceed with me. In the jungle, no one can hear you scream."

"Oh, I know." Santana walked ahead of Valentina.

Valentina watched her for a few paces, hating the feeling of her journey held in another person's hands. She relented and fell in step behind as they approached the group loitering on the corner.

Santana showed no signs of concern at their presence, even when a woman stepped in front of her and blocked her way. The woman was short, but muscles corded her arms beneath her jacket. Valentina could tell she worked out. She'd also shaved the sides of her head. She pulled a drag from a joint in her mouth, and the air filled with the stink of marijuana. "Going somewhere, gorgeous?"

Santana replied, "Isn't everyone always going *somewhere?*"

The woman smirked. "Seems late for two pretty pieces like yourselves to be wandering out in the streets alone. Especially this part of town."

A couple of deeper chuckles came from the shadows. The woman handed the joint to one of her chums.

Santana cocked her head. "We'll be fine, I'm sure."

"That a fact?" a man asked, moving beside the woman. He was a full head taller than her and wore leather pants and a long jacket. Despite the lack of sunlight, dark shades sat on his face.

"That's a fact," Santana replied.

Valentina pulled up beside her, talking to Santana from the side of her mouth. "Don't antagonize them. I've got this."

Santana raised an eyebrow with an entertained expression on her face.

"Way I see it," the man continued, "is we've got two little dollies in the ass-end of nowhere and no one to play with them." He took a long drag, stretching his time between words. "How's about you play with us, little dollies?"

Santana burst out laughing. The man's mirth faded, replaced

with a snap of anger. The woman put a hand on his chest as he took a step forward, her demeanor unfaltering.

"What my associate means," she explained, "is that we could have some fun together." She jerked her thumb at two more men and another woman emerging from the shadows, the five of them blocking the path entirely. "We're good people. We've got a place out back, real comfy. I know my associates would appreciate having two beauties like you to…" She drew a deep breath, eyes narrowing. "Play with."

Valentina spoke before Santana got a chance to. "If you think you've found two women ready to bend over and 'play' with you, then I'm afraid you and your 'associates' are very much mistaken." She moved her hand to her holster. "Unfortunately, we've got places to be, and playtime is long since over."

"Nice," Santana whispered.

Valentina glanced at her.

The woman frowned. The four beside her shuffled, and one of the men cracked his knuckles. "That's a real shame," she commented. "Because we don't take no for an answer." Her eyes flickered to Santana's bullwhip. "And you seem prepared for some fun."

"Hold on…" Santana waved her hands in front of her. "Can we come back to 'associates'? It's 2027, not 1946. Who the hell talks like this anymore?"

The man growled again and tried to take another step. The woman held him back, but only just. "Watch your tone in front of my friend, miss. I can't hold him on his leash forever."

Valentina scanned the group, sensing that things were about to break. Her fingers twitched over the butt of her pistol as a pregnant silence passed between them. "Last chance, *friends*. Slink back into your little hovel before things get…explosive."

The woman spotted Valentina's pistol for the first time. She gave a derisive snort. Then her hand flashed to her gun.

Valentina drew her pistol, then aimed it at the woman's leg in the hope that a severe injury might mute the rest of the group. While she would kill when necessary, she didn't much like the idea of slaughtering five pieces of scum in one sweep. It would be easy, sure. Would it be worth it?

Probably.

Valentina's finger flexed on the trigger, but before she could shoot, a loud *crack* broke beside her.

Before she knew it, the bullwhip lashed out in front of them, sliced a clean red line in the woman's hand, and ripped the pistol free before drawing it toward Santana.

Santana expertly caught the gun on the retreat, then tossed it into her spare hand. Her face was a mask of dogged determination as she snapped the whip again, coiling its lash around the man's neck who had broken from the pack and charged at the pair.

The man's hands rose to his throat as his face turned pink. The three others kicked into action, all reaching for their weapons.

Valentina moved by instinct, discarding the choking man and the short woman nursing her hand injury. Foregoing her pistol, she fished into her pocket and pulled out a handful of small metal balls. She tossed them to the ground around the feet of the two men who now clutched knives in their hands.

Valentina smirked. "What? Can't be trusted with firearms?"

The men's expressions curdled as she drew their attention to her face instead of the tiny spheres surrounding their feet. Valentina laughed, then thumbed the trigger in her pocket. Blue-white light erupted as the bearings sparked and fanned their network of electric pulses. The men grew rigid, and a strange guttural cry emerged from their throats. They fell to the ground, arms clamped to their sides, as a slight stink of urine mixed with what remained of the weed.

"Cool toy." Santana's arm muscles were taut as the large man struggled against her, his face a sick shade of purple.

"Thanks. You too. Maybe try not to let that one live out his asphyxiation dreams, though."

Santana flipped her wrist and drew back her hand. The whip obeyed, uncoiling from the man's throat. He sputtered and gasped for breath. The woman with the bleeding hand glared at Santana, face burning with rage. Behind her, the second woman bared her teeth, looking ready to charge them both.

Valentina deactivated the electric net and turned her attention to the other two. The second woman ran, jumping at Santana as she drew her whip back ready for the strike.

Another *crack* split the air.

Something warm and wet hit Valentina's face.

Santana gasped, her hand drawn back, the bullwhip not yet thrown into action.

The woman crumpled to the ground, one side of her face missing, drowning in a puddle of her blood.

"What the…" Santana managed before Valentina grabbed her hand and dragged her away.

She pulled Santana toward the building, running as fast as she could until they receded into the shadows and around the corner. Four more shots cracked through the night, then a fifth. Valentina looked back to find the two women dead on the ground and the large man clutching his chest as blood seeped through his clothing. The other two men remained unconscious, unmoving until another three shots fired. One took out the large man's head. The other two found their beds in the remaining men's chests.

"What the fuck is happening?" Santana leaned around the corner to try and get a look at their attacker.

Valentina looked past Santana to where a dark figure emerged on the rooftop of the building across the road. Backlit dimly by the moon's glow, she recognized the shape of the man. She didn't linger as two more shots sped toward them, narrowly missing her feet.

"Run," Valentina urged, a word that she hated to use when faced with danger. "Now."

They skirted the edge of the building, clinging to the shadows. The pebble-dotted paving led them between the building walls and a corrugated iron fence. As they emerged at the back of the building, a floodlight activated, bathing the area in light.

Agricultural machines stood sentinel over pallets stacked in towering piles. Beyond them was a chain-link fence topped with barbed wire, easily twenty feet in height.

"Only one way out," Santana commented.

Valentina scoffed. "You're kidding, right?" She glanced up at the pallet towers. "They'll topple the moment we get higher than ten feet up."

A shot rang out. Metal *pinged* nearby.

"You got a better plan?" Santana asked.

"We could face them," Valentina replied. "Take them by surprise. You've got firepower, right?"

Santana tapped the small pistol holstered to her waist. Valentina didn't recognize the model but assumed it would only help in a situation where the target was within twenty feet.

Santana looked longingly up at the tower. The floodlight switched off, not sensing movement in a few moments. Valentina thought she could make out the sounds of someone climbing nearby.

"He's coming," she commented.

"He?"

Valentina shook her head. "Not now."

"Not to be pedantic, but if you plan to face him head-on, why run in the first place?"

Valentina's jaw clenched. *Why does this girl insist on questioning my every move?* "Do you trust me?"

"No. Do you trust me?"

"No," Valentina admitted.

They stared at each other for a long moment. The sounds of climbing faded. Valentina heard footsteps on the rooftop.

Santana narrowed her eyes. "Look, we're about to dive into *my* territory to get to a place that *you* want to go. You hired me to get us there, and I will do that by any means necessary." She glanced at the tower. "You want to get into the jungle? Let's fucking go."

Valentina conceded, running to the side of the tower. Santana ran to the other side, and soon they were both climbing.

The tower wobbled precariously, swaying with each urgent move.

Santana called, "In sync. We need to keep balance to stop it from toppling. You're going too fast."

Valentina tutted. "In case you hadn't noticed, if we don't go fast, we may die."

Santana grumbled but sped up. The fence fell away before them, and soon they rose above the barbed wire.

Valentina glanced at the rooftop where the dark figure silently stood, watching them both with interest. The rifle rested in his hand by his side, a large one with a scope.

"Ready?" Santana asked. "On the count of three, we jump. One…"

The man lowered his hood.

"Two…"

The man brought up the rifle, lining up the shot.

"Three!"

Valentina raised a middle finger to the man and leaped over the fence. The pallets shook under strain, the tower leaning beyond the point of balance as wooden squares crashed and clattered to the ground. Among it all came another sharp *crack* as the report from another gunshot sounded.

Valentina heard the bullet whistle above her. The muddy ground rose to meet her. Trees lined the way a few feet ahead, and as both she and Santana landed, they tucked into a roll to soften the blow before sprinting into the cover of the trees.

A final shot found its way toward them, catching the side of Valentina's ankle as she lost herself in the foliage, the thick, wet stink of the jungle waiting to meet her.

Santana ran beside her. The pair raced forward until the city vanished, and all that remained was trees.

CHAPTER THIRTEEN

The man watched the pair disappear into the undergrowth with a dark glint in his eyes.

Was he worried about Valentina's escape? No. Not one bit. Many things in this world concerned him, but there were also many things to relish: the scent of freshly poured petroleum, hungry for the spark of the match, the first gasp of panic as the cold steel of the knife met the throat of your victim...

...and watching your target run as a fresh buzz surged through your body at the excitement of the hunt.

Where was the fun in a static kill? You had to earn the pride of your trophy. You had to incite the challenge and overcome the adversity as your target worked to escape or hunt you in return.

A shiver ran down his spine.

Others had warned him not to antagonize Valentina. When the wasp's nest was larger than a Volvo and heaving with danger, the best approach would be to sneak up and take it out in one quick flash. Valentina had earned her title as one of the greatest mercenaries ever seen, and he knew the risks in kicking that wasp's nest.

Still, how would he earn his title as the greatest if he simply snuck up and took her out in one blow?

He could have shot her. When she was on the roof of the opera house, he could have ended her then and there—he liked to think. Instead, he laughed, relishing the panic and the retreat as she melted into the shadows and faded from view. He had even left his token deliberately, letting her know who she was dealing with. Life was a jumble of board games, and he was in it to win it.

He stayed there for some time, high in the air, occasionally shooting randomly into the trees. Birds took wing in droves, and somewhere behind him came cries of alarm and declarations that the AJS were on their way.

It would be too late. It would always be too late. Just as it was for his fresh kills as their blood seeped into the cracks in the pavement below.

Five minutes passed. He stared up at the moon, a mask of triumph on his face as he soaked in its light. When he was sure they had a sufficient head start, he climbed down and worked his way into the trees. Their imprinted footsteps left tracks for him to follow.

He wondered how far they would take him before they faded or he lost their path.

He supposed it didn't matter. The challenge was on. The hunt was in motion, and for a man who hadn't yet braved the jungle, the thrill of the challenge set his blood blazing.

Ready or not, Valentina Winters. Here I come...

CHAPTER FOURTEEN

"Who the hell was that?" Santana asked.

They had run for some time, side by side, the darkness taking over as Valentina placed her trust in the jungle girl and hoped a bullet wouldn't penetrate her back. Eventually, they slowed down. The cloying heat of the jungle air caused her clothes to stick to her body. At last, Santana stopped by a sudden break in the trees as the roaring rush of a river blocked their path.

Valentina rested her hands on her hips but soon regained her breath. Santana was less fit—likely not stimulated by experimental serum—and bent over with her lips pursed, taking in huge lungfuls.

"I don't know," Valentina replied at last.

Santana turned on her. "Bullshit. What mercenary doesn't know who's got a target on their back?"

"A mercenary facing another mercenary." Valentina narrowed her eyes. "You know our entire job is to hide our identity and not let our targets find out who we are?"

Santana sat by the waterside. She scooped river water into a flask and took a long draught. Some of the liquid spilled and moistened her t-shirt. Valentina chuckled.

"What?"

"You look like every man's idea of a perfect beer commercial. Only with water instead of beer."

"I'll take that as a compliment." Santana glanced across the river, a thirty-foot span. The water foamed and frolicked, moving faster than Valentina cared to guess. "How're your swimming skills?"

Valentina laughed. Santana looked at her evenly. Valentina's face dropped. "You're not serious?"

"We have to cross the river," Santana insisted. "How else are we going to get to the other side?"

Valentina touched her chin theatrically. "Let me think...boat? Bridge? Helicopter?"

Santana broke into laughter. "You're in the wilds now, princess. None of your gadgets or gizmos will help you across the rough terrain. It's all about survival out here. Do you have the slightest idea how to start a fire from tinder and rock? Could you identify the edible fungi from the poisonous? How do you counteract the venom of a brown cave tarantula?"

Valentina frowned.

Santana rose to her feet, one hand rifling through her backpack. "I mean it, princess. It's you and me and the elements now. Better get used to it. This isn't going to be an easy ride."

"Life never is." Valentina stepped to the river bank and stopped by Santana. "Go on then."

Santana pulled a length of rope from her pack. The coil was thicker than the whip, and one end of the line had a weight bound to it. She took a step back and spun the weight around her head, flicking her wrist to gain momentum as a *whooshing* sound followed. With a graceful hurl, she flung the rope across the river toward a tree trunk on the far bank. She let the line slip between her fingers. It unraveled rapidly, stopping only when the weight *thumped* at the base of the tree.

Santana chewed her lip. "Sometimes takes a few attempts."

"Grappling guns don't."

Santana pulled the line back in, fighting against the current as the rope slipped beneath the water. "Get yours out then and show me how to do it."

"I didn't bring it with me." Valentina frowned, annoyed at the oversight.

"Then keep your mouth shut," Santana retorted.

Valentina bit her tongue. This woman was helping her. She didn't need to make things more awkward than they had to be. Valentina sat on the bank, watching as Santana retrieved the line and went for a second toss.

Valentina glanced over her shoulder, keeping an eye out for anyone who might be following. She was almost certain there would be no way he could track her and Santana through the undergrowth, but she could never be one hundred percent sure. A one percent discrepancy could be the difference between living and dying in the jungle.

Santana made the catch on the third attempt. The line whirled around the trunk and caught itself, anchoring the weight between the tangle of roots. Santana pulled the rope taut and crafted a loop around a nearby tree. She tied a knot that Valentina hadn't seen before, and after a minute or two, she was satisfied with her work.

"Ready?" She nodded at the far bank.

Valentina stared across the water. Even with the rope, this was going to be a treacherous path.

Valentina took one step into the current. The water froze her toes through her boots. "What about devices?"

Santana held up a plastic bag. "Put everything in here. I'll carry it in my backpack."

Valentina looked skeptical.

"Waterproof," Santana confirmed. "Don't worry. I'll double bag it."

Valentina waited.

"Fine, *triple* bag it." Santana held open the plastic pouch.

Valentina removed her cell phone and placed it inside. She also put the triggers for the various devices inside the bag but made an educated guess at the paraphernalia that could withstand getting a little bit soggy. When she finished, the bag was half-filled with an array of devices that caught Santana's interest.

"Should I be worried?"

Valentina smirked. "Stay on my good side, and you won't have to be."

Santana led the way into the water. The first few steps were okay. The bank was a little slippery, but the current wasn't too strong. On the fifth step, the bank sloped down, and Santana hung expertly onto the line, her body disappearing beneath the water, only her head and arms poking out.

Valentina took a leaf out of Santana's book and prepared herself for the drop. Her hands gripped the line as water rushed against her body, freezing every cell. The pressure was tremendous, and Valentina was impressed by Santana's resilience. Their bodies floated behind them, caught in the torrent as they shimmied with only their hands, moving fist over fist until they were halfway across the river.

"Still with me?" Santana called over the rushing roar.

Valentina told her she was and refocused her attention on ensuring her hands didn't slip. One over the other, then one over the other, they went. Valentina tried to bring her legs down but discovered that the current was too strong. She had no idea how deep it was, only that it seemed she kept feeling the pressure of objects floating by her. A fish leaped out of the water by her head, startling her before it splashed back under.

Santana chuckled. "Yellow-bellied trout. Beautiful things, ain't they? Don't like to be disturbed though." Another three leaped out of the water, one soaring over Santana. She laughed. "See?"

Valentina rolled her eyes. When they finally reached the far bank, Valentina felt the current's grip lessen. Another few feet and she could stand again. She walked the final distance and caught up with Santana, who was shaking herself off and beaming. "Refreshing, huh?"

Valentina shrugged. "Something like that, I suppose." She held out a hand.

"What?"

"My items, please."

Santana nodded as she realized what Valentina was asking. She took out the plastic bag of Valentina's items and handed them over. "No screwing around with you, is there? Don't even want to pat yourself down before you arm yourself to the teeth again."

"You got a towel?" Valentina cast a doubtful look at Santana's backpack.

"No."

"Well then…" Valentina pocketed her effects, but not before checking her cell phone was still in working order. The screen illuminated and worked with no problem. She held it up to Santana. "Thanks."

"Don't mention it." Santana busied herself with wringing out the loose parts of her clothing, although much of it would remain damp as they continued their march and gained ground on Merchant's Grove. She poured the remaining water out of her boots and finally squeezed the water from her ponytail. "Surprised your wig didn't fall off."

Valentina, who had been busy removing her items of wet clothing, looked up. "Excuse me?"

"The wig," Santana repeated. "If that's your real hair, I'd think about getting a new hairdresser."

Valentina's blood heated. "Not that it's any of your business, but yes, this is a wig."

"A disguise," Santana interjected. "I get it. Must be tough doing what you do, having to hide who you are for the sake of your career. There's a certain duology with mercenary work, isn't there? Daylighting in one guise, moonlighting in another?"

You have no idea. Valentina settled with, "Something like that."

"Don't worry," Santana continued. "I won't interrogate you at all. You have your secrets. I have mine. Let's gain some ground and get some height, shall we? Heat rises, and the land is drying on the incline. If I remember correctly, there's a hill a few clicks from here where we'll be able to get a good vantage point on the rest of the jungle."

"If you remember correctly? Doubting your abilities?"

Santana laughed and brushed off the comment. "Not really. It never hurts to appear modest. Come on, before your friend works out the quicker route across the river."

"Quicker route?" Valentina looked up and down the river. Now that they were on this side, she had a perfect view of the bend. A short distance upriver was a long wooden bridge arcing atop the torrent, wide enough to allow a single car passage.

She turned to glare at Santana, but the woman was disappearing into the forest, a flashlight in her hand illuminating the path ahead.

CHAPTER FIFTEEN

Santana panted as she led the way up the endless hill.

The endless hill. That's how Valentina thought of it in her head. She'd climbed many hills in her life, trekked up many inclines, but those were mostly out in the open, where you could see your progress. Now she was surrounded by towering trees, ancient forestry that long surpassed the years she'd spent on this Earth. Their boughs and branches twisted around each other, trapping the dense heat and blocking the world from sight. All was green —and tree trunks.

And there were bugs.

Clouds of them flew around the pair. Valentina grew steadily more irritated as she slapped her skin and killed dozens after dozens of the tiny black things. Occasionally one would bite. Valentina's neck and hands were soon covered in small red marks that itched and burned.

Santana strode on, never batting an eye at their presence. Valentina growled. The path upward still showed no sign of relenting. "Aren't mosquitoes and midges supposed to gather near water sources? There's no bog or creek around here, is there?"

Santana laughed, her carefree attitude starting to grate on Valentina. "They must have followed from the river. With the air so warm and wet, they can follow anything warm-blooded. Maybe we'll be lucky enough to pass some hogs or even a wild-cat, and it'll distract them."

Valentina slapped her hands in quick succession, then waved away a bug that flew in her sight. "Don't they bother you?"

Santana shrugged. "You kind of get used to them after a while. Spend some time in the jungle, and you learn not to get so worked up. The warmer you are, the more likely they are to suckle from your flesh. Keep it calm and cool, and they'll leave you alone eventually."

Easier said than done.

A short while later they had to climb over a fallen log. It was so large and thick that it was a wonder it was ever able to stand without crushing itself under its weight. Santana used her whip to make a handhold from a snapped piece of branch, then offered Valentina a helpful hand. She accepted it begrudgingly, her temper simmering close to the boiling point as they landed on the other side and there was still no sign of relief.

Valentina asked the question she hated to voice. "How much farther?"

Santana looked ahead. "Twenty minutes, maybe? This log marks the final stretch of the hill." She put her hands on her hips and gave Valentina a funny look. "Don't tell me you're tired."

Valentina's jaw clenched. "No. I'm not tired physically. I'm tired of this cloud of assholes following every move I make. You said the top of this hill is open, right?"

"Right."

"Then let's get out into the goddamn open." Valentina lowered her head and increased her pace, sweeping past Santana, who merely watched her with an amused expression. Santana rolled her eyes and carried on.

At Valentina's increased speed, that twenty minutes became

fifteen. Finally, the trees thinned as the incline lessened, and soon Valentina had an uninterrupted view of the night sky. The veil of fog was still present, but it was thinner up here, and for the first time in a long while Valentina could see clusters of stars, distant swirls of galaxies, and even a few constellations that she hadn't encountered since her years away from Atlantica.

"Beautiful, huh?" Santana appeared through the trees. Her hands clutched the straps of her backpack as she looked skyward. "You sometimes forget that there's more to this world than Atlantica."

Valentina's mouth stayed open, her eyes tracking and attempting to count the stars. "How is this possible?"

"Easy. Even the tallest buildings in the city are less above sea level than we are now. The mountains and hills of Atlantica climb for thousands of feet, giving a much greater vantage point." She slid her backpack off and stretched out her arms. "Not only that, but the light pollution from the city aggravates the veil, bouncing back additional light that blocks any view of the night sky. Look."

Santana pointed back the way they had come. Although they couldn't see any real definition of the city from here, it was clear to see where it stood.

A large dome of pinkish-yellow light shone in the distance, the city held under a bubble of light pollution. Valentina looked on either side of it, then behind her, surprised to find that there was only one bubble. The rest of her view was of more forest, fading into denser fog far in the distance and the canopy of stars above them.

Santana moved to the center of the open space, toward a makeshift firepit with charred edges. She drew out a stack of sticks from her backpack—presumably collected as Valentina stormed ahead—and placed them into a conical shape in the center. "It's amazing what you miss living in the heart of the city, right?"

Valentina was speechless. She had spent most of her life in

cities, learning the intricacies of their streets, subways, alleys, and politics. Her clients were power-hungry, overly rich bastards with grudges to win and points to make. The city had beauty, the warmth of hot air blown from the subway into the street, the sweet stink of doughnuts and confectionary on street corners and carts, the neon lights of the busier districts at night.

This was different. Valentina looked up at the sky and remembered doing the same thing all those years ago in a dojo outside the city proper, in a place where the light couldn't touch and night could rule supreme.

Countless nights in training flashed before her, numerous runs around the building…

She thought of the dark figure.

Warmth reached Valentina's back. She turned as something crackled into life and found Santana nursing the growing flames. "For a girl with a mean mouth, you sure are quiet." Santana smirked, a playful gesture.

Valentina took one more look at the stars and the surrounding trees, then wandered closer to the flames.

"You'll notice the bugs have gone now," Santana highlighted. "They don't stick around much for fire. Those who do get lured in and there they build their final Viking funeral." She tossed a long, thin bundle to Valentina. "Here."

"What is it?" The bundle was the length of Valentina's forearm and wrapped in cloth. Something hard was inside, and it rattled around as she loosened the drawstring.

"A place to dry your clothes." Santana presented her bundle and showed Valentina how to set it up. When she finished, two triangular ends were connected by a long pole, forming the shape of an extended tent. Santana removed her socks and top and laid them over the rod. "If you shift it nearer the fire, you'll dry out in no time. I know how uncomfortable it can be to walk around in soggy clothing."

Valentina set up her frame. "Then why make us swim?"

"Testing your mettle. The river is the first of many obstacles in this place. Those who can't handle the river won't get far. Figured if you tried to drown, I'd save you. If you gave up after reaching the shore, it's an easy walk back."

Valentina couldn't fault her for that. The logic made sense in a twisted way. She removed her jacket and shirt and laid them over the line. "Still…it's not like we could have gone back the way we came."

Santana was now busy with a metal pot and unsealing a bag of food. She poured the contents into the pot and placed it on a frame she had built over the fire. "Yeah, I was going to ask you about that. Care to explain what happened back there?"

Valentina considered this as her hands hovered over her pants. Her thumbs tucked into the waistband, but she didn't feel entirely comfortable presenting herself to this near-stranger.

Santana rolled her eyes. "Get over yourself, princess. We're in the wilds now. No one but the mosquitos gives a rat's ass if you strip naked and roll around in the mud."

Valentina drew a breath.

"Here." Santana stood and stripped down to her underpants. She threw the remaining clothing onto the frame and returned to her cooking. "They'll be dry quick enough. Then you'll be back to your gussied state."

Valentina removed her pants and folded them over the frame. She dragged the poles closer to the fire, mindful of Santana's eyes lingering on her. "What?"

"Maybe I'll take back what I said. You have a body carved by the gods. You'll have to share your workout routine when we get rolling in the jungle again."

Valentina sat beside her clothes, watching the fire.

"Careful, princess," Santana remarked. "Might want to pull those away from the heat a touch." She pointed at a corner of the fabric where embers licked it. "Stay there any longer, and all your clothes will burn to a crisp." Santana looked her up and down again. "Not that anyone out here would complain."

Valentina rolled her eyes, then reached for her pistol. The safety clicked off, and she casually aimed the barrel at Santana.

Santana continued stirring the pot, not in the least bit fazed. "Stand down, princess."

"About that. Just because you have me in your homeland and you think you rule this roost, let's refrain from pet names and forgetting for one moment that, whether we're in the jungle or the city, I could kill you in a heartbeat."

"Did I touch a nerve?" Santana looked up and let out a tired breath.

Valentina cocked her head. "I'm no princess."

Santana nodded. "Noted. Anything else?"

Valentina considered this. "Since you ask, how about no more trials, no more tribulations, and no more games with your character or mine. I've only been in your company for a few hours and your Jack-in-the-box approach to nurturing some kind of working relationship with us has me exhausted. You be you. I'll be me. We work as a team until we get to where I want to go, and we go our separate ways. Deal?"

Santana nodded. "Deal."

Valentina held the gun steady at her forehead, wondering what kind of predicament she'd find herself in if she took Santana out now. She didn't want to. Santana was her guide and seemed to be a good friend of Dick's.

Still, some instincts never die.

"You finished with that?" Santana pointed her spoon at the pistol.

Valentina waited a moment longer, irritated by the lack of fear in Santana's eyes. Any time she pointed her gun at people, they knew she meant business. To be under the watchful eye of Valentina's barrel was akin to withering as an ant under the concentrated light and fire of a magnifying glass.

This girl…

Valentina lowered the pistol and placed it on the ground within reach. "What have we got?"

Santana raised a spoonful of orange and brown slop. "Reconstituted meat, beans, and sweet potato mash."

Valentina brought her hand to her head and sighed.

"Problem?"

Valentina shook her head. "Sounds delicious."

Santana chuckled. "You might want to tell your face that."

CHAPTER SIXTEEN

Santana shaded her eyes with her hand and swept her gaze over the forest.

"Down there." She pointed toward more of the green canopy. "About four clicks north and we'll reach our next checkpoint."

Valentina scraped her bowl clean. The reconstituted meal was surprisingly delicious. Santana had packed their bags, and thankfully their clothes were considerably dryer although some of the creases and crevices were still a touch damp, and she was now eager to get the pair moving.

Valentina set her bowl beside the bags and joined Santana. "How can you tell? Everything out here looks the same." She pointed east. "There's some trees." She pointed west. "There are some more trees." She pointed north. "More trees over there."

Santana raised an eyebrow. "You get familiar with things over time. Look, over there is where the river bends. See that slight break in the trees, where a shadow presses in an 'S' shape? The leaves are slightly darker, too, because of the mangrove clusters. The water is deeper there as well, but you can't *see* that from here. Just note that if you ever find yourself in the mangrove spots, you *will* get attacked in the water."

"By what?"

"I'd rather not say." Santana pointed elsewhere. "Over there where the trees rise, that's the road to the Wagner Bunker. It's aptly named because the first discoveries salvaged an entire Nazi German troop and their effects. The sergeant in charge, Walter Wagner, stationed his troops there, but no one ever found the bodies. The only evidence of who was left was a series of notes and some carvings on the wall."

Valentina counted on her fingers. "Watery death, Nazi ghost house, what else have you got?"

Santana laughed. "More to the east, where that dome of leaves rises from the sea of green? That looks like a hill, but it's a mother tree rising above its children. Beneath the canopy, it's an isolated trunk for meters and meters, but above ground, we see only more green." She pointed slightly off-center from the mother tree. "That ribbon of smoke curling to the sky is likely another set of explorers searching for ruins or the supposed hidden treasures in the jungle."

"You've spent some time out here, haven't you?"

Santana turned back to their items and bagged the last of their utensils. "You didn't hire me for nothing, did you? The wilds are my second home. They're so much more interesting than the city. There's so much out here to discover, things to do, plants and animals to find. Once you get a whiff of nature, you might find that you never want to return to the city."

"Do you?" Valentina nudged.

"What?" Santana asked.

"Ever go to the city?" She thought about her first encounter with Santana, a girl in expedition gear standing outside a modern, metropolitan dessert house.

"Of course. Even a girl like me has to live among regular folk from time to time." She shouldered her pack. "Are you ready to get going?"

"As I'll ever be," Valentina replied.

Santana laughed and patted Valentina's shoulder as she strode past and led them deeper into the wilderness.

An hour passed in relative silence. Santana blazed the way ahead, though with every step the bushes and plants seemed determined to trip them up and block their path.

Santana dipped into her bag at a wall of thorns, soon revealing a broad machete wrapped in cloth.

"A woman of many tricks," Valentina commented.

Santana waggled her eyebrows. She hacked at the brush and soon cleared a path wide enough for them to pass, though the thorns continued to snatch and clutch at Valentina's clothing.

The jungle was alien to Valentina. Led only by Santana's flashlight, the trees and the darkness behind pressed in on her. The jungle calls were many, with insects chirping, birds whistling, and larger animals scuffling and snorting out of her vision. On a couple of occasions, yowling from a big cat broke the air, and Valentina tightened her grip on her pistol.

There was little to mark their progress. While Santana clearly recognized where she was heading, all Valentina knew was that they were passing through an untidy tangle of vines, trees, and flowers. Only on a couple of occasions did the density of the trees open up to allow them to breathe, and in those tiny pockets of the forest, Valentina couldn't believe what they found.

Ruins, built with crudely carved stone, stood erect and silent. The corners were crumbling, and the ivy was fighting to claim back the land. Some were outposts, small stations of salvation that explorers and presumably soldiers once occupied. Others were significant structures with multiple rooms and carvings of German swastikas on the side and crooked wooden doors that barely clung to their frames.

Santana explained the brief German occupation in the 1940s,

detailing how the Nazis believed they had found something special when they stumbled across Atlantica. In the dying years of the Second World War, American troops had picked up on the island's location and sent in their forces. Though they were able to find the Germans, they never fully discovered their fascination with the little hunk of island cast out in the middle of the ocean.

"From what I've read, the end of the occupation is still a mystery," Santana informed her. "One minute, there was a battle. The next…" She pulled her hands apart, miming an explosion.

"A bomb?"

"No." Santana hacked at a thick vine that blocked their passage. "Just…nothing. One minute they were there, the next…gone."

Valentina looked up into the boughs as something jumped above her head. She caught a glimpse of something large and black with long arms. Then it was gone. "Mystery seems to covet this island."

"You can say that again."

The path ahead sloped down, the air growing progressively cooler with each step. After another hour of walking, they crested yet another hill. The smells in the air changed as they entered trees that bore clusters of fruits and stray pockets of flowers that furled their blooms under the moonlit sky.

After a stretch, the ground grew rocky. Crude steps snaked ahead, giving Valentina the occasional view of the forest. She had no idea how far they had come, but she couldn't see the city anymore. Even the faint dome of pink light had faded behind the mist, and now all that remained was trees.

Valentina didn't know Santana had paused and was watching her until she spoke. "Glad you bought a guide now, aren't you?"

Valentina hated to admit it, but she was right.

"Many people try to survive the jungle." Santana continued to lead. "Few succeed. It's intimidating, the wild. Everything looks the same unless you know where to look. You have to understand your compass, learn the map of the sky, hone your skills in bushcraft, survival, creatures—"

A loud yowling came from nearby. Santana flinched. It was the first time Valentina had seen her grow genuinely tense, and the sight of it made her uneasy.

"What was that?"

Santana put a finger to her lips, tilting her head to listen better.

Only the jungle was talking.

Valentina opened her mouth to speak, but the yowling came once more, louder and furious.

Santana turned to face up the hill. Her hand reached for her whip. "Stay close."

Valentina looked ahead into the darkness. Their flashlight only stretched so far, and beyond all was in blackness. Santana didn't wait. She was already moving, eyes fixed on the black.

Valentina ran to keep up, casting only a brief furtive glance over her shoulder. Her skin prickled as another yowl rent the night.

What the hell is that?

Santana moved fast, her feet making barely a sound. Around them, columns of stone leaned precariously above piles of rubble. The stairs were intermittent with mud and the tracking of feet. Trees wove around them, and at one point, Santana hopped over the rotting carcass of a feral hog.

The breeze rushed past Valentina's face. The path led to an opening where the trees parted and made way for a campsite of sorts. A handful of stone buildings provided shelter, built like primal cabins, some with holes in the side, others shrouded with vines and ivy. A frayed rope ladder hung from an outpost that looked out over the forest and rose above the trees. Its platform looked precarious at best. In the center was a fire pit that looked recently used. A couple of stray embers glowed dully among the charred wood and ashes.

"Light," Santana barked.

Valentina turned her flashlight ahead, struggling to find where Santana had gone. A dense shape moved and heaved, and it was there she aimed the flashlight. Santana appeared in shades of dancing shadows as she wrestled with something large.

Valentina watched for a moment, unsure what she was seeing. It was only as another yowl came from the edges of the light that Valentina understood.

Santana was wrestling a man.

A jaguar was sprinting out of the darkness, making a straight line for Valentina.

Valentina threw herself back, avoiding the leaping cat. She rolled to the side, hand moving to her pistol. Nearby, Santana gasped, grunting as she held her arm around the throat of the man, squeezing tight as his face grew red.

The jaguar skidded to a standstill. In the light, Valentina saw that the creature was already in a state. Its eyes flashed. It bared its teeth. A large gash ran down its flank, blood pooling at the bottom of the tear. It limped on one leg as it stalked toward Valentina, eyes unblinking.

Valentina brought the pistol up and tensed her finger.

The sound cracked around the clearing.

Valentina snapped her hand back, a clean, straight cut along the back of it.

"What the fuck are you doing?" Santana roared.

Valentina flashed her a look, conscious of the advancing predator as it reared back and readied another strike.

Valentina leaped sideways, twisting to roll on her shoulder for a cleaner rise. She closed the distance between her and Santana, the man in Santana's arms eyes slowly beginning to close as he lost consciousness.

"Saving myself from becoming lunch," Valentina shot back, eyes darting to her fallen gun. She reached in her pocket, but another whip crack with Santana's spare hand made her recoil once more.

The jaguar roared. It sprinted toward Valentina. It was quick, and this time Valentina was less prepared. She twisted to avoid its brunt, but the weight of the beast knocked into her side and sent her sprawling.

The jaguar turned once more. It wasted no time in running at Valentina. *What the hell is this creature's fixation with me?*

The jaguar pounced. Valentina kicked back and grabbed her pistol. She was about to aim it at the beast when a muzzle flash illuminated a second man at the door of a nearby cabin.

The jaguar howled in pain as the bullet hit its rear and lodged in the flesh. Santana cried out. Valentina rolled away as the jaguar crumpled not too far away from her.

"For fuck's sake, Val. Do something about *them*," Santana commanded.

Valentina was confused. Her primary enemy was the spotted cat beside her. Why was Santana so eager to help the animal over the men?

As she turned to the man by the cabin, she realized that maybe she had made a minor error in judgment, for his gun now aimed at her.

Valentina shot first, hand moving lightning-fast. Her expert fingers stroked the trigger, and her aim was true. The bullet caught the man dead in the heart and knocked him back toward the cabin wall. Blood colored the rocks as he slid to the ground.

Santana relaxed her arm around her target. The man was now unconscious on the ground. "Jesus. I didn't mean to kill them."

Valentina gave an indifferent shrug. "It was him or me. I chose him."

A twig *snapped* nearby. They shone the flashlight at a cabin to find a man leaning out from behind a crumbling wooden door. He was large with dark skin, wearing only a pair of short briefs. In his hands was a hunter's rifle.

Santana managed to whisper, "Shit," before Valentina shot twice. One bullet went into the man's head. The other went into someone in the cabin.

Santana gave Valentina a look. Valentina ignored her, shining the flashlight in an arc around the clearing. They parted ways without a word. Valentina examined each cabin in turn to find any missing enemies. Santana strode toward the jaguar.

The cabins were large enough only for a bed and a side table. Each looked as if Tarzan himself had made them. The sleeping bags, lanterns, and rucksacks were the only things in here that looked modern and out of place. At the fourth cabin, she found a woman asleep in her bed. A dozen empty beer bottles lay beside her and a bottle of pills without a label. Valentina's lip curled into a snarl as she aimed her pistol at the woman. After a moment of consideration, she removed the guns and knives that lay haphazardly on the floor, then paused by the cabin door.

"Santana," she hissed. "Come here."

Santana waved a dismissive hand without turning. She crouched over the jaguar, the creature now fast asleep, though Valentina had no idea how. Valentina growled, not appreciating the brush-off.

"It's not like I'm trying to prevent more bloodshed," she muttered.

She stood by the woman's bedside, a coil of rope in her hand that she fished from the nearby rucksack. Her face hovered inches from the woman's. Stale beer bloomed with each breath. Valentina tapped the woman's shoulder.

The woman grimaced but didn't wake.

"Wakey wakey, sunshine," Valentina crooned, this time pinching the woman's nostrils shut.

After a silent few seconds, the woman sat up, gasping for air. Her eyes were wide, glancing around the room as she tried to get her bearings. When she saw Valentina, her eyes darted to the floor, searching for her weapon.

"I'd stay very still and cooperate if I were you," Valentina warned.

"Aaron!" the woman shouted, eyes struggling to focus, the heavy-headed effect from the pills and liquor still weighing her down. "Grant!"

Valentina drew her pistol and pushed the muzzle against the woman's temple. "Last chance. Cooperate. Now."

The woman's breathing quickened. Her lips clamped shut, and she gave an eager nod. "Good girl." Valentina held up the rope in her other hand. "I'm going to bind you now. You're going to remain still and let me do so. I have ten men outside waiting for my order. Make one wrong move, and they'll open fire on your sorry ass. Got that?"

The woman nodded. Valentina wasn't sure how much she truly did understand at that moment, but she obeyed and allowed the mercenary to tie her hands and feet.

When Valentina finished binding and gagging the woman, she helped her up. The woman hopped toward the cabin door as Valentina led her by the arm. She grunted, the rope tied around her mouth to hold the cloth gag enough to muffle the sound. As they emerged into the clearing, Santana turned over her shoulder.

Her eyes widened. "What are the hell are you doing to that woman?"

"Hostage," Valentina replied coolly. "Leverage, in case we need her."

Santana glared at Valentina. "What are you—"

"Relax," Valentina interjected, hands placating. "You didn't want them dead, so she's alive and obedient. Isn't that right?"

The woman glanced around, looking for something that wasn't there.

"That's right," Valentina confirmed. "Those ten men were one lady and a jaguar."

The woman saw the man on the ground. She hopped over and dropped to her knees, eyes welling with tears.

"Relax," Valentina soothed. "He's only asleep."

Valentina made her way to the fifth and final cabin. It was a quick search, and by the time she turned, the woman had found the large man at the far quarters, one arm stretched limply in front of him, and the second with his back slumped against the wall.

"Yeah…" Valentina added. "Those are a different story."

CHAPTER SEVENTEEN

Valentina sat beside the campfire, arms folded over her knees. The bound woman sat beside her, eyes puffy and fighting sleep. After her third attempt at hopping around the clearing to escape and sobbing over her comrades, Valentina brought her over where she could keep an eye on her.

Santana sat a short distance away, still hunched over the jaguar. She had made the fire at Valentina's request, a modicum of empathy kicking in as the woman began to shiver and shake. Santana's pack was open, a kit beside her filled with threads and bottles of medicine and several items Valentina had only ever seen in hospitals.

Valentina watched as Santana closed the wound on the jaguar's side. She stitched through the tough, furry skin, the jaguar's chest rising and falling with each breath. Occasionally the creature let out a slow rumbling growl, but that soon ceased with a gentle hush from Santana.

"You do have a way with animals," Valentina complimented.

"Thank you."

"How do you do it?" Valentina asked with genuine interest,

remembering the menacing face of the jaguar in pain as it lunged toward her. "How did you soothe it so easily?"

"She," Santana clarified. "She's not an 'it,' she's a 'she.'" She nodded toward her bag. "It's not all that hard when you know how. She was in pain, struggling to stand. That asshole over by the cabin made sure of that. By the time I got to her, she was ready to lie down and sleep."

"Just like that?"

Santana nodded at a nearby syringe. "Dormicum helps."

"Dormicum?"

Santana finished the stitching. "Tranquilizer."

"Oh." Valentina studied Santana's back, wondering what her background truly was. How did she have all of this knowledge? How was someone like this born into the same world that Valentina grew up in? She gave Santana a curious look. "You said sleep? She was dying."

Santana glanced over her shoulder, letting out a deep breath. "Yes. She's not going to die anymore."

"You're sure of that?" Valentina asked with genuine curiosity.

"No." Santana pulled out a series of bandages and worked them around the jaguar's leg. "No, I'm not. She has a severe laceration in her side, I've had to fish out a bullet from her flank, and her rear femur has a mild fracture. Jaguars are powerful beasts, but if they can't hunt or run away from their predators, they won't last long at all." She looked longingly out in the direction of the city. "Ideally, I'd get her to a vet, but…she's wild. We're lucky that we—"

Santana stopped sharply, rising as if she'd forgotten something very important. She stomped over to the bound woman beside Valentina and slapped her on the side of the head. The woman's eyes snapped open, her head rocking drunkenly back as the blow pulled her back from the edge of sleep. "You assholes. What the fuck did you think you were doing up here?"

Valentina watched, entertained. Santana slapped her again, the woman unable to answer with her mouth gagged.

Santana drew a blade then hooked it under the rope. She sliced through in one clean sweep. "Answer me, bitch." She grabbed the woman's cheeks and directed her gaze to the pitiful jaguar, asleep and on its side, covered in its blood and Santana's bandages.

The woman snapped at Santana's finger. Santana moved it just in time. She slapped the woman again. The woman grunted, "I don't know! I was asleep. I was asleep! I don't know what the fuck happened."

Santana and Valentina exchanged a look. Santana grabbed her collar, then dragged her closer to the fire. She leaned the woman closer. With her arms bound, she was off-balance. The only thing preventing her from falling face-first into the flames was Santana's grip. "Speak."

The woman was sweating, droplets drying as they fell to the ground. "You know what we're here for!" the woman exclaimed. "You wouldn't have attacked us otherwise."

"Say it," Santana grunted.

The woman moaned, swallowed dryly. As she was about to speak, a voice rose from behind them. "That pussy wandered into our camp. She was asking for it."

The man sat with his back to the cabin, arms bound in the same fashion as the woman. His face was still red and flushed, and his voice was weak and raspy.

Valentina eyed him curiously, a pudgy man with thinning grey hair and a feeble mustache. She raised an eyebrow at Santana.

"She just wandered into your camp?" Santana challenged. "No traps, no bait, nothing?" She dragged the woman back and threw her on the ground, then strolled closer to the man and loomed over him.

"What can I say?" the man continued. "We knew what we

were after, but it's not often the gold seeks the miner." He coughed and tried to reach a hand to soothe his throat, but his bonds stopped him. "We got lucky, I guess."

Santana's face flushed with heat. She kicked the man, her boot catching the side of his face. He flopped onto his side, unconscious once again. Snores sounded from his lips.

Santana's fingers curled in frustration as she flopped onto the ground beside Valentina. She grabbed some items from her bag— food, cooking equipment, and a frame for the fire—then busied herself with preparing some grub.

The woman's eyes were fixed on Santana, her sleepiness gone. Valentina cleared her throat. "Santana?"

Santana finished emptying a packet into a silver tin then sat back. "They don't get it. They don't get how beautiful the natural world is. How it's not a resource they can tap at any point to sell a fur coat to the highest fucking bidder."

Valentina raised an eyebrow.

"Poachers." Santana waved an arm. "They're poachers, killing animals for their selfish gains."

"I know what they are," Valentina declared. How could she not? A group of assholes out in the jungle, stacked with rifles, scrapping with an endangered creature…

Santana put her head in her hands, composing herself. She drew a long breath, then stared into the fire. "I'm sorry, Val. It's just…I've traveled this world, seen what the natural world can offer. The whole ecosystem lives in a delicate balance, beautiful creatures thinning in number because humans want the latest fashion item. It makes me sick to my stomach. These creatures…" she gestured at the jaguar, "didn't ask to be born into our world. The jaguar has already been hunted to near extinction once, with deforestation and poaching, and they've only just started rising in number. I want to help the natural world where I can."

"Some humans are monsters." Even Valentina wasn't sure whether she was talking about herself at that moment. The two dead poachers remained where they had fallen, untouched by either Santana or Valentina.

"Yeah. An eye for an eye. That was always my father's motto. If these fuckers feel the need to hunt defenseless animals, they deserve it themselves, in my opinion."

Valentina grinned. "Hold on, two things. One, you barked at me for shooting them."

"To take someone's life is an irreversible act," Santana replied. "Okay, okay. Despite it all, I hate the idea of ending life unless necessary. We could have roughed them up a bit. You're pretty eager to the bullet, aren't you?"

"Yes." Valentina didn't expand. "Secondly, that creature was not defenseless."

"Against a gun?" Santana asked.

"Point taken." Valentina rested back on her hands, eyes meeting the woman's for a moment before the woman turned away and stared at the floor. "So, what's your plan with these guys? Leave them tied up here? Offer them as food to the jaguar? An eye for an eye?"

Santana stirred the food. The air filled with the scent of beans and vegetables. "We send them out into the wild."

A grin crept on Valentina's face. "Jungle girl, I like your thinking." She looked at the woman. "Hear that, sweet stuff? You and your boyfriend have a long walk home with very little equipment."

The woman seemed as though she was going to protest, then thought better of it.

Santana smiled. Valentina smiled back.

They ate their dinner in the quiet of the night. By the time they'd finished, Valentina had spotted the first faint glimpse of dawn in the distance, the blacks and purples melting into a soft mauve. She looked up at the rickety observation post. "What's up there?"

Santana followed her gaze. "One of my favorite spots on this side of the island. I can't count the number of times I've watched the sunrise from that ledge. On the right day, you can see for miles. Feel free to take a look."

Valentina rose to her feet. She gathered the frayed rope, held it between her hands, and tugged. The rope creaked slightly. There was a lot of give—more than she'd like—and she looked back at Santana questioningly.

"Don't worry," Santana called, throwing some water from a flask over the pans. "It's quite safe."

Valentina took the rope and hoisted herself up. She placed her feet on the trunk of the tree and began her climb. After three steps, the rope groaned. The line went slack, and Valentina hopped onto her feet just before the rope snaked down to the ground, pooling around her feet. She frowned.

"Sorry," Santana laughed. "I had one more in me." She pointed. "The other side of the tree. There's a stronger rope. That one *might* take you to the top."

Valentina scowled, growing used to Santana's hijinks but still not enjoying them. She found the rope—considerably stronger, as promised—and within moments she was forty feet above the ground.

While the platform looked precarious from below, up here, it was clear that whoever built this had been careful with their construction. The boards were thick if a little angled. They were fixed solidly into the trunk's upper reaches, nesting around the many arms and branches of the tree. Valentina held a nearby limb for balance and as a failsafe if something *did* go wrong and advanced to the edge of the platform.

The sky was beginning to lighten. She sat, legs dangling over the edge of the boards. While Santana busied herself with tidying up and at one point found more rope to re-gag the woman, Valentina studied the surrounding forest, her mind drifting to ask the question: *how did I get here?*

It was no wonder that Deng had struggled to reduce the

search radius for Archie. From up here, this place seemed infinite. Minute by minute the forest grew in expanse, the farthest canopies catching the light of the rising sun. Soon the distance was emblazoned in pinks and oranges until the harsh circle of yellow appeared and washed away the night.

She looked for clues or signs of where they were or where they had been and found none. Without Santana, she would surely have been lost out here in the wilderness, hunting for days on end without a clue about where she was going. Deng had been right to send a reconnaissance group. Valentina wondered where they could be.

"She's pretty, isn't she?" Santana appeared behind Valentina.

Valentina nodded, eyes fixed ahead. "You weren't wrong."

Santana sat beside her. "I rarely am." She tore the seal of a protein bar and handed half to Valentina.

Valentina accepted, gaze drifting to the ground and the absence of something near the fire. "Where's the jaguar?" Her eyes flicked to their two hostages, who now sat side-by-side next to the cabin, unable to move.

"Gone. Woke up. Helped her off into the jungle."

"You weren't worried she'd attack you?"

"No." Santana's face hardened. "Predators only attack when they're hungry or scared. It's rare they hit back when they're weak unless they have to. She knew I was no threat."

Valentina turned back to the view. "How much farther is there to go?"

"At our pace..." Santana chewed this over. "Another day or so, I'd say. Depends how eager you are to walk and forsake rest. You seemed pretty desperate to get ahead in your messages."

Valentina was. One thing held her back from continuing straight away, though. The little voice beginning to wake in the back of her head. She could feel her rolling around, stirring. Soon Isabella would wake. Then what?

"Val?" Santana asked.

Valentina drew a long breath. "I'll need a moment to myself first. I have…something to address."

Santana raised an eyebrow. "I mean… Okay? Everything all right?" She made to stand.

"I don't mean now." Valentina motioned for Santana to sit once more. "Soon. For now, you can talk me through what I see in front of me. I'd love to learn a little more about this place if we're to spend the next few days here."

Santana warily resumed her seat. "Sure thing, Countess. Tell me what you want to know."

Valentina's eyes drifted toward the sun as a thick layer of fog rose from the trees. It hung above their highest reaches, forming a blanket of white that was interspersed only occasionally with the mother trees of the forest. Valentina thought of airplane rides and soaring above the clouds as the sky lit up in bright pastels and dappling sunlight.

The warmth touched her face. One she hadn't felt from the sun in years. As they sat there, side-by-side, Valentina asked her questions, all the while waiting for Isabella to wake up and wondering where in this labyrinth of green and cloud Archie could be hiding.

CHAPTER EIGHTEEN

The knocking reverberated around the cavern walls, the sound bouncing an endless tune as its rhythmic tempo repeated endlessly.

Around him, LEDs powered by only small charges dealt a great deal of harsh light into the cave. The walls were rough, the tunnels crudely carved, clearly a rush job that hadn't intended to be prepared and inhabited yet.

Archie was thankful that it was.

He had drawn up grand plans, an underground manor with smooth marble walls and tiled floors. Sconces would illuminate the building. A hundred rooms would spoke off the central reception hall. There would be a gym and a theater, a pool and a topiary. His researchers had found alternatives to sunlight that could be maintained and regulated, and it would all be his, his little kingdom under the jungle. In the place where only the daring trod, he would be the island's greatest secret—a trapdoor spider, claiming the core of the island as his.

For the core was where the secrets lay, wasn't it?

Archie laced his fingers behind his back and strolled along the rudimentary walkways, picturing what this place would one day become. Wires trailed from light to light, and dust and rubble settled on the floor. There was a smell of burning in the air, and as he passed the teams of workers with tools used to shape and refine and reinforce their build, he grinned.

None would meet his eye.

The journey into "The Deep"—as he'd later come to call this place—was precarious. On his descent into the island's underground, Archie and Friedrich initiated the commands and sent the little transporter pod speeding through the underground network. This had, until recently, only been used to transport his workers to their hidden location. The tunnel was blocked at intervals by dozens upon dozens of automatic doors, which opened only upon sensing the speeding carts and closed swiftly after.

Archie wasn't worried about the pursuit, even if he knew that Deng was one hell of an opponent and he shouldn't underestimate her.

Still, we strive to be the best, and what could be better than dominating the center of the island?

A loud *crash* sounded farther along the tunnel. Archie made his way closer and peeked around the rough door frame. A group of three miners hacked at the walls with pickaxes and a jackhammer. A pile of rubble reached six feet in height nearby.

One of the workers turned at his approach. "Nothing to worry about, just a softer bit of rock is all. Happens from time to time."

Archie narrowed his eyes.

"We're on track," the worker added hurriedly. "Just a minor blip."

Archie left without a word.

The truth was that Archie was feeling a little cooped up. It had been nearly a week without any sunlight or fresh air, and there was little to do down in his construction site than to stroll between the doors, talk, and study. A short walk and a brief transport hop later found Archie in one of the only rooms that resembled a room, and it had been this area where they docked upon arrival down here.

Friedrich stood when Archie entered the room. He grew alert, feverishly strolling around Kit's bedside. He tapped on the tablet screen and occasionally adjusted his glasses, doing everything he could not to meet Archie's eyes.

"Progress report," Archie stated darkly, a satisfaction in having Friedrich so neatly under his thumb.

"Th-there's progress," Friedrich replied, looking at Archie as if he had only now noticed his presence. "Synaptic communication seems to be restoring in the major extremities—eight toes, now, and three fingers. Monitors are tracking the recalibration, and the AI's algorithms appear to be doing their job in cracking the biological code that we may never understand."

Archie swept closer until he was leaning over Kit's bed. There was a touch of color in Kit's cheeks, something that hadn't been there before, yet he remained stationary in his coma.

"Any prediction on—" Archie cut off as a resounding crash came from somewhere in the tunnel. He grimaced, eyes flashing dangerously. When the sound faded, he continued, "Any prediction on how long we may be looking at for results?"

Friedrich ran a hand through his hair, stray strands standing out in all directions. He looked as if he hadn't slept in weeks. Archie *knew* the man hadn't. He was driving him like a mule because what else was there now but work? He had laid his cards bare with Deng. It would only be a matter of time before the others—Atlantica's proud and elite—would catch his scent and realize what he was doing.

What needs to happen.

"Well?" Archie nudged, his words low yet cutting.

"It's impossible to predict," Friedrich replied. "The human body is an intricate system, and the AI is a code unto itself. It may take days, it may take weeks or months, or years...I just..."

"Don't you *dare* say you don't know," Archie warned. He advanced, low simmering anger in his gut. "You have one job and one job only, Friedrich. Your job is to know the things that I don't. I don't keep you around for 'what ifs' and 'I don't knows.' I keep you around so you can give me answers. So you can take the work that needs doing and get it done. Where else are you guaranteed the safety of life in Atlantica? Where else are you given the salary I give you? Where else are you given these opportunities to have your name down as a pioneer of one of the greatest applicable discoveries of modern time? *When* this fucking thing works, your name will be in medical journals across the globe. You'll have an everlasting legacy you can hand down to your children. Who else gives you these opportunities, Friedrich?"

Friedrich's gaze fell to the floor.

Archie smirked. "That wasn't rhetorical."

"Nowhere," Friedrich replied. "Here and here alone."

Archie patted his cheeks. "Good boy. Now hurry the fuck up and get it done. We don't know how much time we have."

He swept out of the room without a second glance, leaving Friedrich to rub his tired eyes and continue with his analysis. Archie felt only a twinge of pity at Friedrich's loss of his assistant. After making their way down into the tunnel and the boy having seen too much...

Well, the bloodstain on the floor never quite scrubbed clean.

As Archie ran his fingers through his hair, his throat yearning for the calming embrace of liquor, footsteps approached from behind. He spun, meeting the young worker in her tracks. The worker stopped, her forehead sheened with sweat. Her hair was short, presumably to make life down in the tunnels easier on herself. "Mr. Fontana..."

She doubled over, hands on knees, gulping in air.

"Yes?" Archie asked, his disinterested tone making her shrink before him.

"There's something you need to see, sir," she managed. "There's... Well, you've got to see it for yourself."

Archie straightened his back, enjoying the slight tremble in her body as she held his gaze. "On whose authority are you asking?"

"Captain Ki—I mean, Kirk Connors, sir." She licked her dry, cracked lips. "He's asked for you."

Archie gave an agreeable nod then followed the woman through the tunnels. The layout was familiar from the sketches the architect had drawn for him, though with the mass of unrefined rock, it was far from feeling like home. They snaked through the rooms, the workers fixated on the job at hand, paying little attention to Archie and the woman leading him into the farther realms of The Deep.

They descended a spiral staircase—one that would soon boast timber and rich oak, the walls lined with fluorescents and murals. Archie loved the idea of a contemporary underground dungeon, with more levels than anyone could care to count, more rooms than could be filled, bedecked with...

"Watch your head," the woman warned, just in time. Archie ducked under the low roof. The woman crouched at the bottom of the stairs and grabbed a bright yellow hard hat. She offered one to Archie. A steely gaze gave her the answer. She left the second helmet on the floor.

The roof was lower here. The lights were fewer and farther between. The walls were narrower. Archie was barely able to walk straight ahead without the walls rubbing his shoulders. After a short stretch that descended a shallow gradient, the tunnel opened enough to offer a pocket of room at its end.

Two workers stood beside Captain Kirk Connors. They were some of the beefier of Connor's team. Wheelbarrows and pick-axes and drills were scattered around next to mounds of dirt and rubble.

"Mr. Fontana," Kirk greeted. "I hope your descent was smooth."

Archie's mouth straightened. He glanced around the cramped and filthy space and brushed the dust off his shoulders. "As smooth as it could be, considering the work yet remaining on our project. I'm assuming there's a reason you summoned me into this pit other than simple pleasantries?"

Kirk grinned. It was contagious. His smile could light up the room, though Archie couldn't show that in front of the other workers. It would only come off as weakness, and if he were to succeed, he needed to rule with an iron fist.

"There is," Kirk confirmed. "Let me ask you a question first, sir. What is the one currency in Atlantica that all Atlanticans strive to acquire?"

There was a multitude of answers to this question, Archie thought. Power, money, sex, power, command, respect, power…

Something shook above. Dust rained down on those gathered. Archie grimaced as he felt the dust settle on his hair and shoulders again. "Kirk, do you think that now is the time to plague me with riddles? Either be straight with me, or you'll find yourself otherwise assigned."

Kirk glanced uneasily at his colleagues. They were double his width, and he knew who they worked for. One click of Archie's fingers, and he might die down here, buried and lost forever in the muck along with the ghosts and ghouls of Atlantica's past.

However, Archie knew Kirk, and he knew the answer he was about to receive.

"One guess…" Kirk stated, knowing that Archie held at least some favor for him.

Archie drew a calming breath. "Atlanticore."

Kirk nodded as his face broke into a smile.

Archie's gaze bored into his. "What's your point?"

Kirk chuckled. "Why, this, of course."

He took a step back. The two meathead workers moved into

the place where Kirk had been standing. Archie now noticed a chunk of rock that appeared as though they'd replaced it in its hole. One of the meatheads grabbed the rock and removed it. The other picked up a pickaxe from the ground. A faint blue glow came from the porous holes of the rock's surface on the wall. The second meathead brought the ax back and swung it into the wall.

A fissure opened from the ax's steely point. The ceiling shook slightly. Archie glanced up, worry clouding his face. The woman standing behind him tapped his shoulder. He turned as she offered him a helmet again. He placed it on his head, not having time to secure the strap before the fissure on the wall ruptured and collapsed. Archie spotted that the wall crumbled from particular points where they must have pre-drilled, creating weaknesses in the surface. The room stopped shaking. The wall fell away in a rain of stones and rocks and mud.

A violent blue glow harshly illuminated the hungry look that fell over Archie's face.

CHAPTER NINETEEN

Valentina sat in the quiet of the treetop platform alone. Santana left her to it, climbing down to the ground a short while ago. Although there were cabins around the clearing, Santana opted for a sleeping bag on the hard earth. Her gun rested near her head, and her body faced their captives in case she needed to make a sudden attack.

Valentina rested with her back to the trunk. The sky was turning blue, and the sun dazzled her eyes. She leaned her head against the rough bark and waited as the little voice inside her began to grow, the familiar sensation of conflict rising within her as Isabella woke up.

As Isabella rose to consciousness, Valentina had to fight to keep herself from falling. Often in times like this, she felt as though she were being dragged into an endless pool, only able to watch another rise past her and surface to safety. As much as she fought the sensation, the pair were interlinked, and neither one could surface at the same time. To meet in the middle, both would have to remain below the water.

Valentina felt her arms being taken from her. Isabella rubbed her eyes, a cold wash of panic setting in as she realized she wasn't at home.

"Simmer down, princess," Valentina cooed. "You're not in any danger. Just appreciate the view."

Valentina slipped back, the clarity of the setting around her fading behind a vignette of shadow. Her world was at the end of the tunnel, and it was pulling her backward.

"Where am I?" Isabella asked with Valentina's lips. "Where are *we*?"

The jungle, Valentina replied in Isabella's head, the transition difficult to fight. *Where did you think we were?*

"I don't know," Isabella replied. "We're certainly not at home."

Valentina pulled herself up, fighting the tug to disappear and quiet herself. She needed this moment. She needed Isabella to relent, to allow her to continue on her quest—a quest to save *Isabella's* brother.

Isabella crawled over to the edge of the platform, knuckles turning white at the strength with which she gripped. "Why are we here, Val? What are you doing in the jungle? I can't..." Valentina's head began to spin, the jungle blurred, the definition of the leaves and sky lost. "I can't be here, Val. I can't..."

Valentina swam upward. She tried to grab Isabella to stop her spiraling. The girl kicked back, shoving herself toward the tree, fear taking over her body. Valentina needed to take control before things turned dire.

How did I not know you were afraid of heights? Valentina asked. *Jesus, girl. Calm down for a moment and breathe. Look at the view. Forget the fall.*

Isabella closed her eyes, her body tensing up.

Please, listen to me, Valentina soothed. *You are safe. We are safe. But only if you listen to me, okay? You need to listen to me if we're going to get this over with. If we're going to find Kit, you have to trust me.*

Isabella's eyes opened at the mention of her brother's name.

Can you do that? Valentina asked.

Isabella nodded. She closed her eyes and tried to regulate her breathing. As she forced her body to calm, Valentina found herself more able to meet Isabella, the pair of them swimming in the murky dark.

Can you trust me? Valentina asked.

Isabella contemplated. *I don't know.*

Why not? Valentina pushed.

Isabella was quiet for a moment. Valentina knew why, though she didn't want to admit it. Isabella didn't want Valentina to be a part of her any more than Valentina wanted to be a part of Isabella. Still, it's what they had, and the only way to deal with this situation was to keep on pushing forward.

Isabella, you have to listen to me, Valentina soothed. *You are safe. We are safe. But, we have to work together here. Just like back at Deng's place, you need to know that we're going to be okay. I need you to rest. I need you to hibernate. Close your eyes and surrender to me, okay? It's the only way we're going to be able to get Kit and Bradley back.*

Isabella swam before her, a metaphysical blob in abstract space. *You can get him back?*

I can, Valentina replied. *We're en route now. Just a little longer and he'll be back with you, I promise. I can do this—I need to do this. Can you deal with that?*

Isabella paused. *I can. Will work—*

Valentina growled. *If work is your priority right now, we're in a completely different headspace. You have the next two days off, correct?*

Isabella told her she did.

Valentina continued. *Then please... Shut down, Isabella. Let me finish what we started.*

Valentina felt Isabella slipping down as she began to rise. Isabella called up to her, *Who's Deng? What was that place?*

Valentina had never truly explained what had happened that night, but she promised she'd come through on all explanations in the future once they had their prize and could finally put an end to all of this.

Okay. Isabella plummeted into the dark. Her body flopped, and Valentina rose to the surface, claiming her place inside Isabella's body. She flexed her fingers, screwed her eyes shut, shifted against the trunk.

She squinted against the vibrance of the sunlight. When was the last time she'd felt such heat? When was the last time true sunlight had left white blossoms in her retinas? She rested her head against the trunk, exhausted, yet geared up for the road ahead.

She took out her cell phone and snapped the sunrise. With a faint smirk on her face, she slid down the rope and took her place across the dying fire. Soon she was fast asleep.

The man hacked at the undergrowth, his expression sour and eyes narrowed. Mud painted his face. All around was green, and all beneath was brown.

He paused, sliding his sleeve across his forehead to soak up the latest batch of sweat. The salt sting was painful, but it would all be worth it.

Yes. It'll be worth it soon.

Taking his canteen from his waist, he downed the last water he'd acquired at the river. Since crossing the bridge and rediscovering the path where the women had trod, he found he could follow with relative ease, tracking the heavy bootprints in the mud. Animals watched him as he passed, smart enough to stay out of his sight as he pursued the two and strode on through the jungle.

All was well until it wasn't.

He hit a snag.

The wall of vines was the obvious clue, the two halves and the careless handling of the plants indicative that they had been through here. Rough hacks at the greenery were unmistakable, certainly not the work of an animal, but from a human forcing entry. Coils and ties and knots littered the ground, the detritus covering the mud through the hewn alley and a little farther beyond.

That was where the tracks stopped.

There was shrubbery all around. Twigs and bracken lay on the forest floor. The hacked castoffs from the brush masked whichever way the two women had gone.

Dammit, he cursed. He had expected some kind of difficulty, but he was also a man of nature, a man of the world, and he hadn't expected this to happen so quickly.

Something grunted in the brush. He glanced right, picking up two red eyes watching from the shadows. He shot without hesitation. The silencer masked the sound of gunfire but not the hog's dying cries.

Birds took wing, fluttering into the air in a great cloud. He shot them, too. A couple of stray feathered creatures plummeted impotently to the ground.

He smiled.

The smile faded when he looked at the ground.

The search was frustrating. It took longer than he could afford. At last, sweaty and covered in bug bites, he found them. They were difficult to make out at first but clearer as they led him away from his location. An ape of some kind swung overhead. He aimed his pistol, then thought better of it. There were only so many bullets remaining. All he needed was one, in theory. Still, he knew who he was hunting.

He knew her very well.

The sun was past its zenith by the time Valentina awoke.

She was groggy, the sun still blinding from way up high. She wasn't used to waking at this hour, much less in this intense climate. Somewhere deep down she felt Isabella in slumber, more pronounced than she usually was at night, but pacified, nonetheless. She was thankful for Isabella's cooperation, though in the same way that Isabella didn't truly trust Valentina, she didn't trust Isabella either.

Santana was awake, stoking the fire and occasionally glancing at the man and woman bound by the cabins.

"They still sleeping?" Valentina asked. "Should probably give them *some* food and water."

Santana shook her head. "They tried to escape."

Valentina spotted the pieces of rope littering the ground. "Bitch crept up to me in my sleep. Tried to take my gun. Managed to get my knife first."

"What did you do?" Valentina was unsure how she could sleep through such a thing. She wondered how much it truly affected her having Isabella on the edges of her consciousness. It concerned her that she hadn't awoken, but she wouldn't show that to Santana.

"Check out her face."

The woman's head lolled down, her chin touching her neck. A violent red slash marred her cheek, and a few drops of blood had trickled until they dried.

"Whip?"

Santana poked the sausages. "Not at first. That came later. Something to remember me by."

Valentina nodded, impressed. Santana certainly knew how to handle herself.

She didn't press it further. They sat side-by-side, eating from their metal pots until they were clean. Valentina scraped every last mouthful, the food coursing through her body and bringing her strength. When she put the pan down, Santana was watching her.

"Problem?"

Santana considered this. "Who were you talking to?"

Valentina raised an eyebrow.

"Up there," Santana clarified. "You were talking to someone."

Valentina weighed the pros and cons of several answers. She settled with, "My business."

"Fair enough." Santana finished her food, then wiped her mouth with a tissue. She offered one to Valentina, who declined. "Shall we let these fuckers go?" Santana nodded at their captives.

Valentina exhaled. "I suppose. How do you want to do this?"

"Without fuss."

They kicked the pair awake. Valentina caught the man in the shins, Santana catching the woman's ankle. They grunted in pain as they came to. The man showed no fear while the woman cowered under Santana's hand flexing against her whip.

Santana crouched, her gaze holding the woman's. "You have one chance to escape, assholes. I don't know why we bother letting you live when we know what you're capable of, but my mother always taught me about redemption and change. Consider this your moment. The turning point in your life that guides you toward better pastures. Because if I find either of you fuckers in this jungle again, doing what you were doing, then…" She pointed toward the dead man laying half out the cabin. Flies hovered around him, his skin turning ashen.

The woman nodded eagerly. The man offered no sign he had heard.

Valentina crouched, joining Santana. She held the man's gaze, eyes boring into his. "Did you hear her, sunshine?"

The man remained stoic.

Valentina grabbed the man's hand, poking out through his rope. She gripped his finger, and a small pair of pliers found purchase at the end of his nail. With one quick movement, she pulled.

The nail came clean away. The man's finger bled.

He grimaced, unable to maintain his apathy any longer. "You bitch," he grunted.

"I said, did you hear her, *sunshine*," Valentina repeated.

The man looked between the women, then nodded. "I heard her."

"Good." Valentina released the nail from the tiny pliers and dropped it in his lap. "On your feet."

They guided them to the edge of the clearing until they were facing in the direction of the city, Valentina assumed. They cut the pair's ropes, then gave them a sturdy shove.

"You can't just leave us out there," the woman protested, finding her voice now that her limbs were free. She rubbed her sore wrists. "We'll die."

"You'll be fine." A smirk appeared on Santana's face. "As long as you don't come across any jaguars."

CHAPTER TWENTY

"Are there more like you?" Valentina asked.

If Valentina had thought the jungle was wild before, it had been nothing compared to what now surrounded them.

She had heard of virgin forests before—natural reserves untouched by man, allowed to grow wild and free, twisted and knotted, completely unexamined by people walking through—but she had never experienced this herself.

The ground was uneven. Every step was an obstacle. The brush fought for dominance, and this far from the city, the animals grew curious. They were cautious of the women trudging through the trees but unaware of the dangers of humans and their tools.

Valentina spied marmosets in the trees. Birds flew down to rest on the branches nearby. On more than one occasion, Santana had made use of her whip, dealing a warning crack to hogs, lizards, and snakes that Valentina couldn't name.

Insects flocked around them, though Valentina was thankful that they had passed the mosquito phase. She spied mantids patiently waiting on broad leaves. Santana called behind her, warning of a trapdoor spider's nest underfoot. At one point a bouncing marsupial ripped by at speed, akin to a kangaroo, but in a color and size Valentina had never seen before.

"More like me?" Santana examined a compass she clutched in her palm. Night was falling above them, though the canopy was blocking the stars, making it difficult for Valentina to understand how Santana knew her direction.

"Solitary explorers. Seems like a risky profession. Most hunts into the Atlantican wilds I've heard tell of seemed to be mostly groups." Valentina flicked away a shiny crimson beetle that landed on her shoulder. "Seems like a dangerous place for a lady to run solo."

Santana shrugged. "I don't know what to tell you. I like alone time. I like the call of nature. The thrill of discovery drives me."

"I mean, that's all fair enough," Valentina pushed. "But there doesn't seem to be a whole lot of coin in this kind of life. You seemed pretty eager to accept my price, considering you profess not to lead expeditions like this."

Santana pocketed the compass, then took a soft right. "You mean you'd have paid more?"

Valentina grinned. "I'm certain I will. If you see us through to the end."

Santana glanced over her shoulder. "Give me a challenge." She hacked her way through a bush laced with thorns, Valentina's flashlight catching the shine of her sweating forehead. "Honestly, there's quite a lot of money in discovery. If you can uncover the secrets that the rich and lazy bastards aren't willing to hunt for themselves, you can make a pretty penny. I can't count the number of items I've brought back from this jungle. Ruins yield armor and weapons and coin. Even coloring in a little bit of the map can be enough to make a pretty penny."

Valentina stretched her leg over a fallen log, the bark covered in an array of colored fungi and crawling bugs. "So you do have an employer?"

Santana stopped, then spun to face Valentina, a tired expression on her face. "You have your secrets. I have mine."

"I'm just trying to understand it," Valentina replied. "It seems like a lonely profession to be out here all the time. Is it truly about the thrill of discovery?" The slight falter in Santana's eyes told her it wasn't.

Santana frowned before she turned back and continued forward. "What about you?" she asked.

"What about me?" Valentina felt a knot tighten in her stomach.

"How does mercenary work...well, work?" Santana asked. "I can't imagine you can just accept requests for murder and thievery on Facebook."

Valentina glanced up at the canopy as something leaped above them. "Yeah...I refer you to your answer. You have your secrets, and I have mine."

"Fine," Santana replied.

Though Valentina felt a strange urge to share with this woman of the jungle, she was glad that Santana pressed no further.

The darkness fell like a thick blanket around them as they made their miles. It pressed in, an ever-present gloom that stole the light from their flashlights. Shadows danced and waved as they bobbed around, and eyes shone at them in the dark. They walked for another hour before the sound of a single shot rent the night.

Birds flocked into the sky, out of sight, but not all that far. Their wings beat like heavy flaps of canvas, and Santana ordered Valentina to shut off her flashlight.

Valentina obeyed. The second the light was gone, another world appeared, a world in which darkness was everything, and all that existed were the other four senses.

They heightened as Valentina's nose, ears, fingers, and tongue worked to compensate for the loss of sight. Santana's fingers closed around her wrist, and she had to resist the instinct to respond. Ordinarily, an unwarranted grab would have her victim twisted and out cold on the ground. Instead, she allowed Santana to lead her forward.

Santana whispered commands. Valentina listened. Though Valentina had no idea how Santana was guiding her, they made slow progress. Soon the sound of voices met their ears. Another gunshot broke, followed by the raucous laughter of men and women.

"Steady," Santana whispered. "Watch out for this rock."

They crept a little closer, and soon the darkness yielded as the orange flickering of flaming torches appeared ahead. The movement made Valentina dizzy since the trees interspersed it to form a strange kind of zoetrope. A dozen or so figures wandered through the trees, and mixed in with the light of the flames was a gentle blue glow.

One of the figures fired another shot. Laughter rose again as birds took wing. The figures delighted in scaring the animals, making no attempt at a quiet passage through the land they assumed was theirs.

Santana took a position behind the trunk of an enormous tree. Valentina moved behind her.

"Who are they?" Valentina murmured. She squinted, trying to recognize some kind of uniform or outfit, but nothing came. She hoped Santana's eyes would be sharper than hers.

"Don't know," Santana replied softly. "There are a lot of them."

"You say that like it's an unusual occurrence."

Santana considered this. "A large group of people carting something through the jungle and shooting at animals for the sake of it?" She shook her head gently. "I can't say I've seen all that much of this, particularly this deep into the jungle."

The group continued walking, their pace slow but steady. The men and women laughed with each other, one or two occasionally breaking out in song. Valentina wondered if any of them were drunk, though this was soon confirmed as bottles raised to lips and more gunshots rang out.

"What are they carting?" Valentina's gaze homed in on the wheelbarrows that three of the group were pushing. Thick cloth blankets covered the contents although the blue glow shone through.

Santana leaned out a little more and gave an affirmative nod. "Atlanticore."

"Atlanticore? I thought the island had been tapped dry."

"Apparently not. This deep into the jungle there's a lot we have yet to explore. Troops of raiders will sometimes stray this far, though not many manage to make it back to the city alive. I've only ever seen one group with any Atlanticore, though."

"What happened to it?" Valentina asked.

Santana raised an eyebrow. "Hell if I know. You think my job is to interfere with miners and cash-hungry assholes digging for the bright blue?"

"Maybe if they kicked a jaguar along their journey..." Valentina muttered.

Santana looked back with a coy grin on her face. "Easy, tiger."

The group carried on their way, blissfully unaware of the pair watching them from the shadows. Their path brought them closer, though Valentina and Santana remained at a safe distance. They wore no uniform, only the smug expression of pillagers who were proud of their catch. Valentina wondered where in the city they'd be heading and what purpose the Atlanticore would serve.

Santana darted ahead, breaking from cover momentarily before ducking behind another tree. Valentina waited a moment, then followed suit.

"Why are you getting closer?" Valentina asked.

Santana's eyes took on a curious glint. "They must have raided that Atlanticore from somewhere nearby. Or, if not, they've left a track straight through to the place where they found it. Imagine what they might have missed inside. They might have carved the entryway to a great underground ruin."

"Underground ruins?" Valentina rolled her eyes. "Focus on the prize, Santana."

Santana chuckled softly. "They exist, Valentina. I know it. I've seen carvings and buildings akin to those built by the Mayans and the Aztecs. The deeper you go, the more common they appear. Paintings on the walls. Carvings and runes. Though I've yet to snag any substantial treasure, who knows what this group has unlocked."

Valentina's fingers stroked her cell phone. Her mind cast back to the strange images and decorations she had found in the underground city cavern as she lodged herself into fissures and upper levels to escape attack.

The group faded away, shrinking into the distance. Soon they were lost from sight. Valentina couldn't forget the blue glow, but this far into the jungle, it was for the best that they continue with their mission.

Santana appeared to have other ideas. "Come on," she instructed and took Valentina's wrist again.

They sped through the brush in near enough darkness. The ground was firmer where the group had trodden, and Santana's senses were keen. She followed the rudimentary path, only stopping when another group appeared in the distance, this one with only half a dozen to their troop, lit by flaming torches and another cart of the blue.

"They've found a new reserve. Val, imagine the secrets."

Valentina's face hardened. "No. Imagine the coin..."

She felt Santana glance her way, but neither said a word. Santana led Valentina off the track, and the pair hid in the brush —closer than before. As the group neared, they got a better look at the bunch.

An athletic-looking man in his thirties led the troop. He sported a grizzly beard, yet the top of his head was balding severely. A rat-tail hung from the back of his head and fell to his shoulder blades. He carried a rifle in his hands.

The cart was behind him, wheeled by a woman with thick arms and a grim expression. Her eyes were dark, her brow low. Flanking her on either side were two more men with rifles, and two women brought up the rear.

A shot sounded in the distance, echoing from the other group.

"No qualms about wasting bullets, do they?" the grim woman chided. "Not like we have unlimited supplies."

Rat-tail grinned, answering the shot with one of his.

The rest of the group flinched.

"Really?" one of the men asked.

Rat-tail chuckled. "Hush your lips. You think anyone gives a shit about a couple of stray bullets? Worst we can do is knock an orangutan out of the trees and cook us some dinner."

Valentina felt Santana tense up.

"Ain't no orangutan in this jungle," one of the women called. "They're off somewhere in the east. You'd be lucky to get a gorilla here."

Rat-tail's face grew dark. He gripped his gun tighter.

"Oh, fuck off, won't you?" one of the men answered. "He was just making a point."

"Yeah, suck up to the boss." The woman made no attempt to soften her voice. "See if he'll let you suck his cock."

Rat-tail whirled. Now that he was facing the torchlight, Valentina was certain she could see something crusted around his nose. Was that white powder?

He aimed his rifle at the woman at the back with a demonic glint in his eye. "Listen now, bitch. More of that and you'll find yourself painting the jungle with your insides."

The woman's jaw clenched. "Shoot me, and you'll have the boss to deal with—"

Rat-tail shot. The bullet sped through the woman's face. Her head exploded like shattered fruit as the others cried out in alarm. The woman fell to her knees, then onto her front. Her torch rolled from her hand, landing dangerously close to a large bush with long leaves.

"What the fuck did you do that for!" the other woman called.

Rat-tail grimaced. "I *won't* stand for insolence. I'm head of this command. You're with me, or you're fucking not." He swung the rifle to the other woman. "Got it?"

A shot sounded in the distance, a call and answer from a clueless troop.

The woman remained silent. A tear rolled down her cheek as she tried not to glance at her comrade. The grim woman with the cart stared at Rat-tail unblinking. The man flanking her right opened his mouth to speak, hand moving slowly to the pistol at his side. "You can't think that—"

There was no mercy as Rat-tail shot again. This bullet landed in the man's shoulder. He howled in pain as blood exploded from the wound. His arm went limp, fingers unable to grab his gun. The group flinched again. This time the woman and the other man jumped to the side as they went for their weapons.

Rat-tail scowled, swinging his rifle to the woman. He fired but missed. As he went to try again, Santana burst away from Valentina, whip in hand.

A second shot fired, narrowly missing the woman as she scuttled into the trees. Santana cracked the whip, and the lash coiled expertly around the rifle's muzzle. She yanked back, tugging the weapon free of Rat-tail's grasp.

"The fuck?" he roared, anger etched into every line of his face.

Valentina groaned. Santana had no tact. Who rushed into fights, all guns blazing like this?

The man turned on Santana, but she was ready. The whip trailed behind her, then snapped through the air and coiled around the man's throat. She dragged him toward her, rat-tail flying behind. As he neared, she hooked an uppercut at his chin.

His head wrenched back. Spit flew into the air. His eyes rolled back into his head.

She drew the whip away, loosening it with an expert flick of her wrist. As she looked up, the man and woman pointed their weapons at her. The man with the injured shoulder lay on the ground in agony. "You're welcome," she offered.

Their faces implied they didn't reflect the sentiment. Meanwhile, behind the woman, sparks rose from the dropped torch and licked the bush's leaves. The ends charred and the flame grew.

Santana raised a placating hand. "I saved your asses."

"You killed the head of our troop," the man countered.

Santana's forehead wrinkled. "You're kidding me, right—"

A shot fired. Santana threw herself to the ground. The man howled as he fell to the earth with his comrade. Valentina emerged from the bushes, pistol aimed at the woman. The grim-set woman with the cart watched on motionless, hands still gripping the handles.

"Weapons down before you join your boss," Valentina spat.

The grim woman glanced at the Atlanticore in the bed of the cart. "You can't have it."

Valentina scoffed. "We don't want it."

Was that true?

"Back the fuck up," the other woman warned. "We have places to go. People to see."

"We saved your fucking lives," Santana replied. "Show at least a modicum of respect. We don't want your shit. We want to know where it came from."

"So you *do* want the shit?" the grim woman growled. "You can piss off." She turned and nodded at the woman, who flexed her finger on the trigger.

Valentina dove at Santana, knocking her out of the way. She twisted, pushing quickly to her feet. She fired without wasting a beat, the bullet speeding toward the woman's chest. Blood blossomed through her shirt. She gasped, then folded to the ground.

The two men offered no help as the grim woman stared at them, eyes flickering between the pair. "No," was all she offered.

Valentina shook her head. "Whatever. My only question is are you going to let us pass peacefully, or are you going to be a problem, too?"

The grim woman wrinkled her nose, indecision in her eyes. The strangers outnumbered her. That much was clear. How could she possibly protect herself?

Something rustled in the bushes. The grim woman's eyes glanced behind them. Valentina knew the situation before her eyes confirmed it as the large troop appeared on the edge of the torch's light.

The flames on the bush progressed along the leaves. They multiplied, the light increasing as the fire sought the dry patches and expanded.

"Well, well, well…" a voice cooed. A woman broke free from the pack, wearing a grey tank top that sported dark patches of sweat. Mud coated her arms, and a satisfied grin stretched across her face. "What have we here?"

Valentina shuffled closer to Santana. Her fingers flexed on her pistol. The woman noticed. "You can kill one of us, but you can't kill us all."

"Wanna bet?" Valentina replied.

Santana straightened her back, her fingers flexing over her whip.

The woman looked over their shoulders. "Mind telling me what's going on here?"

The grim woman motioned at the ground around her. The two men rolled, attempting to crawl to the other group. They only made it as far as Valentina and Santana before the woman loosed two bullets and put them both out of their misery. "We have no time to help the weak. Casandra," she nodded at the grim woman, "bring your cart up here, and we'll have you join our troop."

Valentina slowly eased her hand into her pocket.

Casandra nodded, the cart wheels squeaking as she curved around Valentina and Santana.

"And you two…" The woman theatrically tapped her chin. "We don't need any more baggage."

Valentina let the orbs drop to the ground.

Without a hint of empathy, the woman met their eyes. "Sorry, ladies."

The explosion was swift, set off by Valentina's trigger. Smoke erupted into the jungle, masking them from view. The orange from the growing flames was absorbed into the smog making the white cloud pulse and throb with light.

Shots fired. Valentina dove out of the way. Santana launched herself in the opposite direction. Valentina shot. Someone grunted. Another shot caused another casualty.

Valentina ducked low, then ran toward where Santana had been. She called for her, but that drew the attention of the others, and the bullet narrowly missed her shin. She heard someone scurrying nearby and hoped it was Santana, but as the others broke into a run, the sound was soon lost.

Shit.

Valentina ran toward the flames, hoping they might give her a clearer field of vision. The smoke was doing its job to confuse the enemy, but what would Valentina be in the jungle without Santana?

Someone shouted in triumph. Another shot split the air. A sudden creaking sounded as if a giant machine had awoken and was shaking the rust off its hinges. Then rumbling rocked the ground.

Valentina moved to the nearest tree. She dug in her toes and climbed, getting away from danger while trying to restore her view of what the hell was happening. More voices cried out.

Something *cracked*, and the sound of boulders racing down a hill met her ears. She climbed until she was above the smoke and looked down at where she had been but could see nothing.

The voices stopped. The rumbling faded.

It would be another few minutes before the smoke parted, and Valentina saw a sight she'd never expected to see.

CHAPTER TWENTY-ONE

The stink of rotting flesh was thick in the air. Blood still stained the man's clothing from the two he had encountered along his path.

They were crazed and desperate.

A deadly combination.

Alone and abandoned in the jungle with none of their equipment or faculties. They babbled something about two women shooting their friends.

Now the man looked down on those two friends.

A large man lay half-in, half-out of the cabin door. His eyes were glazed, and his skin pecked at by creatures that had long since gone. The man examined the cabins and saw that someone had tossed the sheets and equipment into the fire in the clearing's center. No embers remained, only ash.

He didn't care. At least it was a sign he was heading in the right direction.

He looked out over the trees, the stars and moons casting a silvery glow that caught the soft veil of fog and lit up the scene like a ghostly graveyard. Beside the clearing was a tree. He scaled it, finding his vantage as he scoured the treetops in the hope of maybe glimpsing his target.

He remained there for a short while, resting his limbs. He drank from his canteen and ate from his supply of Power Bars. The moon shone brightly, beautiful over the top of the haunting forest.

A few clicks over in the distance, a thin ribbon of smoke rose followed by the dull glow of torches.

He shaded his eyes, more out of habit than necessity, and wondered if that could be them. The two he had encountered had thrown him off the scent, causing him to question whether there truly were others out in this wilderness who were crazy enough to wander at night.

Still, it was the only sign of life he could see, and as he climbed down and approached the edge of the clearing, he found their footprints.

He oriented his compass to the smoke, then trundled onward.

CHAPTER TWENTY-TWO

Santana's head throbbed. Grit and dust filled her nose and eyes. She could smell water, moss, and rock.

All was dark.

She levered herself into a sitting position and placed a hand to her head. Something sticky met her palm. She was certain that it was blood, but there was no way to know for sure. The absence of light saw to that.

Around her, something moved. She detected fabric on stone, the sound of someone shifting in their sleep. She thought back to her last memories of smoke and fire. Valentina's contraption caught her unaware, and Santana leaped from harm's way. In the edge of her vision, she could make out the fuzzy shapes of her attackers, then...

And then...

Santana coughed, and the sound echoed around her. There was no doubt in her mind as to where she could be. The problem was identifying how far down she was.

What was the trigger?

The floor had cracked open beneath the group. What was

once sturdy sagged and buckled like heavy weights over worn-out fabric. They tumbled into the darkness. Rocks and soil and brush crashed around them...

Then the darkness. That'd explain the itchy scrub of dirt lodged inside my shorts.

She stood, wobbling a little as she did. She kept a hand above her, feeling for a ceiling, but found none. She tested the ground around her with the toe of her boot and found a steady mass of uneven rock made the floor.

There was more movement beside her. Someone else sat up, groaning. Another person coughed. Another remarked, softly asking where they were and what happened.

I'm one step ahead of you.

Santana crouched, feeling around for her backpack. She was quiet, delicate with opening it. She reached inside and found a lighter. The fall had smashed it, and the liquid had leaked into the material.

She sighed.

Someone groaned in pain, the steady awakening of the group growing louder with every passing moment.

Santana fished around and found another lighter.

She spun the wheel.

The spark flashed, momentarily illuminating the space around her. She only left the flame lit for a second, using the flash of light to gain her bearings. Eyes turned toward the source. People scuttled away, startled by her sudden apparition.

She moved. She'd burned her vicinity into her memory and used it to take a careful few steps ahead. The rocks descended a gradual decline. The ceiling was twenty feet above, though behind them was nothing but stone and large patches of mud.

Voices called to Santana, alert and fearful. Santana flashed the lighter again, a short distance from where she was, leading their gaze and attention like a will-o-the-wisp.

Someone pushed to their feet, crying out in pain as their leg buckled. Someone else feverishly grabbed for their weapon, surprised to find it was nowhere nearby.

Santana used the burning image of her surroundings and moved another twenty feet. The outline of an underground river snaked ahead of her. Beyond that was a dark hole into a cave.

Santana flashed the light.

Four people were on their feet, eyes desperately seeking Santana.

Santana moved again. Another flash of the light.

This time a gun was waiting for her.

The light lasted moments.

Santana jumped out of the way, foot landing awkwardly on a stone. Her ankle threatened to sprain, but she kept it together as adrenaline drove her forward.

Another flash from her lighter. The river was close. It was only six feet across. Santana knew she could jump that on a normal day.

She cut the light, this time not glancing behind her. She made the jump, feet slipping as they landed on smooth, damp stone. A shot fired. The ceiling crumbled above. Dust rained down. Rock shook. Someone shouted, wrestling the gun away, fearful of more noise and what it could do to the cave's collapse.

Santana pocketed the lighter and ran, heading in the direction of the tunnel, unafraid of the dark and not wanting to draw their attention any further.

Something rushed beside her. Wind stirred. Santana lowered her head, held her hands before her, and ran.

Straight into a soft, fleshy mass.

A mass that grunted and grabbed her wrists. "Where do you think you're going, sunshine?"

Valentina hopped down from the tree as the blaze continued to grow. Now it had spread, and a few pockets of other fires were steadily increasing.

She grimaced, then slipped out of her top. It was damp from her sweat, and she used this to attack the nearby flames, attempting to quell the worst of it. She reduced the size of the nearest fire, creating a track around it where the fire wouldn't spread thanks to the ashen ring. She eventually managed to stamp it out.

That did nothing to help the others. Across the track, another fire was steadily growing. There was only one solution Valentina could think of, and there wasn't a river in sight nearby. She arched her head to the sky and looked for clouds or any indication of rain. Luckily the damp of the forest reduced the speed of the spread, but it would still find a way to grow.

Valentina put her hands in her hair, then looked at the sinkhole where the others had disappeared. She quickly examined the ground, a large crater where once there had been trees and shrub and brush. The land was uneven, a mass of rocks and dirt. It sank inward, and as far as she could examine, there was no way inside.

Fuck. Fuck. Fuck.

She wondered if Santana was with them. She had to be, otherwise wouldn't she be here doing something about the fire?

Valentina frowned, then made her decision. She turned up the path where the troops had appeared and sprinted through the jungle. Her only option was to either find help or run from the raging inferno that might soon grow.

She wound through the trees, the path not in the least bit straight. The fire's crackle soon receded, but the light and the smoke did not. She ran for what felt like miles until eventually, the path descended into a small pocket in the ground. A tunnel appeared like a mineshaft entrance. There was no one nearby, only trees and quiet.

Valentina drew a breath and headed inside as the first drops of rain began to fall.

CHAPTER TWENTY-THREE

The way ahead was dark, but Valentina refused to allow any kind of light. She felt naked and exposed now that Santana was gone, and all that she had on her person was ballistic explosions, gadgets, and her pistol.

I mean, still not a bad bag, though.

She had no food or water. She only had the darkness. She tentatively crept on, using her hands and feet to guide her way through the black. The walls were rough earth. They crumbled at her touch, her fingers occasionally knotting in roots. There was enough space above her that she could stand tall, and only when she came across her first split along the tunnel route did she draw out her cell phone and light up the screen.

A dark corridor opened to her left. The tunnel continued straight ahead.

She closed her eyes and listened, seeing if she could detect any notion of anyone nearby. Satisfied that she was alone, she thumbed the flashlight app and lit the tunnel in brilliant white.

The opening to her left was a small den, its floor flattened and its walls fairly smooth. A couple of sleeping bags lay in untidy bundles, and the signs of a makeshift fire long burned out were visible in the corner. She shone the light ahead through the tunnel, which seemed to stretch on forever. Tracks in the ground indicated that this was where the carts had come from.

Valentina shut off the light and continued ahead.

The dark pressed around her. Soon she was lost again. She paused, then flashed her light, allowing the image to burn into her brain. She had no idea that, at that very moment, her lost comrade was doing the same.

The tunnel took a hard right. She followed around the corner, only stopping when she met resistance.

A wall stood before her. The tunnel ended at a solid block of packed earth.

Valentina took a step back, snarling at the sudden blockade. She switched on her flashlight and shone it at the barrier.

"Where did you all come from?" Her voice echoed gently around her. She glanced at the ground and discovered that the tracks were gone.

"Curiouser, and curiouser." She spun and tried to detect where the last of the tracks had ended. She retraced her steps, no longer concerned about anyone finding her since there was no one around.

She walked back thirty feet or so, switching direction and going back the way she had come. The tracks were there one minute, then they weren't.

Valentina crouched and examined the ground. She ran a hand over the dust, palm scratching against rocks and fallen roots. The earth was compacted, pressed hard with the weight of bodies and traffic. Where had it come from?

The rain increased in strength outside. The sound of the droplets pattered against the earthen roof. Trickles of water snaked their way into the tunnel, creeping along like sentient vines as it fell down the gradual slope. From where Valentina stood, she could make out the dark, silvery glow of the entrance and see the rain falling in angry white lines.

At least that should do something to quell the flames. She hoped but didn't fully believe it could.

She examined the walls, the ceiling, and the floor again. There was no sign of entry or where they could have come from. It was a mystery and one that she pressed herself to uncover. She stood there in the darkness for five minutes, then fifteen passed. Soon another five minutes had gone, and the water was slicking the floor, making the compact earth smooth and slippery. The rain pounded outside and the trickles of water built into something greater. The water reached her feet even this far down the tunnel, darkening the soil, slowly increasing until it was half an inch deep.

Guess this is what monsoons look like in the tropics. Nothing, then a lot all at once.

She shone the light around her feet, wondering whether she should find somewhere else to wait out the storm. The water built around her, swelling, until…

A line appeared at the bottom of the nearby wall. A faint dark crack of an opening that the water seeped through, wearing away at the mud. Valentina crouched and prodded the seam. It yielded beneath her finger. Some of the water trickled off in the tiny crevice, and with each milliliter that passed, the hole grew.

Valentina stepped back, then kicked the wall with the sole of her boot. The wall didn't break, but it did budge. From the small crack grew a much larger one.

Valentina scooped water in her hands and ran them along the line, tracing where it led until it was six feet in height. She drew her knife and hacked away at the seams until her knife fell cleanly through. When she was satisfied, and the entrance's outline was clear, the water was licking the tops of her toes. She stepped back, pressed her back against the wall, jumped with both feet, and kicked the door again.

It moved slightly.

She kicked again.

Water rushed inside.

She kicked once more.

The door opened, enough to slide inside. Darkness met her on the other side.

Darkness I can deal with easily. An ambush might have been trickier.

Two things occurred to Valentina as she entered the opening. The first was that no one had entered this chamber in some time. The second was that this hadn't been the hidden entrance the others had used.

Either way, the path led down, and she would somehow find a way to use it to her advantage.

Santana's wrists were sore.

They knew how to tie their rope. The coil was rough, binding the wrists and cutting into the skin. No matter Santana's protests, they tied harder than she'd have preferred.

Her legs remained free, and one of them held a length of rope tightly in one hand. She felt like a dog on a leash, except a dog had the dignity of all four limbs being free.

"Shine over here." The woman in the grey tank top was authoritative, yet there was a little warble in her tone that betrayed a fear she tried to swallow. Still, she composed herself well.

Casandra obeyed, pointing her torch in the direction of more of the rubble. Three of them had managed to light their torches with Santana's assistance, and they now illuminated the damage before them. Bodies littered the rubble, many covered in blood, most lying limp and lifeless. Only a handful of the group had survived, and two of them were worse for wear. A lank man with patchy stubble and a permanently sour expression groaned and pawed at the piece of bone sticking out of his thigh. A woman with a short crop of dreadlocks lay nearby, her top covered in blood, her breathing shallow and faint. Santana knew it wouldn't be long before she took her final breath.

The torch shone on yet another victim of the collapse. One of the men who Valentina had shot in the shoulder lay on his back, his body twisted in a way it was certainly never meant to go. The woman in the tank top shook her head. "Fuck."

Casandra nodded solemnly. "Fuck," she repeated.

"How many dead?" The cave carried Santana's soft voice.

The giant behind her grunted and nudged her as if to say, "Shut the fuck up."

Santana ignored him, looking at Tank Top for the answer.

Tank Top hopped down the rocks. By all accounts, she was okay. There was some bruising and a few mild lacerations, but the worst that had happened was the giant tear in her pants. Her knee and most of her thigh were on show, but compared to everyone else, she'd been lucky.

She hopped the final rock and landed close to Santana. Her fingers danced over her pistol strapped to her waist. "You want to be very careful about speaking out of turn in a situation like this."

Santana raised an eyebrow. "I asked a simple question."

"Here's the simple answer." The woman turned back to the wreckage. "Enough." She whirled and prodded an angry finger in Santana's chest. "All because of you and your friend and your bullshit. We should be halfway out of the jungle by now, ready to claim our cash prize. But no. I'm stuck down here with you, and half my crew is dead."

Santana chuckled.

The woman drew closer. "Something funny?"

"That's why I laughed," Santana shot back, enjoying the fire that grew on the woman's face. "Your guy didn't seem that concerned about saving lives when he was shooting at your gang."

The woman scoffed. "He was a fucking idiot. I told them not

to trust him, but would they listen to me? No. They wouldn't." She advanced, closing the final inches of their gap. Her breath smelled of mushrooms. She pinched Santana's cheeks. "We need to make something very clear, Jane. You're ours now until we can find our way out of this catacomb. One word out of line and we'll punish you." She jerked her thumb at everything behind her. "You think these guys suffered awful deaths? You haven't begun to see what we can do with you."

Santana spat at her. The woman jumped back in surprise, face burning red, screwed with fury.

"Why keep me alive?" Santana asked. "Just kill me if you don't want the burden."

"As tempting as that is," the woman wiped the spit off her face and attempted to compose herself, "I have a feeling you might prove useful. Plus, we have evidence of our situation I can show the boss in case he refuses to believe what happened here today."

"Found it!" Casandra called from the rubble.

The woman addressed the giant behind Santana. "Grip her tight. Punish her if she speaks again."

"Just like that—"

Santana stopped as a rush of air expelled from her lungs. The giant's fist found her side, burying itself deeper than she cared for. She doubled over, seeing stars for a moment.

The woman laughed, then wandered over to where Casandra was busy digging in chunks of rock. As she removed a medium-sized stone, a pulsing blue glow appeared.

"Good," the woman stated. "We're still in business."

CHAPTER TWENTY-FOUR

Tunnels, tunnels, always more tunnels.

Valentina scoured through the darkness, passing through a series of small, empty chambers. There was nothing remarkable about any of them. The rooms were no larger than fifteen feet by fifteen feet with open mud doorways that led into yet another room. Maybe they had once been bedrooms, a place for people to get out of the jungle and find some solace and protection from the elements. Perhaps they had been something else entirely. Valentina had never been that much of a historian.

All she knew was that curiosity drove her forward. The rooms continued to slope down, and down was where she needed to go. The air smelled wet, although she'd left the water from the rain far behind her. Her flashlight app shone the way, and she no longer feared an ambush.

By the time she entered the twentieth chamber, she'd grown impatient. One thing was different in this room, however. There were three doors instead of one.

Decisions, decisions...

Valentina examined the entrance of each and finally settled on east. If her internal compass was right, that one would take her toward the place where Santana and the others had fallen into the earth. Her mind drifted to Santana, then Kit, and Bradley. Once again, her internal rage stirred.

This ends soon. One way or another, this ends.

The next room was like the others. The next was like the one before. She wandered alone in the darkness, seeking some kind of differentiator, anything to tell her that things were different.

Finally, that sign came.

The room was the same shape and size, but one feature stood out.

In one corner was a patch of green. It was no larger than a dinner plate, but the moss grew proudly and bright. Valentina examined it and ran her finger through the growth. It was damp, which could only mean one thing.

A hidden doorway was nearby. Valentina went through the visible entrance and found another room, sans moss. She returned to the patch and felt around the green. The wall was colder and a little softer. She pressed on it to see if it would yield, but no luck.

Valentina looked back into the darkness, then made up her mind. She took a round device from her pocket. There were no distinguishing markings across the metal surface to communicate what kind of device it was, but Valentina knew. She had spent years crafting and learning the weights and feels and temperatures of her gadgets. She could pick them out in a lineup of identical copies, her fingers grown sensitive to their touch and feel.

She placed the orb in the patch of moss and walked back into the other room. *If this goes wrong, I can always go back.*

But she couldn't go forward.

Valentina ducked around a corner and initiated the device. A second passed, then the concentrated ballistic explosion came. The walls rumbled, and dust fell. The doorway threatened to collapse but held its structure. After a few seconds of waiting, she peeked around the door and examined her work.

A hole the size of a wrecking ball was now in the corner. The wall was gone, and where the moss had been was only dirt.

Beyond that was new darkness, and it led down into the belly of the earth rather rapidly.

The wheels squeaked, but the barrow held.

It was an irritating addition to their journey into the dark. Every rotation punctured Santana's mind and caused her to wince. Tank Top led the procession, torch in hand, a grin on her face when she threw the occasional glance to Santana and spotted her discomfort. There were only four of them remaining. Santana, Casandra, the giant—who she heard Tank Top call Johnson—and Tank Top, who preferred to be called Boa.

Boa. Santana laughed in her head. *Because you're so badass, you had to name yourself after a snake.*

The tunnel stretched on for what felt like miles. Cavern walls, rough and littered with holes and entrances to other places formed around them. Santana took it all in, trying to remember each tiny detail in case her expeditions ever led her here. She wondered if they were heading in the right direction toward the Atlanticore mine and supposed she'd find out soon enough.

A pool appeared on the right, its surface deadly still and mirroring the ceiling. Boa peered over the top, torch in hand, and claimed she could see the bottom. Santana knew that while the bottom of cave lakes and pools was mostly always clear to see, it was impossible to know its depths. Untouched water had its mysticism, and a quick look could leave you thinking you could touch the shallows and stand, while the reality was that the water stretched a hundred feet beneath you.

Casandra threw a stone. The "plop" echoed in a strange pattern around the walls.

Boa glared at her.

Casandra's smile slipped off her face.

The Atlanticore throbbed with power in the barrow and seemed to hum in the call of the sound. Santana had never witnessed them shine so brightly. She had seen plenty in her time in Atlantica, powering the AJS's vehicles, and contained within the power grids and facilities across town, but never had she seen them shine this brightly.

Boa walked ahead. They hardly spoke. The pool passed, and the chamber opened, revealing a large hole belowground the size of an amphitheater. Their footsteps echoed, but there was something else, too. Something that Santana's ears picked up long before the others.

Casandra rested the wheelbarrow on its stand and gave a heavy sigh.

"What are you doing?" Boa asked, venom in her eyes.

"A rest," Casandra declared. "Just for a minute. Sorry."

Boa looked as if she was going to protest, then saw the exhaustion on Casandra's face. Though she hadn't taken too many injuries, Santana had noticed her limping along with the barrow. Not only that, but it was now almost double the weight than before considering the amount of Atlanticore they had to salvage.

They set up a small camp. Johnson took the bag he had recovered from his dead comrade and laid out some food and bottled water. They sat and ate, Boa, Casandra, and Johnson munching happily while Santana merely watched. Of course, they wouldn't let her eat. Why would they? It's not like she was the only one who would soon be able to save them.

The scuttling continued, gentle tapping on the hard ground. Santana glanced toward the pool. Its mirrored surface rippled from the creature's emergence. It was sneaky, camouflaged to blend with the rock. A hooked tail behind it.

"Think we'll be able to find them?" Casandra asked amid a mouthful of food. "We close?"

Boa swallowed, gaze focused on her food. "Sure. We just keep moving in..." She drew out a compass and waited for the needle to stop. "That direction, we should be fine. Can't be that far, now."

Johnson grunted, zeroed in on his food. Santana remained silent as the creature worked its way toward Casandra, the gentle tapping nearly inaudible.

She grinned.

The scorpion was tiny, the size of Santana's thumb. It approached Casandra's rear and paused, waiting in her shadow. She shifted, trying to get comfortable, one leg out straight in front of her to account for her ankle, which had rapidly begun to swell now that they had stopped.

The scorpion reared up, its tiny pincers snapping. The tail hooked over its body, elongating, a black droplet of venom at its dark tip.

Casandra finished her food and took a long breath. She leaned back, resting her arms behind her, the weight of her body pressing toward the scorpion.

The scorpion stung.

"Fuck!" she exclaimed, a hand swatting at her back. She twisted around, looking for what had caused the pain, but her flurry of movement batted the scorpion several feet away. "What the hell?"

Boa shot her a look. "Problem?"

"Something just bit me," Casandra complained. "Ouch, it hurts."

She twisted, trying to see the site of her pain, but no amount of turning helped. She asked for help, which Boa reluctantly gave. She examined the location, running her fingers over the bright red spot on her back. The center point had begun to bleed, and a strange yellow pus bubble was forming over it, the area of the wound multiplying.

"That can't be good," Boa stated.

"What?" Casandra asked. "What is it?"

Boa glanced around, looking in the air as though a mosquito or insect had caused the problem. Santana tilted her head. "Permission to speak, captain?"

It was facetious, but she didn't care.

"What is it?" Boa replied.

"You might want to look lower," Santana informed her. She nodded to the edge of the pool where the scorpion was nearing the water.

Boa's eyes grew wide. "A scorpion?"

"A what?" Casandra bellowed. Nearby, a stalactite wobbled precariously on the ceiling.

"Shhhh," Boa instructed. She rushed over to the water to get a better look, but the creature had slipped away into the deep.

The wound grew larger. Casandra groaned in pain. The redness had now swollen to the size of her hand. It rose into an angry mound, and with each throb, Casandra bellowed. A spear of rock fell from the ceiling and slipped into the mirrored pool.

"A black-tailed cave scorpion," Santana stated matter-of-factly. "First discovered in 1943 by David Myers in Argentina. They're tricky beasts, having evolved to develop a camouflage that makes them ridiculously hard to detect. The only giveaway is the black mark on the end of their stinger. Aggravated easily, and with enough toxic venom to knock out a fully grown elephant in five minutes." She tilted her head. "I'm not sure how long someone like you would have left."

Boa spun on her, eyes blazing. Casandra wept on the ground, curled into a ball, one hand massaging the rapidly growing swelling.

"What's the antidote?" Boa asked.

Santana grinned. "Antidote?"

Boa shook her violently. "The antidote, Poindexter. How do we fix her? What's the cure?"

Santana nodded at her bonds. "Untie me, and you'll find out."

"Tell me!" Boa roared.

Another stalactite fell. The water rippled.

Santana grinned. "Only one way to help your friend, and that's to untie me, bitch."

Casandra turned white. Her lips lost all color. Her back was the only thing that was in any tone other than red. Boa glanced her way, then looked at the cart. Santana knew what was on her mind. Even in that moment of peril, her concern was with the core. Who was going to lift it if not Casandra? Johnson, perhaps? But Johnson had been set to watch Santana, so who was going to look after their captive?

Santana repeated. "Untie me if you want her to live."

Casandra howled. A dozen more stalactites fell. One dropped nearby, its fragments of rock reaching Boa's feet. She growled, then sliced her knife through Santana's bonds. She drew her pistol. "You so much as think about running, and you're dead."

"I'd like to see the effect of a gunshot in this cave," Santana muttered as she sprinted back the way they had come.

Where are you? Where are you? Where are you? She chanted in her mind as she skirted the pool and looked for what she thought she'd seen. The pool was less clear now that the surface rippled from the stalactites' entry. Still, she could make out the bright crimson glow of the plant she was looking for on its wall. She called, "I need better light. Now."

Boa grimaced, then nodded at Johnson. He came behind her, holding up the flame as though he were offering an umbrella. The light illuminated the swirls of plant she was looking for, and without a second wasted, Santana dived.

The water was freezing. Her skin prickled. She opened her eyes, feeling no sting from the fresh, clean pool. She swam down toward the patch of red, on the surface looking as though it was within arm's reach, realizing now that it was meters beneath her. She continued, keeping an eye on the critters that scuttled and swam, strange things that were colorless or pale. Crabs with large eyes to see in the dark. Fish the length of her finger with no eyes at all. She swam ever deeper, the spores looking as if they were moving further away with every stroke.

Still, she went down, not counting the seconds or the minutes that passed. Something rubbed her arm as it swam past, but Santana focused on the plant. Soon she found it, just as her body was beginning to gasp for oxygen. She grabbed a fistful and pulled it from the root. The leaves were long but spongy, the color of blood. She kicked from the wall and sped upward, the surface playing with the illusion that she'd never make it, that she was here forever now, encased in the watery depths.

Her lungs ached. She kicked her feet. The torch's flame rippled the surface.

She breached the water just as her lungs shouted and burned from oxygen deprivation. She clawed her way onto land, then ran to Casandra.

Boa and Johnson watched with fascination. Casandra had stopped screaming—which was a true blessing, giving the debris that had crumbled and broken around them. Santana screwed up the plant in her hand, rubbed her palms together until the water that dripped from the leaves turned red, then placed it on the wound.

She rubbed the plant roughly into the skin, all around the zone of infection. Where the scorpion had stung, in that tiny little nodule of blood and pus, she pressed the fronds against her back, then formed a suction cup with the wet leaves and her hands. She pumped her hands as though she were giving chest compressions. Thick, red liquid oozed between her fingers, and it was impossible for Boa to tell if it was blood or the plants doing their work. Santana knew. It was both.

The swelling was boiling against her hands, but it soon started to reduce. Santana took another chunk of the plant and shoved it into Casandra's mouth. Her jaw was lax, and she was unmoving, but Santana knew it would do the job.

"Get her some water," she commanded of Boa. Boa bristled against the direct order, then grabbed her bottle. She raised Casandra's head and dribbled the water along her lips. It combined with the plant and turned pink, then red. Casandra spluttered as the water clogged her airways. She sat up, coughing, eyes clenched shut as she expelled the plant from her mouth.

"Chew. No questions." Santana handed her another fistful of the plant.

Boa enforced this lot, making sure it stayed down. She wasn't delicate, clamping Casandra's mouth closed until it was gone. The larger woman bucked and convulsed against the food, but eventually, it was gone.

Santana waited a few moments, then removed some of the leaves from her back. The swelling was half the size it had been. The head of the pus bubble had popped and mixed with the red liquid.

"It's on its way down," Santana declared. "I'll compress this for a little longer, but we should be in the clear."

Boa eyed her suspiciously. "What was that stuff?"

"Draconius Sporidius," Santana explained. "It's a rare root that only grows in the depths of cave pools. It has antitoxins to aid with severe stings, and you can often find it in the places where aquatic scorpions dwell. No one quite knows why. The plant draws out the toxins and also acts as a bandage to the wound site. It actively sucks it back, a little vampiric in its properties." She shook her head. "Amazing, isn't it?"

"Where did you learn to do that?" Boa asked.

Santana waved dismissively. "It's a long story and one that you probably don't care about. All you need to know is that your answer to getting the fuck out of here has been tied up behind you all along."

Boa turned to Johnson, then looked back at Santana. "Who are you?"

Santana grinned. "Your exit strategy." Her eyes roamed to the whip that Boa had stolen and kept around her waist. "May I have my effects back, please."

CHAPTER TWENTY-FIVE

Voices came from up ahead.

Valentina ducked low. The hole had led her farther down into the depths, though this time there were more signs of sophisticated life. Stones and steps interspersed the darkness. She was in a cave that seemed to have no ceiling. Even her flashlight couldn't illuminate what was overhead. Occasionally she passed stone structures with ancient faces half worn off from the passage of time. Once she passed through a large archway inscribed with strange runes that matched those she had found in the ceiling of the city cave.

"What the hell was this island?" she muttered.

Now she stayed low, the voices of two men in polite chatter making their way to her. She couldn't see the source, and knowing a little about cave acoustics, she wouldn't dare to guess where they were coming from or how far they could be. They could be miles away, or they could be beside her.

She shut off her flashlight and let her senses guide her. Progress was slow, but soon she came to a structure that might once have been a fountain of some kind. The stone basin had cracked, and the water had long since drained, yet a golden ornament decorated the rock in the center.

Well, well, well. What a surprise to find one place that people haven't yet looted.

Valentine entertained the notion of grabbing the gold, only for a fleeting second. She had no easy way of excavating or carrying it out of the cave. The voices grew louder, appearing after a short silence, and Valentina turned her head in their direction.

In the far distance, a dim light glowed—a circle of vision in the cavern's darkness. Two men stood side-by-side, standing on what appeared to be a smooth, carved path.

Interesting.

Valentina snuck toward them, careful of where she trod to avoid disrupting the rubble and loose debris. As she drew closer, their conversation became clearer.

"...they're really throwing it in the trash this year." The man wore a thick jacket with a fur collar. He had a pistol strapped to his waist, and he'd folded his arms around himself as he shivered.

The second man sported an AR15, holding it in both hands. Its muzzle pointed at the ground, neither of them sensing any apparent threat. "They did well a couple of years back. When Jose Burkenstein was leading the charge. Ever since he got jailed for some kiddie touching thing, the club's gone downhill. Ain't never been able to recover."

"God bless the Atlantica Avengers," the first man scoffed with a headshake. "One day they might actually stand a chance of making it to the playoffs. You'd think that with the amount of money they pipe into this city, they'd invest in some decent players that could do the job and hit the World Series."

"Hmmmm..." the second man agreed.

Valentina drew closer, finding a place to hide that was out of reach of their light. The path they stood on had parallel markings that showed tire tracks along its length. Valentina wondered what kind of traffic passed through here because they sure as hell weren't wheelbarrow tracks.

"Still..." the man with the AR15 stated. "Hopefully things will change. Lesley Voss is supposed to be a damn sight better than the shitty managers they've had since Burkenstein."

"One can only hope." The first man scratched his head. "Any update on when they're coming back through?"

"None," the second man replied. "Still, easy money for a piss easy job, don't you think?"

"Mmhmm," the first man agreed.

"I'd rather be sentinel in the quiet than harvesting the blue," AR15 commented. "Imagine if that shit blows. Whole place will go down."

Valentina had heard enough.

Working quietly, she took her pistol and screwed on its short, stubby silencer. She rummaged in her pocket again and found a tiny vial of liquid, which she shook to activate the agent. She ejected the magazine, then dripped the liquid down into the golden casings. Satisfied, she eased the magazine back into place and seated it, then aimed.

With one eye closed, she lined up the sights with AR15. She pulled the trigger.

The bullet spat out of the gun, the silencer forcing the report into a tiny *pop*. The bullet whizzed at AR15, slicing through his shirt and grazing his neck.

He growled, alarm and surprise brightening his face as he brought his rifle to firing position. Before he had the chance to steady himself, his eyes rolled back in his head, and he collapsed.

The first man held his pistol aimed into the darkness. He glanced down at his fallen comrade. "Leon?"

Valentina shot again. This time it ripped the pistol from the man's grip. He recoiled, shaking his hand as though electrocuted. Valentina swept out of the darkness, appearing like a vampire from the gloom. She sped at the man, lunging at him before he could raise his fists.

She socked a blow to his cheek, then twisted his hand behind his back. With a bit of pressure in the right nerve centers, the man folded. She pressed him against the floor, her knee in his back, his cheek bunched up as he turned his head sideways.

Valentina leaned in close, whispering delicately into his ear. "Hello, friend, sorry for the intrusion. I have a couple of questions for you, and I think the best thing you can do is answer them before you end up like your friend over there."

His gaze moved to the unconscious man beside him. "What did you do to him? Is he dead?"

"Stupid question," Valentina reprimanded. "If he were dead, he wouldn't be breathing. See how his body is still moving? That's the first indicative clue that he's not quite ready for the grave."

"Then how…" the man started.

"Sleeper agent. A simple dose of chemistry on a bullet. A couple of drops absorbed into the bloodstream and you're out like a light. Pretty neat, huh?"

The man muttered incoherently.

"So," Valentina urged. "What's it going to be? The easy way, or the hard way?"

The man thought for a second, then relaxed.

Valentina smiled. "I thought so."

She helped him to his feet, pistol pressed against his temple. With some carefully worded instructions, she got him to sit against a nearby rock outcropping. She crouched before him, gun in her hand as a reminder as she asked her questions.

"Where are we?" Valentina asked.

The man's face clouded. "Hell if I know."

Valentina's gun twitched toward him.

The man waved a hand, protesting. "I don't mean it like that. I mean that I have no idea. We're under the jungle. They haven't put in many names or territory lines down here. We came down with the team, and they stationed Leon and me in this section."

"Why?"

"I don't know." Lines creased his brow. "We do as told and get paid well for it. Saw some carts come through this way a couple of days ago, but nothing has happened since. It's not like it's a commonly used road."

"How far away is the rest of the expedition team?"

The man's eyes said, *How did you know it was an expedition team?*

Valentina answered without him asking out loud. "Because, as you've so rightly declared, we're beneath a jungle, in a cave, and your team would likely be down here to dig. I'm sure it's that or playing poker around the stone table. How far away is the main group?"

The man looked down the path toward the darkness. "A mile? Maybe two?"

"That's quite a distance to protect." Valentina narrowed her eyes. "What's down here? Why so many of you?"

The man's lips thinned. There was genuine fear in his eyes.

Valentina moved closer. "You have two things to fear in this world right now. Number one is your employer, and number two is standing in front of you. My guess is that if your employer is anything like the rest of the shitbags in Atlantica, they'll kill you quickly. A bullet to the temple and..." She fanned her hands away, miming an explosion. "But, if you go for the option of me killing you, things will take a different turn. I *will* test your pain threshold. I will find every part of you that screams. I will search and seek and discover the darkest bits of you, the deepest fears you hold, and I will exploit them. You think you know the darkness, but you haven't even knocked on its door."

The man gulped.

"Have I made myself clear?"

The man nodded. He drew a long breath, then spoke. "The

truth is that I don't know the full extent of things in here. They keep it all pretty under wraps. All I know is that the project is large. It's revolutionary. It's something that the city has never seen before." He nodded at Leon. "All I know I learned from him, and all he tells me is that this will go down in history as one of the greatest creations of all time. A sight that historians will write about in history books."

"So you're talking about a maniac with an ego? Okay, I think I know something you don't know." She glanced down the tunnel, wondering if she could be that close to Archie by now.

"Which direction is the exit?" She knew the response as he pointed back the way she had come. "What's your best means of transportation?"

The man pointed in the opposite direction. "SUVs. Enough to bring the team down. Most tunnels are only large enough for one to pass through at a time."

"Interesting." Valentina stroked her chin. "Well, you've been more than useful, and your country thanks you for your service." She aimed the pistol at the man.

"Wait, you promised!" he managed, but Valentina had fired, and the graze on his neck trickled with blood. His head flopped to his chest, and he was out like a light.

"Poor kitty," Valentina crooned. "You thought I'd let you stay awake through this all, didn't you?" She patted his cheek. "Baby, Valentina Winters works solo."

She strode off down the tracks toward the heart of it all. A heart that hadn't yet begun beating but soon would. She kept her ears pricked, listening for further signs of conversation. The cave stretched around her. Darkness covered her. Valentina strode on along the path.

CHAPTER TWENTY-SIX

A mile in the darkness was equivalent to ten miles in daylight—Valentina assumed. She didn't often walk that far in daylight.

She had never felt more alone. While she was used to working in isolation, her mind kept flicking back to Santana. She had to be down here somewhere, around this area underground. Valentina wasn't familiar with the network of underground tunnels and caves, but she assumed one should lead to the other...surely?

Santana had grated on her above ground, but now she missed her guide. The woman had proven herself a worthy ally, and though Valentina rarely played with others, she knew she'd benefit from Santana's help now. She felt bad for her, too. To be lost underground, surrounded by enemies was never a good state.

Still, what was Valentina to do?

Her mission was to find Kit and Bradley. Now she had her first inkling that they were in the right direction. What other egomaniacal tyrant would be building some kind of colossal contraption beneath the jungle?

Archie Fontana. That's who.

The path wound ahead, smooth and reliable. Now and then, Valentina would use only the dull light of her screen to confirm her direction. After nearly a mile of walking, she came across more voices, and her heart lifted. She had nearly approached the end of her long walk.

Something very pretty caught her eye.

There was electricity in the tunnels. As she rounded the corner, the light hurt her eyes. Great LED panels decorated the walls, strung together by thick black wire. A group of men and women were hacking at the walls, shaping the rough rock into something smooth and presentable. Valentina thought about the Bat Cave and the large open sections interspersed with modern corridors and rooms and wondered if that was the effect that Archie was going for.

She took another step ahead, and the SUV gleamed in the harsh glow of the LEDs. There were three of them, neatly parked to the side of the construction, although it didn't matter where they sat here. No traffic control was going to be monitoring the situation.

Valentina tried to work out her path.

The group was in a tunnel that opened out into the cave. A large expanse of wall towered above them. Pockets of rock were missing, and there were many places for handgrips and toeholds, but wouldn't it be more fun to shoot her way forward and wipe out the enemy?

No. Be smart. Despite how much longer it'll take.

Valentina made her way to the wall and shrank against it. As the chatter of voices and the *clank* of metal on rock covered the noise she made, she gripped the wall and began her climb.

The rock was rough, and some of the edges were sharp, but Valentina's hands were calloused and thick from her years of training. She pulled her way up, rising twenty feet above the ground before she shifted to the side and moved over the mouth of the tunnel. She glanced below, keeping an eye out for wandering enemies, and luckily only once did someone appear in her sight. They smoked their cigarette and stretched. The smoke rose and filled Valentina's nostrils. The scent reminded her of Dick, momentarily clouding her vision as her body reacted to the feelings.

The man soon left. Valentina continued crossing the cave. She'd started lowering herself when her hand slipped. A chunk of rock tore from the wall and fell to the ground. She lost hold, clinging on by one hand, her feet slipping in the surprise of it all.

She found another hold and composed herself. She waited a few moments, glancing down in case someone had heard the ruckus. It soon became clear that no one expected the intrusion.

That works out well for me.

Valentina made the final descent and rushed to the SUVs. She ducked behind them, keeping out of sight of the tunnel where she could make out a woman hacking at the wall. Her tank top was dark with sweat, and her bulging arms shone with moisture.

Valentina rounded to the door of the nearest SUV with its tinted windows. She dug into her pocket and found a lock pick. She raised the pick to the lock, but as she did, the SUV started rocking.

Valentina shrank back. A hand appeared at the window, and soon she could make out the sounds of amorous activities from within.

You've got to be kidding me.

The SUV rocked rhythmically in time with their grunts. Valentina rolled her eyes then rounded to the second SUV. She paused, wondering if this would be a one-off or if she had just accidentally wandered into an underground dogging site. She tried the handle. They'd locked the vehicle. She put her lock pick to work.

It took longer than usual to get the door open. These latest models of SUV had updated protocols to ensure their security, but nothing bypassed Valentina. She opened the door and slid in, closing it gently behind her.

The SUV reeked of new leather. The seat cradled her ass. She felt strange having just walked through a cavern with rough, ancient walls, the air possibly undisturbed for decades, to now sit in a modern machine. The comparison was jarring.

She crouched beneath the steering column and examined the façade. Hooking her fingers beneath the surface, she revealed the panel beneath and the wiring connections. She studied the cables for a few moments, familiarizing herself with the gadgetry before making her move.

She touched the wires together.

The car thrummed into life. Headlights exploded light into the cavern. The hum of the engine drew the attention of the workers.

A group came to the tunnel entrance. Someone called through cupped hands. Valentina couldn't hear them as she slammed the SUV into reverse and pulled out from the parking spot. She slipped the gearshift into drive, then sped on down the track.

She wanted desperately to find Archie, but first, she had an adventurer to locate.

The lights were bright, forming a large cone of vision before her. As she drove away, careful to stick to the winding road and make her way safely where she needed to go, she monitored her speed carefully. One wrong move could have her rolling over and exposing herself to the others. Headlights erupted behind her, and Valentina knew for certain that others were following her.

She curved along a sweeping left arc, eventually passing the two men she had left at the side of the road. They were still unconscious, snoozing away in the dark. She drove on, the great expanse of cave finally brilliantly lit to expose the ceiling ahead. Another mile gone, and she found another cave wall.

The road veered toward a small hole, far too neat to speed straight toward. The SUVs behind crept up with a muzzle flash of gunfire as bullets *dinged* off the metalwork. Valentina sped up but knew she'd have to do something dramatic before even attempting to navigate through the tight space.

She slammed the hand brake and spun the vehicle in a half-circle. A press of a button rolled the window down, and she extended her arm and shot back. The first bullet neatly penetrated the SUV's tire.

The vehicle swerved, the force of the pop enough to rock them off balance and send the SUV careening off the track. She watched as it sped toward rock and crashed. Dark shapes emerged from the badly damaged vehicle.

The second SUV continued its path, bullets cracking the windscreen, yet it held its place. Valentina shot a few more rounds, narrowly missing their tires as they slalomed back and forth, making it hard to track in her limited visibility.

Valentina sighed. "Fine." She shot her windshield, creating a gap she could see through. She continued to roll slowly backward while the SUV in front of her sped at her.

Another round of gunfire hit her vehicle. She shot and heard someone exclaim. As the car zeroed in on her, she slammed the shifter into drive once more and yanked the wheel to the left. She curved away as the other SUV sped to the place she had been. Its body clipped her vehicle, but they bypassed each other. Valentina grunted, then shot, managing to get a clean line of fire to the driver, who slumped against the steering wheel and set the horn blaring.

Valentina kicked her SUV into a donut, then drove to the hole in the wall. She slowed on approach, far enough away that she knew the remaining figures that shot at her wouldn't be able to do proper damage. As she poked the nose through the hole, she held her breath. The tunnel was narrow, and she would have to be careful for a short while until it opened.

Wherever that may be.

CHAPTER TWENTY-SEVEN

Santana might have her whip back, but that didn't free her from the overwatch.

Johnson pushed the cart, with added weight piled onto the load of Atlanticore since Casandra rested on top. She was no small woman, but Johnson handled it well. Santana walked beside Boa, the pair not exchanging a word unless it pertained to direction and navigating through the caves.

Santana was impressed with the wildlife that managed to make the cave their homes. Bats fluttered in the stalactites. There were frogs and crabs and glow worms and a host of other insects. The human interlopers made good progress walking between the caves and tunnels until they finally emerged onto an outcrop of rock.

Darkness spread before them, below them, and above them. Boa held out the torch, but the flame only lit so far.

"Dead end," Boa muttered.

"Only if you give up," Santana replied. She found a rock, then tossed it gently into the darkness. It faded from sight as she counted the seconds. When they finally heard the clatter of the rock on the ground, she nodded. "About sixty feet down, I'd say."

Boa shot her a look. "You say that as if we're going to climb down there."

"It's either that or head back the way you came." Santana waited for a reply.

Boa snarled. She glanced at Johnson, then Casandra. Some of the color had returned to the grim woman's skin, but she still looked pallid. "You think we should?"

Santana rolled her eyes. "You knew this wouldn't be an easy journey. I know this place as well as you guys do. Either we take the way ahead, or we spend hours searching for something we might never find. You said your expedition team was due east, correct?"

Boa reluctantly nodded.

"Then east is where we go." She leaned over the edge. "Pass me the torch."

Boa did.

Santana extended an arm, squinting into the darkness. The next thing they knew, the flame was pinwheeling toward the ground, great licks of fire trailing behind as the orb of light fell and broke the darkness.

"What are you doing?" Boa exclaimed.

Santana held up a placating finger, which only made Boa turn a deeper shade of crimson.

The light illuminated the chasm, only stopping when it crashed on the solid ground below. Where it shone, they saw a rudimentary path and an abandoned wheelbarrow on the edge of the light.

"Look familiar?" Santana asked.

Boa's eyes narrowed, not wanting to accept Santana was right. "That's one of ours."

"How do you know?" Johnson broke his lengthy silence with a gruff voice.

"Because one handle is missing," Boa replied. "That's where

we stashed it to keep it out of the way. See those tracks on the dirt?"

Johnson nodded.

Santana gave a satisfied nod. "Still want to go back the way we came?"

"There has to be another way," Boa commented. She glanced along the wall on either side, only lit by one torch now, and that was the one half-sticking out of the glowing pile of Atlanticore. "Another ledge, a ramp down? Something…"

"Unfortunately, the world doesn't work like that," Santana replied. "The natural world isn't full of convenient staircases, ramps, and houses. You have to make your path if you're willing to survive." She shook her head. "Honestly, why even attempt work in the jungle if you haven't got the skills to survive out in the elements?"

Boa's hand tightened around her weapon, but she didn't draw it. "Just help us get down."

"Very well," Santana replied. She pivoted, then took her first step onto a jutting piece of rock.

Boa grabbed her wrist. The sudden jerk caused her foot to slip. She hung onto Boa and Boa alone.

Boa lurched forward onto her stomach. Santana dug her feet into any space they could find purchase. Her weight lessened. She grimaced. "Problem?"

Boa stared into her eyes. "What makes you think you're going first?"

"Because I'm the one who can do this," Santana replied. She fished into her pocket and found a snapped chalk pencil. "I can mark the way down for you. If I get down there, I can find resources to help you get down."

"Yeah, like we're going to trust you," Boa replied. "You'll run the moment your feet touch the ground."

Santana considered this. "Perhaps. But if I've led you this far, don't you think I'd help you the rest of the way?"

Boa held her stare.

"Besides," Santana continued. "You have guns. The moment I try to break free you can shoot me."

"And I will," Boa replied.

"I have no doubt," Santana commented. "Now, what are we going to do? Because even though your friend over there was relieved of her toxin count, she still needs medical help to assist in recovering from it."

Boa groaned as her face soured. She released Santana's hand, then held up her pistol. "I'm keeping this trained on you."

Santana saluted. "I'd expect nothing less."

She climbed down the rock face without issue, marking the best route along the way. Some rock pockets were large but too smooth, and others looked perfect but crumbled beneath her touch. Soon she had everything marked, and her feet touched gently on the ground.

She looked up at the others, tiny figures above her head. The mix of the torch and the Atlanticore made a strange green glow. Santana cupped her hands and called up. "I'll find some rope."

She picked up the nearby torch, then made to leave. A bullet ricocheted off the ground nearby. "You'll do no such thing."

Santana sighed. "Your choice, Boa. How are you going to get down without me?"

Boa called back, "There's a container unit thirty feet to your left. A storage capsule with some items that you can use."

Santana sighed. "Could've told me sooner," she muttered to herself.

"Keep that torch with you," Boa instructed. "I want to know where you are at all times."

Santana held the torch high and walked in the location Boa had instructed. Sure enough, a wide, steel container appeared before her. She raised the container lid and examined the contents.

There was a whole array of gear in there, from pickaxes to helmets, to flashlights, to high-vis jackets, plastic buckets, and....

Santana's eyes flickered toward the pistol. She couldn't see if it was locked and loaded, but she knew she wanted it to replace the one she had lost.

"Found anything?" Boa called down.

Santana looked up at the ledge and waved. "Some useful gear in here. Bear with me while I work out what I can do." As she spoke, she masked her arm behind her body and lowered it into the container. She felt around for the pistol. "I'll fashion something to help with the Atlanticore, too."

She slipped the pistol into the back of her shorts.

Bundling up the rope, cloth, and a series of hooks and ties she found in the container, she returned to the rock face. She climbed back up, this time attempting to work the hooks into the surface, checking they would hold their weight. It was precarious work and not ideal compared to doing this with proper equipment, but as she threaded the rope through the various pegs and hooks she had wedged into the crevices, she felt satisfied with her efforts.

She returned to the top, then tied the rope around a nearby boulder. "There. You should be able to climb down the rope. Some of the hooks may feel a little wobbly, but it will hold."

Boa turned to the boulder. "What's that for?"

"Backup," Santana replied. "No sense relying on one anchor when we can use two or three."

Boa glanced at Johnson, then back to the rope. "How are you going to get the Atlanticore down?"

"With this." Santana unfolded the large canvas. "We tie this tightly around the barrow, ensuring it holds everything in place. We double-wrap, ensure it's strong, then using another set of ropes I'll fix on my next descent, we can tie them around the barrow and lower them on a makeshift pulley system."

Johnson frowned.

"You disagree?" Santana asked.

"That thing has to weigh at least two hundred pounds."

"We hope and pray, then," Santana replied. "Let's test the rope on *you* first. If it holds for you, we should be fine. You have to be at least what? A hundred fifty pounds?"

"One-sixty," Johnson replied.

"There you go," Santana remarked.

Although Boa wasn't happy with it and cast mistrusting gazes at Santana, Johnson was allowed to descend. The rope groaned under his weight. Halfway down, one hook wrestled free and caused the line to judder. He reached the bottom, head peppered with sweat, and quickly let go. He shot a thumbs-up to the top.

"Atlanticore next," Santana instructed.

Boa nodded. They set to work tying the canvas around the barrow. When they finished, and Boa was certain it was secure, they looped the rope around the frame of the barrow and ensured it was tight. Santana climbed down to join Johnson. She handed him the rope, then climbed back up, ensuring everything was fixed and in place.

Working with Boa, they managed to shove the barrow to the brink of the outcrop. Boa glared at her. "This better work."

"I know," Santana replied dryly. "Because if this doesn't, your friend may erupt into flames from the impact."

She gave the final shove.

The barrow rolled over itself, falling sharply down. Though Johnson held the rope at the bottom, it dragged him forward, its weight causing him to buck. He pulled hard, regaining control as the barrow reached the end of its slack. It bounced a couple of times before swinging in the air.

Johnson's arms knotted with strain. His muscles flexed as he gently allowed the rope to slip through his grasp. The barrow lowered in stuttering jerks until it finally touched the ground.

Johnson released the rope. Boa called for him to check the

contents. He cut away the canvas—a waste of material in Santana's eyes—then gave them a reassuring thumbs-up.

"Me next," Boa announced.

"No," Santana contradicted. Boa shot her a glare. "Casandra next."

Boa's hands balled into fists. "You can't tell me the order, bitch. This is my squadron."

Santana shrugged. "You asked me to help. We need to help Casandra get down. She can't do this alone."

Casandra sat nearby, her breathing heavy, her eyes half-closed. She looked as though she was on the edge of sleep. There was no way she was going to climb.

"Your suggestions?" Boa asked with an edge of exhaustion in her voice.

Santana looked down at the cart. "Same technique. How you feeling about that, Cassie?"

Casandra glared at her.

"She doesn't like nicknames," Boa commented.

Santana chuckled. "Good thing she's in no condition to fight, then."

Maneuvering Casandra down was simple enough and a much easier weight for Johnson to bear. They were slower with her, careful not to knock her head against the wall as the makeshift strap frame that Santana built creaked under the weight. Finally, she landed on the canvas that Johnson had laid out for her.

She was asleep when she reached the ground.

Boa clapped, then shimmied to the edge. She sat, spun, and began her descent. Santana raced past her, speedily finding the crevices the others hadn't discovered. She hopped to the earth half a minute before Boa did.

"Proud of yourself?" Boa asked.

"I am." Santana beamed.

"What's the smile for?" Boa asked.

Santana shrugged. "I don't know. Maybe it's because you fuckers are weaponless and now I hold the power."

Boa's eyes widened. She looked at her side, hands patting her empty holster. When she looked up again, Santana held a pistol in each hand. The one she'd found in the container pointed at Johnson, while the one she'd managed to take from Boa on the descent pointed at its previous owner.

"Smooth," Boa snarled.

"I know. Now you fuckers are going to show me the way to your Atlanticore stash, mmkay?"

Johnson and Boa exchanged a glance. Casandra snoozed peacefully on the ground.

CHAPTER TWENTY-EIGHT

The steady, rhythmic drip of water was agonizing. For a length of time that was indeterminate, he closed his eyes and gritted his teeth, attempting to block out the irritating droplets.

The world was dark, and it smelled of river water. His hands were sore from the metal chains that bound his wrists, and the blood had left his legs some time ago. All Bradley Pepper knew was pins and needles, the ache of thick metal on wrists...

...and that repetitive dripping.

He raised his head. It was a Herculean effort and one that he was doing less and less often. His hair was greasy, occasionally jabbing into his eyes, and he knew that he stunk, although he'd grown used to the scent.

What is my crime? he asked himself for the hundredth time, wondering when this kind of torture would end. If only he knew how much time had passed, it might make a difference, but the only way to know would have been by counting the steady dripping of droplets from the start. Now it was too late.

He was hungry. He was thirsty. He could feel his stomach sinking.

The last thing Bradley remembered was being in his bed. He

hadn't long fallen asleep when he became aware that someone was in his room. He thought it was a dream at first. He raised his head, still lost in the fog of his mind as something stalked nearby. He muttered something, couldn't have been words, but the next thing he knew, he had taken a punch to the gut.

He hadn't even had time to recover. Before he could breathe and fill his lungs again, the sack was over his head. Someone lifted him, then crudely dragged him out of the building.

It was organized and well-executed.

He had yet to discover the rationale behind it all.

It had to have something to do with Harvey. It just had to. It couldn't be a coincidence that the moment he took a new job, something like this would happen. Isabella warned him. She told him not to get involved with dark sorts.

He had, anyway. Cash and kind words and the Atlantica smile had lured him in.

His head dropped, neck struggling to support him anymore.

Someone had delivered his food what felt like a day ago. Some nobody in dark clothing had shoveled dry wheat toast into his mouth, and the crumbs had scratched his throat. They threw the water at him, letting him catch any droplets that made it into his gaping mouth, but it wasn't that much.

He couldn't go on like this.

He couldn't cry anymore. He wouldn't cry anymore. Nothing remained to cry about. He wanted out. He *needed* out. It was bad enough to be held prisoner for days on end, yet it was worse not to know *why*.

Someone moved outside. A door handle twisted. Light spilled into the room, burning his sensitive retinas.

A figure stood in the doorway, black against the harsh, stark light. "Mr. Pepper... Good news."

"Hmmm?" Bradley offered.

"You're free to go," the voice returned.

A moment stretched before them. Bradley stared at the figure, unable to determine anything special about their characteristics. His heart thumped at the notion of the words uttered to him. He offered a weak smile before a man's voice burst into laughter.

"You should see your face," he stated before pointing the gun at him.

The man pulled the trigger.

The world filled with noise.

Pain.

Darkness.

CHAPTER TWENTY-NINE

Valentina cruised through the tunnel. The radio *hissed* at her, so she shut it off. The way ahead was tight, reminding her of a dream she once had but refused to assess its Freudian qualities.

It curved on ahead, tracking miles below the ground. When the tunnel shifted, and the cave appeared, Valentina slowed down. She was certain that those who had been behind her were gone, but now she had a decision ahead of her.

There was a fork in the road. One track led left toward an unknown destination.

And one turned right, with the same results.

Valentina rested her head against the steering wheel. *Everywhere I go, it's just more and more mazes. What the hell have you gotten yourself into, Val?*

She closed her eyes and thought of the city. The scent of fumes, the sting of the neons on her eyes, and the salivating stink of fast food. She missed it, her body aching to return. Instead, she was...

Wherever the hell I am.

She stared in either direction, then did something she hadn't done for years. She recounted the rhyme she had once spouted in kindergarten many moons ago.

"Ip dip sky blue…"

She wagged her finger with the rhyme, eventually settling on the right-hand path. She crept forward in the SUV, aware that anything could be waiting on the road ahead of her. She eased the gas, the lights casting great dancing shadows on stone columns and rocky teeth. She shook her head in disbelief, discomfort creeping into her stomach at the idea of being lost beneath the jungle. Was it here that all those people had gone missing? Would she soon come across the mass grave of a thousand wanderers lost beneath Atlantica?

Occasionally she passed structures with that same artwork she had witnessed on the way in. Sometimes they would be painted on the walls, faint, but there. She hit more forks and made more decisions until she was all but certain she was lost.

She pulled over.

She stood next to the cave lake and scratched her head. The headlights remained on to allow her the grace to see, and that time she looked up at the cave's ceiling.

"How do I get up there?" she pondered. That would be the preferred way out. If she could gain some height, excavate herself through the ceiling, she'd be able to emerge into the jungle. Sure, she'd still be lost, but she'd be a damn sight closer to freedom than she was now. At least out in the open air she could return to the city. Here…

Here, I'm buried alive.

She spent a few minutes pondering an escape plan. The lake beside her caught the headlights' glare and dazzled the cave in color. The engine was a constant companion in the dark.

"Fine." She walked back to the SUV, then jumped in the driver's seat. She got the vehicle rolling again and drove on.

She had only gotten a few meters when she saw the figures approaching ahead.

"Keep walking," Santana ordered the two conscious ones as they walked ahead.

Johnson pushed the Atlanticore. Casandra lay on top of the barrow, snoring loudly. Now and then, Boa looked over her shoulder, reaffirming that Santana was there and the gun was indeed pointing at them.

She pushed them on, taking their cue as to which direction to go. The barrow squealed beneath the weight, the wheel wobbling precariously against its moorings. Santana wondered how much farther they'd have to go. She was tired and hungry, and that didn't put her in a good mood, but she wouldn't show weakness to the group.

Boa led her through a series of tunnels. Although more domestic items appeared, they seemed to be nowhere near other people from their group. How far did this cave stretch? Could this have been the cave where...

No. Not now, Santana.

"You're going to regret this," Boa warned, breaking the silence sometime later.

"I'm sure I will," Santana replied. "The same way I regret skipping breakfast and choosing the wrong lippy."

"I'm just saying," Boa continued. "The moment you reach our camp, what do you think's going to happen? They're going to swarm you. You'll be on the other side of our weapons before the day is through."

Santana looked at the ceiling, wondering what the sky was doing. *What time of day was it? How long had they been down here?*

"We'll see," Santana returned. "Or, I can make sure I execute you all before you even think about running off to mama. I could tie you up. I could leave you in a lake or pool. Truth be told, there are a lot of things I could do with you. Do you know why?"

Johnson glared at her.

"Because I have the guns," Santana shot back. "Now get your ass in gear and enough stalling. How far to go?"

Boa refused to reply.

Santana let the issue drop, her attention drawn as they took a sharp left and met with an explosion of light. Boa raised her arm to shield her eyes. Johnson squinted against its beam.

"I told you it was only a matter of time," Boa smirked. She turned to face Santana. "The cavalry has arrived."

Santana couldn't make out anything beyond the light, but she pointed her weapons straight ahead. With careful precision, she shot into the center, discovering that the light was two lights, and one beam remained.

The side of a vehicle glinted, more visible now that half the light had gone.

Boa clapped her hands excitedly. She ran toward the SUV. Santana jumped out of the way, hiding behind an outcrop of rock as the group sprinted to the vehicle.

They cheered and clapped. Boa made it there first. Santana watched from her cover, waiting for the bullets to fire. Instead, a resounding *gong* of metal reached her ears, and it was then she saw that Boa had run into the car door.

Santana frowned. Upon closer inspection, the driver had opened the door into Boa, who now rubbed her head and protested to the person climbing out.

The woman was beautiful, even more so given the current situation. Her flaming red hair caught the light of the one remaining headlight as she loomed over Boa and pinned her under the gaze of her pistol. Johnson stopped in his tracks, the jerk of the cart so sudden that Casandra rolled off and woke herself up when her head hit the hard floor.

"I remember you," Valentina offered, eyes narrowing on Boa. "You're the bitch with the ego, right? Tried to catch us in a cross-fire. What was that…" she tapped her chin, "only a few hours ago. What a happy coincidence this is."

She crouched low, pistol in Boa's mouth. "Where is she?"

Boa mumbled.

Valentina grabbed a fistful of her hair. "I don't think you understand. I said, where the fuck is she?"

Johnson growled then, spurred on by the threat of his boss. He raised the cart off the ground, then shoved it toward Valentina. The frame at the back caught the rock, and the barrow toppled, Atlanticore spilling over either side. Some of the rocks rolled, their blue pulse trailing behind them. Others flashed a dangerous white.

Valentina hopped back, aiming the gun at Johnson. "You idiot. You realize they're highly explosive? It wouldn't only be me you killed. It would be all of us."

She shot at the big guy. The bullet tore into his foot. He howled in pain. Valentina grimaced, then caught Santana emerging from behind the rocks.

"Oh, nice of you to join," Valentina replied. "Could have used some help to stop the elephant from sending us all off into space."

Santana laughed and shrugged. "You looked like you had it handled. Plus, hard to tell who's good and who's bad behind a light. You could have been anyone."

"I'm definitely not anyone," Valentina replied. She hopped back as Boa kicked out and tried to sweep her legs. Valentina aimed the pistol, but before she could fire, Santana had holstered her gun and whipped out at Boa. The coil wrapped around her leg and pulled her away. Another *crack* of the whip and Boa grunted, a violent red line appearing across her wrist. A third *crack* and another line appeared on her cheek.

"Okay, okay," Boa protested. "Enough."

"No," Santana returned. "For someone who names themselves after a snake, you sure crumble quickly under mine." She whipped again. "Besides, it's either this from me, or redhead here is going to blow your fucking brains out."

Boa glared at Valentina.

Valentina shrugged and grinned.

Santana stopped whipping and came closer. "You took your time finding me."

"I could say the same to you," Valentina replied.

"Sweet ride." Santana nodded, impressed.

"It was," Valentina explained. "Until a run-in with your friends' friends, I assume. What the hell is this place?"

Santana took the coil of rope that she had brought from their descent and began to bind Boa. Johnson gripped his foot, his teeth clenched, and his eyes relaying the message that he was coming up with ways to exact revenge. "There are hundreds of them in Atlantica. Underground caverns, places where the pockets of the earth formed. There are lakes, creatures, and secrets to uncover, but no one has ever had the chance to map them all out. I've known some to cover kilometers of space, diving deep into the earth."

"It's a labyrinth," Valentina replied. "I thought I wouldn't be able to find my way out."

Santana finished Boa's knot, then made her way to Johnson. Valentina followed with her gun, causing him to wither beneath its glare. "You were trying to escape?"

"You weren't?" Valentina replied.

Santana shook her head. "Yeah. Only to find you, though."

Valentina raised an eyebrow with a grin.

"Fine," Santana confessed. "I wanted out. If I found you, bonus. If not, then it'd be another day, another victim claimed by Atlantica."

Valentina knew she should have been offended that her guide would have chosen not to pursue her, but she strangely appreciated the honesty.

"Where do we go from here?" Valentina looked pitifully at their hostages. "What's with the sleeping chick?"

Santana let out a derisive laugh. "Long story. I'll tell you about it in the car."

CHAPTER THIRTY

Archie Fontana sat in his room.

It was a replica of his office back on the surface. Or, at least, it would be at some point. The dimensions were the same. The chair and the desk were there, but that was where the similarities ended for now.

He was bored. He was tired of waiting but knew that progress needed to happen. He knew that by now his on-surface clients would know he was missing, and he knew that Deng would be out hunting him. All he had to do was sit and hold tight until the structure took shape.

That was still weeks ahead.

He played with the Rubik's cube in his hand. Once he had understood the algorithms and could solve the puzzle in a matter of minutes. Now, he was struggling. It had been a long time since he had the luxury of time, and he missed knowing the answers— to anything.

A shadow darkened his doorway. "Kirk. How can I help you?"

Captain Kirk stepped inside and cocked his head. "You know they're kid's toys, right?"

"Find me a six-year-old who can solve this." Archie slammed the cube on the table. It shattered into its components.

"Just look on YouTube," Kirk retorted. "I can find you a dozen four-year-olds."

Archie nodded, eyes glazed over. "Did you want something?"

"The extraction of the Atlanticore is underway," Kirk detailed. "Our teams are shipping out and taking the stealth routes back to the city. We should have word on some customer buys in the next few days."

"And the stash we're keeping to power this place?" His eyes grew dark. "We *must* detach from the power grid, Kirk. It's the one link we have back to the city. We need to be independent until the operation is ready and we can carry on. It isn't acceptable to be living as we are."

Kirk raised his hands defensively. "I know. Believe me, I know. We're working on it now. One of Friedrich's guys is hooking us up and getting us independent. He reckons we should be live and online in the next forty-eight hours."

"Make it twenty-four," Archie commanded.

Kirk nodded his head. "As you wish."

A moment of silence passed between them. "Sir, about the items we acquired for you before…"

Archie raised an eyebrow. "Your golden sailor's toy?"

"A sextant, yes," Kirk replied.

Archie smirked. "Filthy name, if I ever heard it. I wonder where that Latin origin came from." He shook his head, remembering the strange object Kirk and Friedrich had uncovered in the caverns beneath the island. "What of it?"

"Friedrich's guys have finished analyzing it and," He paused, eyes cast deep in thought. "They say that there's a missing component, a part required for activation. Kind of like a lock and key."

"A lock and key?" Archie snorted. "If that's the case, break the lock. Pick it. Open that shit up and yield the contents."

Kirk's lips thinned. "That's the issue. We can't open it. There's no way. It...It's stuck fast, and there seems to be no way to access it."

Archie looked at his shattered Rubik's cube. In the same online store where he had made the purchase, the website advertised complicated puzzles that claimed to be unsolvable. Yet, there were videos of reviews of people who had unlocked the secrets. For some, it had taken days, others months, but every puzzle had an answer.

"Keep trying." Archie leaned back in his chair and rested his feet on the desk. Rubik's pieces toppled to the floor.

Kirk nodded. "Of course." He stood there, eyes narrowing.

"Yes?" Archie asked.

"There is one other thing," Kirk announced.

"I'm listening," Archie replied.

Kirk drew a breath. "We've had reports of someone infiltrating the west wing."

Archie sat up straight, hands moving to rub his forehead. "Oh?" His voice was low, but the threat was obvious. "Who might that be?"

"We don't know." Kirk looked at the door. "They say an SUV was hijacked and stolen, someone using it to drive out of the chambers."

"So how is that an infiltration?" Archie asked.

"It's not...technically," Kirk replied.

Archie rubbed his tired face. "Send the team down there to examine. If you need to, flush them out. Increase the security on the perimeter near the west wing. Report to me the minute anyone makes so much as a whisper in the dark."

Kirk nodded and told him he would. He exited quickly, leaving Archie alone with the Rubik's cube. With an angry sweep of his arm, he sent the remaining pieces flying across the room.

CHAPTER THIRTY-ONE

"Thank you for coming back for me," Santana muttered, breaking the quiet. She rested her chin on her hand and looked out the window. The cave here was pretty much the same as it had been for the last five minutes, though it seemed to hold her interest.

"I didn't," Valentina replied.

"Sure," Santana retorted. "I appreciate it, anyway." She drew a long breath. "So, what's your plan?"

"My plan?" Valentina considered this. "I plan to follow through with my original plan."

"Which is?" Santana asked.

Valentina narrowed her eyes on the road.

"Still not going to share?" Santana shrugged. "Keep your secrets. But if you discover a mystical underground chamber that changes the way we understand history and the rest of life as we know it, I demand that you let me claim it."

"You demand?" Valentina chuckled.

"Yep."

Valentina shook her head. "You don't understand who you're trying to boss around, do you?"

"Honey, you're in my territory now." Santana looked ahead,

bags beneath her eyes. In the back of the car, the three captives slept, knocked out by a mixture of Valentina's serum rubbed across their lips and exhaustion from the trip. "You think you're able to hold your own and survive in an environment like this, then go ahead. There's a reason you brought me on this trip."

"You could head home. Your work is over."

Santana shot her a strange look.

"I'm assuming this is Merchant's Grove," Valentina replied.

Santana laughed. "How could you possibly know this?"

Valentina nodded ahead, cutting out her headlights. A short distance in front was the start of a tunnel lit with bright LEDs. "Because I believe I've found the lair of my enemy."

Enemy. It felt funny to say, considering that not too long ago Valentina had trusted Archie with her brother's life.

Not trusted. Forced to trust. That's a whole different ball game.

"Well, then," Santana replied. "I suppose we best make quick work of this. If they've uncovered an Atlanticore mine, and it means you do…whatever it is that you want to do. Then who am I to stand in your way?"

Valentina drew a deep breath, then drove on. She kept the revs low, rolling the car forward until they were near enough to keep the SUV hidden in the gloom.

They exited the vehicle, leaving the others behind. Moving through the dark, they approached the tunnel, staying in the gloom. Valentina kept her eyes pinned on the opening, waiting for people to emerge or for any sign of movement.

But there was nothing.

"Interesting…" she whispered.

Santana looked her way. "What?"

"No workers this time." Valentina scanned the area. Then she noticed the subtle differences. There were no car tracks to where the SUVs had been. "Wait a minute."

They were in a different location, yet the entrance looked very much the same. Valentina tiptoed toward the rock face of the wall, keeping tight and as away from the light as she could. Santana followed behind, pistols ready in her hands. The power had switched, and Valentina was happy. She was leading the charge.

She leaned around the corner. The tunnel was silent. There was no sign of any movement, only the gentle buzzing of the lights.

Valentina entered the tunnel.

She kept her eyes peeled ahead, looking out for any sign of movement. The tunnel bent around a corner. "Cover my six," Valentina whispered.

"What?" Santana replied.

"Watch my back," Valentina clarified. "How have you never heard that expression?"

"Because I'm not an assassin from a TV show or a federal cop," Santana retorted.

"I'm a mercenary, not an assassin," Valentina replied.

Santana scoffed. "Like there's a difference."

Valentina rolled her eyes but didn't pursue the argument further. Instead, she turned her attention to the light panel on her right. After the gloom they'd driven through, the lights were harsh on their eyes. Valentina gripped the sides of the panel and tore one of them from the wall. She flipped it over in her hands and examined the place where the wires connected to the system.

"Is now the time to get a hard-on over tech?" Santana whispered. "I thought you wanted to get inside?"

"What do you think I'm trying to do?" Valentina traced her fingers over the different color wires. They twisted around each other a few inches from the panel, the collection wrapped in black plastic to tidy them and keep them protected. The cable led to the next panel, then the next, and the next.

She twisted one of the cables and removed it. The next light in sequence extinguished.

"Parallel circuit," she mused.

"So?" Santana moved ahead down the tunnel. Her neck craned around the corner, pistol in one hand, whip in the other.

"Why didn't you stay with two guns?" Valentina raised an eyebrow.

"You have your methods. I have mine. Answer my question."

Valentina returned her attention to the panel. "If they were in series, the rest would be affected if one light broke. In a parallel circuit, if one dies, only one dies. Electricity bypasses the broken one and the group can continue to light."

"Why is that important right now?" Santana asked. She gave Valentina a strange look. "You didn't hit your head after we separated, did you?"

Valentina chuckled. "I'm not the one who fell through the jungle floor and into a landslide of rock and mud. How the hell did that happen by the way?"

"Hard to say." Santana turned back up the tunnel. "The jungle is a strange place. Structures weaken over time. The weight of everyone and…I don't know. Sinkholes and fault lines create problems."

Valentina knew enough geography to know that Atlantica didn't exist on a fault line, but she remained quiet.

"Again, I ask," Santana urged, "what's your fascination with the light set up? Don't you want to head inside?"

"I do. But first…"

She slid her hand into her pocket and fished out a tiny screwdriver. She tweaked some of the wires, and the adjacent light turned on. She fished again and found a handful of her ball bearings, then sprinkled them on top of the panel.

"Three…two…one…." she counted.

Electricity crackled. Blue light sparked on the panel Valentina held. She dropped it as the electricity jumped in angry pulses before it snaked along the wires. The first light exploded, shattering glass on the ground. The immediate vicinity darkened. The electricity sprinted along the cables, popping each light as it went. Valentina turned her attention to the lights on the other side of the wall and quickly repeated her actions.

After a few moments and a lot of shattering glass, the cave went dark.

Valentina stood there a moment, proud of her work. She felt Santana move closer to her. "Great. Now, what?"

"Now, Valentina replied. "We walk. Under the shadow of darkness.

Captain Kirk exited the power room with a grim expression on his face.

He hated letting Fontana down. He had worked hard to become his number one guy, and Archie wanted the power separated from the grid as soon as possible. But could they do it in twenty-four hours?

He hoped so. He had barked his instructions and made them aware of the risks, yet it would be interesting to see if it happened.

He sighed. He was hungry, but there was little in the depths of the project stations to sate his hunger. They had to stake out, only able to bring foods that weren't perishable, which left little for the tastebuds.

He strode along the hallway. He'd beefed up security on the west wing, and soon the guards would be delivered to the site. Although the initial plan was to keep their team small, it was quickly swelling. As fast as the construction crew erected rooms, they filled with new workers, new excavation teams, and new deliveries. Truth was that Kirk worried about Archie's mental health, but what could he do about it? Archie had got himself into a tight spot that forced him to flee. Kirk knew he was up to a thousand things that might be considered illegal or morally corrupt, but he paid the bills, and Kirk liked him.

Now Archie had spent a lot of time by himself. He was a man who had been used to freedom and ruled on high. In their city dwelling, Archie could monitor all that was going on, but down here he was restricted. They hadn't yet installed the computers in his office, knowing that they couldn't risk linking to a public Internet network or leaking signals into the air. The only computer in this place was somewhere on the floors below, in the north wings, and that was top secret. Even Kirk had no idea what was going on there, though he was raging that Friedrich was allowed to be a part of it.

He glanced at the hem of his shirt, noticing a small blood spot on the cloth. He hadn't seen it before, and he was thankful that Archie hadn't noticed it. What was the point in keeping that prisoner, anyway? All it was doing was adding more things to Archie's list of concerns. Once he realized the kid was dead, life might be a bit easier for him.

Cut the baggage free.

Who needed the extra responsibility?

Plus, Kirk had a hankering to take out his frustration on someone.

Poor kid.

He looked so sweet, so innocent crumpled on the floor. Kirk remembered how limp he felt when he removed the handcuffs and let him drop.

Poor kid.

Poor Archie.

Kirk made his way toward the west wing, ready to check on his patrol. He only made it a short distance when the power went out, and the site fell into darkness.

CHAPTER THIRTY-TWO

They raced along the hall, guided by the soft light of Valentina's cell phone. It wasn't much, but it was enough in the dense darkness. They gained as much ground as possible, navigating by guesswork, working their way to higher ground.

They heard voices ahead and rushed footsteps. Valentina and Santana shrank to the side as lights appeared. They grew in intensity, flashlights with the power of a thousand candles shining their way.

Valentina growled, adrenaline coursing through her. She had waited for this, had wanted to storm the capital and liberate her brother.

Now the time was here.

She loosed her pistol on them, firing shot after shot. They went down, folding to the ground one by one. The flashlights spiraled out of their hands, turning to strobes. Valentina picked one up and used it to guide her way ahead. The guards weren't organized, which meant she had the power of disruption at her side.

She cradled the flashlight in her arms, the light dizzying as it swayed back and forth while she ran. She clawed into her pocket and grabbed a handful of items. The tunnel banked left, so they followed.

Santana kept pace, their footsteps beating a rhythm in the dark. They passed another corner and met with another group of workers. This batch had flashlights strapped to their helmets and raised guns.

Valentina threw the contents in her hand, scattering the items around the oncoming enemy. They cracked as they hit the hard ground, erupting into a strobe of flashing lights with small arcs of electricity dancing around their feet as the workers jigged and tried to avoid getting zapped.

Valentina shot a few of the enemies, catching their feet and legs and sending them to the ground. Santana's whip cracked, removing gun after gun from their grips with acute precision.

"Nice form," Valentina declared.

"Same to you, princess," Santana shot back with a gleeful smirk on her face.

They passed the enemies, leaping over those who writhed on the ground. They took a hard right, away from more oncoming flashlights. Before they lost themselves in the passageway, Valentina found an orb that fit her palm, the size of a satsuma. She threw it behind her and shut off the flashlight.

"What are you doing?" Santana asked as the darkness claimed them.

Valentina paused, deep enough into the tunnel to be lost from sight, far enough away that they'd be safe as they watched the dancing lights appear.

"Wait for it..." Valentina muttered.

The group appeared, some of them banking toward where Valentina and Santana stood.

"Bingo," Valentina whispered.

The explosion was powerful and contained. Light shone as the tunnel around the entrance collapsed from the force of the small bomb. People yelled in pain, surprise, and anger as a blockade tumbled down and trapped the two women in the darkness.

Santana shuffled. "Great. Now what?"

Valentina rolled her eyes, aware that Santana wouldn't be able to see. "Ye of little faith."

Valentina switched on the flashlight. The tunnel erupted into light. They were at a crossroads, each tunnel empty with no identifying features.

"Nice work."

Valentina nodded. She turned to Santana and punched her in the arm. "That's for the 'princess.'"

Santana laughed, then rubbed the place Valentina hit. "Fair enough."

They strolled ahead until they were in the center of the crossroads. Valentina shone the light down each, noting that these were far cruder in formation than those they'd passed. Valentina wondered if these led anywhere or only marked as yet unbuilt places.

"It's like the inside of an anthill," Santana commented. She searched each tunnel, then took a long sniff. "That way."

Valentina raised an eyebrow.

"What?" Santana continued. "You can smell food from down that one. The others only smell like dirt."

Valentina drew a long breath through her nose. "I don't smell it."

"So that means you don't trust me?"

Valentina narrowed her eyes. "I'm not saying—"

"Look, city girl, you're paying me for this expedition, correct?" Santana tapped her foot, waiting for Valentina's response.

"Correct," Valentina reluctantly admitted.

"Then follow the leader," Santana replied. "Just keep your weapons at the ready." She glanced at Valentina's jacket. "You got any more of those party tricks lined up?"

Valentina grinned.

"Good. We'll need them, I'm sure. We've certainly raised their alarms."

They walked in the darkness for some time, occasionally passing small alcoves in the wall that might soon become doors once this project was complete. One or two arches led into small rooms, some of them littered with abandoned power tools. Valentina kept her eyes peeled ahead while Santana listened and sniffed to ensure they were on track. After a few minutes, the smell of cooked meat reached Valentina's nostrils, and she knew then that they'd made the right decision.

"Down there," Santana whispered. "Shut off your light."

Valentina did so. Ahead of them, a small leakage of light shone from a hatch in the floor. They approached the square hole leading into a brightly lit room below. One day soon it could be an entry vent or a place for air conditioning to sit, but for now, it was a crude cut-out in the dirt.

Valentina and Santana snuck closer. They paused at the edge and looked down.

Steam rose into the air, filling their senses with delicious tastes and smells. The air was warm, and through the blur, Valentina made out a team of workers scurrying about a small kitchen. There were a few high-tech appliances that seemed out of place in the decor below, and occasionally something electric would *beep* to indicate the end of a cooking cycle.

Valentina and Santana exchanged looks.

"...out of food," someone called over to their colleagues. "Didn't realize we'd be holing up for this long without fresh ingredients. Archie fucked us on this one."

Valentina squinted through the steam, trying to get a read on who was speaking.

"Unprecedented circumstances," came another voice, mocking in tone. The sound of a knife chopping on a cutting board accompanied her words. "When the rich are in trouble, the poor save their asses. Ain't that about the extent of it?"

"Not our fault he's in some kind of stick, is it?" the first voice continued. Valentina could vaguely see a large man with his head stuck in a fridge. His rotund ass stuck up in the air as he hunted for something inside. "Now there's sweet FA left to make a decent, wholesome meal for our guys. What do they think they're playing at?"

"I'd heard we're stuck down here now," a third voice contributed. "Stuck, stuck, stuck. Instructions are that no one leaves. *No one*. Not even to see *la familia*. It's bullshit. Haven't seen Margaret in three weeks."

"Five weeks for me," the second voice shot back.

"Cry me a river," the fat man replied, emerging from the fridge with a scrawny piece of meat that appeared to be more bone than food. "Three months. Ain't seen the missus since this project started."

There was an awkward pause. Santana caught Valentina's eye and nodded toward another vent hole farther up the tunnel. They shifted along, Valentina noting the absence of steam from this opening. They glanced inside and found themselves staring at a pantry. Half-empty metal roller racks lined the walls. A chest freezer sat in the corner with a dull blue glow pulsing from beneath it.

There was a door against the far wall.

Valentina scooted to the edge of the hole and lowered herself inside. She landed softly, pausing a moment to listen for any sign of oncoming foot traffic. Satisfied that no one was coming, she crept to the far door.

She opened it enough to face yet another dark tunnel. *Jesus, this place is endless. Let there be light.*

As if to answer her request, in the darkness a long stretch ahead was a dull blue glow. Valentina squinted ahead, able to make out the outline of an archway leading off to somewhere she couldn't see.

Might be a start.

"Psst." Santana glanced down at Valentina.

Valentina waved her down. Santana landed delicately on the floor. Valentina showed Santana what she had found.

"Atlanticore?" Santana asked.

Valentina gave a small nod. "Probably. Could be a start to navigating this place and finding Archie."

"Archie?"

Valentina fixed her gaze ahead, jaw clenched.

"Who's Archie?"

"He's…" Valentina thought about the best answer to give. "He's the reason I'm here. That's all I'll give you. Okay, princess?"

"Wow, way to reverse it." Santana's hand moved to her heart. "That hurt."

Valentina grinned.

They broke cover, leaving the kitchen attendants behind. There were footsteps nearby, but they couldn't identify where they came from. They sped up, then ducked into an alcove when the blue light shone brighter, and someone emerged from the room ahead.

The squeaking wheels of a barrow filled the tunnel. Valentina peeked her head out enough to see a man with a bright yellow construction helmet and noise-canceling headphones. His head bobbed as he pushed the barrow, lips mouthing the words to a song they couldn't hear.

They shrank against the wall, holding their breath as he passed. There wasn't a single moment of awareness as he went along his way, trudging through the tunnel to deliver the glowing barrow of Atlanticore.

"Where do you think he's going?" Santana asked.

Valentina shrugged. "Could be outside. Could be to a repository. Could be anywhere."

Santana leaned out once the man had faded from sight and sped ahead. Valentina kept pace, the pair finding another alcove when a woman emerged with her wheelbarrow.

Valentina glanced at Santana. A smirk appeared on her face.

"What?" Santana mouthed.

Valentina put a finger to her lips.

The woman wore a helmet but lacked headphones. Still, as she passed the dark alcove, Valentina tracked her every move. Once the woman had cleared their spot, she broke cover and moved behind her.

Her hand was over the woman's mouth to stifle the scream. With a well-placed pinch on the woman's neck, she sent her into a deep slumber. The woman went limp in her arms, the barrow dropping gently onto its supports.

Valentina dragged the woman's body into the darkness.

"What are you doing?" Santana asked.

"Keeping a low profile." Valentina shrugged off her clothes. "Help me here, won't you?"

Santana obeyed, but hesitantly. Valentina pulled on the woman's outfit, finding that it wasn't a bad fit.

"Now what?"

"Now, we go undercover." Valentina nodded at a room a little farther ahead. It was one of the only ones with a rudimentary door fixed to the frame. She unraveled a large cloth that poked out from among the Atlanticore fragments and motioned to the cart. "Climb in, please. We have places to be."

Santana's face hardened. She looked set to argue until they heard another worker from the blue-tinted room.

"Fine," she muttered. She climbed onto the rocks and covered up with the cloth.

Valentina turned the barrow, then headed for the room. She passed the new worker, gave a brief wave that the other returned, then disappeared inside.

The moment they were in darkness, she allowed Santana to

exit the cart. They dumped the Atlanticore in the corner of the room, then Santana climbed back inside.

"I hope you know what you're doing," Santana muttered.

Valentina drew a long breath. "Don't you worry your pretty little head about it."

CHAPTER THIRTY-THREE

"What do you mean they've gone missing?" Archie bellowed at the poor guard who was assigned the task of delivering the news. "They're two feeble women amid a fucking beehive!"

The man lowered his gaze. "They were prepared. They diverted us and entered the unfinished chambers. We have workers digging their way inside now, but..."

Archie ignored the fact that several of his employees were dead. The words had hit him, but his attention stayed fixed on the threat. Based on the descriptions they'd given him of the invaders, it was clear that Valentina Winters was in his abode, and she'd brought a friend along with her.

"Send out search parties to every entrance that springs from the unfinished chambers," Archie commanded. "Have every exit and entrance sealed. Cover them. Split the command. Don't stop until you've identified their location and we have them in custody—or dead! I don't care which one."

Archie ran a hand over his face, his eyes stinging from the stack of pulsing blue rocks in the corner of his room. Flashlights scanned around nearby, compensating for the absence of their lights. The timing couldn't have been worse. His team was in the middle of installing the Atlanticore-powered network grid and had only managed to convert power on a few essentials, and now the rest of the lights were out—not turned out but busted from a sudden power surge.

Valentina was clever.

Archie knew her skillset better than anyone.

He knew not to underestimate her.

The guard ran out of the room, quick to set Archie's commands into action. Archie growled, then swept from the room, moving at speed down the tunnels. He knew them like the back of his hand, his head showing images of what the final product would look like. He saw smooth, painted walls, tiled floors, decorations, wood, plinths, plants, and ornaments. He focused on what lay ahead, determinedly pushing all else from his mind as he sped down a set of stairs and encountered the scent of wet earth.

Must be raining outside.

He beelined for a room at the far end of the tunnel, a place that he had made it a point to install as early as possible in the project. There were no windows in it and no way to see inside the thick metal door that blocked free entry. He paused outside, anger coursing through him. He needed a punching bag. He needed something with which to vent his anger. He needed something to leverage against Valentina that she wouldn't expect, an extra token on top of the one lying in the medical facility above. He required a lank-haired asshole who happened to have made the mistake of getting in Archie's way when looking for Isabella.

Archie opened the door. It was dark inside, nearing total pitch black. On the hook outside the door was an emergency flashlight, a small thing that would only light a small cone of the way ahead. He clicked the "On" switch. Nothing happened.

Piece of shit. Archie whacked the flashlight against his palm. He clicked again, and this time the light sputtered to life. He pointed it at the wall ahead, his mind conjuring the images he wanted to see. A man on the cusp of death, gaunt cheeks and greasy hair that covered his eyes. Head hanging down on his chest. Arms stretched to the cuffs pinned to the wall.

Who said that medieval torture and capture should be a dying art?

He stalked into the room, a devilish grin on his face. "I think it's time you served your purpose." His voice was low, the rumble of a predatory dog. "Come, boy. Make me happy."

The boy didn't even glance at him. The shadows hid his eyes. Archie rolled up his sleeves and let the flashlight drop to the ground. His hands balled into fists. He reared back, allowing his anger to consume him, to fill him to the top. He punched, throwing his arm with everything he had, aiming for the boy's face.

Pain exploded in his fingers. Something snapped. He withdrew, shaking his hand as fragments of rubble and dirt fell away from his knuckles. He examined his hand, then looked at the wall, noticing for the first time that the kid was gone.

Where he should have been, there was nothing.

Archie took a step back. His foot slid on something thick and gooey. He glanced down, where the flashlight's beam glided over a pool of crimson on the floor.

He picked up the light and shone it around him. The room was empty, with a faint coppery smell in the air. He lit up the crimson puddle, trying to put the pieces together. Something died here.

So where was the body?

He followed the puddle, a trail of red gore leading him to the chamber door.

No, something didn't die here.

Something got hurt *here.*

And that something is gone.

Gone?

Archie's nostrils flared. His clenched fists shook. He let out a loud bellow of fury as he felt someone picking apart the carefully planned pieces of his operation one by one.

That was when the chamber door closed, and the lock clicked from outside.

Leaving Archie in darkness.

Friedrich saw double.

It didn't matter if his glasses were on or off. Everything was a blur. As a scientist, he understood the restorative effects of sleep and rest, but as a human under the thumb of a multibillion-dollar asshole with power at his fingertips, he knew the risks of trying to catch a few hours of shut-eye.

The lab wobbled in front of him. He gripped the tablet loosely in his hand. He tried to focus on the screen, the numbers and the tiny writing, but it was no use. Although the general trend on the graphs was reading positive results, slowly curving upward on the lines, that was the extent of his knowledge.

His shoulders were heavy. He staggered to the desk and sat in his chair. The litter of coffee mugs would have been precarious near so much electrical equipment, but Friedrich drained every last drop of caffeine he could get his hands on. He reached for the one cup with anything remaining, a few small dregs at the bottom, and slammed the contents into his mouth.

Coffee fell from his lips.

A brown stain joined the others on his jacket.

He let his head flop back and took a moment to stare at the ceiling. He closed his eyes.

He opened them, aware that time had passed.

How much time?

It was impossible to tell. To do that, you needed an accurate base for when you first sat. You needed the control, and he was all out of that.

He glanced over his shoulder, head spinning drunkenly on his neck. Kit lay in his glass chamber, the color restoring to his cheeks. Beneath him came the blue glow of the Atlanticore cell. They had made significant progress in the last few days, and it was amazing. Friedrich was amazing. Archie was amazing. The AI was amazing.

Things were happening that shouldn't be possible. He didn't want to tell Archie that he thought the chances of recovery were zero, but that was all he knew from modern science. Now, this process was testing his beliefs and understanding. Before him was the impossible, and in the challenge was the discovery. In the challenge was the excitement. Science wasn't about proving new theories. It was about attempting to disprove the theories everyone knew to be true. The smaller the margin you can make that something is disprovable, the stronger you make your hypothesis.

But nothing was foolproof.

The margin of error on this impossible sight presented before him was narrowing. Kit was a miracle of science. The AI was *the* miracle. Friedrich couldn't comprehend it. Even on a day when he was rested and could focus on what was in front of him, he'd struggle. Computers had long passed the comprehension of human understanding, with smart systems performing duties and evolving their coding to the point that they were self-sufficient.

How long before the rising of the robots? How long before the future is here and all ends. Asimov's three laws of robotics were great, but even they had their loopholes. How long until...

All went black.

Friedrich had the strange sensation that someone was watching him, a little niggle in the back of his mind. Fog covered his vision, his heavy eyelids barely able to process anything around him. Images of his ex-wife rose and fell like whales breaking the ocean's surface before diving back down to the depths. He saw his daughter, Molly, her smiling face before the world had turned cruel and fate had taken her. He saw the life he once had in the days when his hair hadn't begun to gray and thin.

A strange pressure pressed on Friedrich's chest. He lurched, for a moment riding a rollercoaster he couldn't see. His arms flopped down, his stomach pushed upward, and he was bobbing on the ocean waves. The rowboat was small, only enough to contain two people. It led him across open waters, the figure handling the oars a person with no shape or defining features. The face was blank with a wide-brimmed hat low over their face. They rowed with quiet grace. Friedrich wasn't afraid to be in the figure's presence but thankful, thankful for the release that it gave.

Friedrich smiled.

A small drop of drool leaked from his lips and stained the man's back.

Friedrich stopped fighting and closed his eyes.

CHAPTER THIRTY-FOUR

Valentina entered the room.

The cart squeaked, causing her teeth to grind with every full rotation. She composed herself, following behind a line of workers with their wheelbarrows, waiting for their payload to transfer somewhere in the tunnels.

They were a miserable bunch. Sweat and dirt glossed their arms, and their faces were grim. Valentina thought back to Casandra, unconscious and bound in the back of the SUV. It was like all of these workers were doing their best imitation of her.

"West wing. Power center." Valentina followed the voice and found a man with no shirt and rippling abs standing at the front of the line. The blue glow from the Atlanticore gave him a sickly hue, while the tablet in his hands lit up his face in a harsh white light. He tapped the screen, then addressed the next worker. "You're a city mule. Meet Garrison near Exit 4 and prepare for your trek."

The surly-faced worker nodded, then wheeled his barrow ahead.

Valentina looked past the workers, a considerable gap between the front of the line and where a team of excavators extracted the Atlanticore. Jackhammers and pickaxes were scattered around while workers switched and changed and pulled out large chunks and small pieces of Atlanticore. Valentina had never seen this in real life, and there seemed to be no end to this goldmine of energy. She placed an estimate on what the amount still stuck inside the earthen walls could be worth, and more zeroes than she could count popped into her head.

Valentina made it to the front of the line. "You're west wing. Power center." The man didn't even look up from his tablet.

Valentina wheeled ahead. She glanced at the lump beneath the cloth in the barrow, growing nervous. When she arrived at the wall, a series of workers took turns to ensure the barrow was full. As they loaded rocks into the barrow without a second glance, Valentina watched the shifting package below uncomfortably. She wasn't sure how much Atlanticore weighed. She had heard that it was one of the lighter energy sources, but still...poor Santana.

When the barrow was full, Valentina quickly wheeled away and made room for the next worker. She stopped by the shirtless man and gave him a tentative glance. "Remind me where the west wing is again?"

The man looked out from under his eyebrows.

Valentina smiled. "Sorry, last time I was city. This place confuses me still."

The man drew a deep breath, then tapped on his tablet. He opened an image of the floor plans and showed Valentina the screen. "Just follow the mainline down to the kitchen, then head right. If you reach the lavatories, you've gone too far." He pointed to a woman leaving the room. "If you get lost, follow her."

He rolled his eyes then called his next order.

Valentina headed out of the room before she drew any more attention to herself. She followed the tunnel, heading through the darkness, following the faint pulsing blue light ahead. When she reached the end of the tunnel, she took the right turn, then proceeded toward the room she had seen marked on the map.

The Atlanticore shifted in the barrow. A couple of rocks tumbled out. Santana's head emerged as she swam to the surface, coughing and gasping for air. "Are you kidding me?"

Valentina stopped. She bent down and picked up the Atlanticore fragment. It was light, able to be placed back with one hand, though there was a strange heat to the piece that seeped through Valentina's fingers and got her adrenaline pumping. She felt very awake until she placed the rock back on the pile. The extra energy vanished instantly.

"I don't see what the problem is." Valentina picked up the handles and continued pushing, aware of the worker some distance behind her.

Santana's eyes were wide as her skin prickled with energy. "You didn't tell me you'd bury me under...these things." She pushed the rocks away, trying to clear some distance, but every time she thought she had room, they adjusted and folded around her again.

"Keep your head down," Valentina hissed. "You don't want to draw attention to us."

"No, of course not." Santana frowned. "I also don't want to be buried alive. Why was this part of your plan? Why couldn't we have just kept the old core and wheeled along in this anyway."

"We didn't know the floorplans," Valentina replied. "Now we do. Our assignment is the west wing, power center." She glanced down at Santana. "That can't be too far from Archie."

Santana narrowed her eyes. "Still seems I could have waited in the other room or something."

"Call it revenge for almost letting me drown in the river," Valentina shot back.

Santana considered this. "Fine. We're even."

Oh, we're far from even, Valentina thought.

The floor rose steadily, climbing a gentle gradient until the hum of machinery caught Valentina's attention. She covered Santana with the cloth, then made her way toward the buzzing.

A cross-section broke their path. Valentina paused as several guards and men and women with firearms ran through the tunnels. Valentina froze, not wanting to draw attention to herself. After a moment, they were gone. She exhaled, then made for the room with that familiar blue glow ahead.

The room was one of the largest she had seen yet. The ceiling was domed, with myriad tubes, cables, and wires running in all directions. Electricians and construction workers ran around feverishly, desperate to restore power to the lights and ensure that the rest of the facility would be operational again. Sparks flew. Atlanticore was stacked and connected to several devices that even Valentina couldn't understand. To her right was a fuse box covered in black soot and still smoking as two workers argued and tried to restore the power.

That must be from the lights.

"Come on, we haven't got all day," a woman barked. There were lines on her forehead, and her lower jaw jutted out farther than her top. She waved them over, practically snatching the barrow from Valentina.

The woman unloaded the rocks, tossing them into a nearby pile that was quickly dwindling. "I don't know how much more of this we'll need, but make sure Adrian keeps sending it down, okay?"

Valentina snatched the barrow back.

The woman glared at her.

"I've got this." Valentina tried her best to sound helpful over irritated. "You get the next one. I can do this."

The woman looked at her doubtfully, deciding whether or not this was a mutiny or a blessing. She eventually settled with the latter. "Make it quick. They'll want you back as soon as possible."

Valentina half-unloaded the barrow, blocking Santana's form from the woman's sight. When she finished, she quickly turned the barrow and wheeled away, the woman thanking her with a wave.

Is that how easy it is to remain incognito here? With all the chaos and scrambling, I suppose that no one will bat an eyelid.

Valentina froze. Standing at the entrance to the power room were two guards with assault rifles. They conversed with one of the workers at the back of the line with scowls on their faces.

Valentina leaned down and whispered, "Stay down. Whatever you do, don't move."

The shape of a thumb pressed against the material. Valentina rolled her eyes.

She moved quickly, giving the guards a wide berth. For a heart-stopping moment, she thought they'd turn to her, but she made it past without interruption. Before exiting, she saw a poster on the wall. She veered slightly closer, allowing herself a second to read its contents.

The poster was yet another floor plan of this floor, although where Adrian's had been pinched and focused on only the path Valentina needed to attend, this one showed the whole layout.

Every room was labeled and identified. While Valentina was certain that most of the rooms were unfinished—particularly given the state of the ones she'd visited—she spotted the bathrooms, a second kitchen, workrooms, gym rooms, and a whole host of spaces with other functionalities.

That wasn't what caught her eye. What pulled her attention was the large room nearby that wasn't labeled. It was one of the only places where there wasn't an identifier on the poster.

Valentina smirked. "Bingo."

"Excuse me!" a voice called. Valentina's hackles raised.

She picked up the wheelbarrow and pivoted to the doorway. She afforded a minor glance as she ducked out of the room, able to see one of the guards waving and looking her way.

Valentina sped out of the room. The moment she was out of sight, she pulled away the cloth and revealed Santana. She was crouched, uncomfortably pressed into the fetal position. Valentina jerked her thumb toward the tunnel ahead. "Time to go."

Santana groaned. Behind them, someone shouted.

"Now," Valentina urged.

Santana clambered out of the barrow, almost tipping it over as she jumped. They walked briskly ahead, catching the eyes of a few stray workers who, fortunately, chose to continue with their work. Another few shouts from behind caused Valentina to speed up.

She kept the floorplans in her head as she took a hard right. There was a series of rooms here, and she ducked into one with Santana. There was no door, but the room was dark.

They waited, backs pressed against the wall, listening for the guards.

"You know," Santana stated. "For a mercenary, you have a long way to go with your stealth."

Valentina's lip curled. "These are extenuating circumstances." She peeked around the doorway, then ducked back as footsteps grew louder. "Ordinarily, I'm afforded the luxury of reconnaissance and a great deal of planning. This situation has proven itself to be rather different. You want my mercenary skills? You pay top dollar. You piss me off and set me in action to topple your tower of injustice, and you get a soldier of fortune."

"I thought soldiers of fortune were—" Santana started.

Valentina glared at her. "Semantics."

People ran past the room. Valentina pressed back against the wall and held her breath, Santana in the dark beside her. They waited until the footsteps had cleared and their flashlights had faded to black, the echoing trail of "She went this way" slowly diminishing.

Valentina poked her head out of the door, then casually entered the tunnel. Santana followed, keeping close to her.

"How come you get a disguise?" Santana asked. "I'm out in the open like a schmuck. Next time you nab someone to play dress-up, think about including your partner, won't you?"

"Partner?" Valentina retorted as they returned to an intersection.

"You know what I mean."

Valentina narrowed her eyes, regaining her bearings. "This way." They strode along, guided by Valentina's phone, not encountering a single soul as they worked their way through the tunnel. A few minutes later, they passed the first worker they'd seen after returning to the open. Valentina answered her curious stare with a thumb jerk and, "To the boss."

The woman continued on her way, not bothering to glance over her shoulder.

They made a right, heading a short distance down a corridor before a thick metal door blocked them. They exchanged a glance, each woman noting the distinct difference in decor compared to the rest of the underground facility.

"They wanted to make sure they set up this room, didn't they?" Santana commented.

Valentina nodded. She examined the keyhole. There was a digital pad beside it, meaning that it was double-locked from intruders. She knelt and held up her phone to examine the circuitry and design. "Fingerprints." She sighed.

"Problem?" Santana asked. "Don't tell me we have to find this Archie character and scrape off the pads from his fingers?"

Valentina ignored her, feverishly tapping through a sequence of digital folders on her cell phone. She found what she was looking for, and the screen went black. A moment later, an imprint of a finger appeared on her screen.

Santana watched, fascinated, as Valentina held the image to the scanner and watched the LED turn from amber to green. Something inside the mechanism clicked.

"How did you...?" Santana started.

Valentina drew out her lock pick, then clamped it in her

mouth. She twisted a mechanism on the lock with her thumb, then placed the lock pick inside. "I've known Archie long enough to know that I needed to have some backup in case anything ever went wrong." She twisted and teased the pick, eyes narrowed on the lock. "Here, hold the phone steady, will you, so I can see." She smiled as the light shone in the right direction. "That's better. Archie has always been a concern, and I always make sure to have some kind of evidence of my enemies and friends, should the occasion ever arise. I extracted these from a whiskey bottle after a particularly interesting night when I learned how easily you can get a man drunk and get him to part with his secrets. Ah, here we go."

The door unlocked. She twisted the handle, and it opened. "Quick, inside."

As Santana entered, she spun, looking at Valentina with interest. "So you're saying you have something of mine? Scan of my eyes? Fingerprints?"

Valentina shrugged. She pocketed her phone, then closed the door. "A lot can happen when one is asleep," she replied coolly.

Before Santana could protest, Valentina held up a finger, eyes growing wide as she took in the room around her. "Holy…"

The space was huge—a large domed room carved out of the earth. The lights were on, all of them undamaged and unbroken by Valentina's surge. Ahead of the pair was a metal walkway suspended over a drop that seemed infinite. At the end of the walkway, taking up a large circle in the center of the room, was a platform that was painfully familiar to Valentina.

Her blood boiled in an instant. Flashbacks of her time spent looking in on Kit's glass casing came flooding back to her. The same computer screens spread around the center. Wires and tubes threaded between each other across the systems. A surgical light hung overhead, casting a bright light on…

Nothing.

Valentina's face fell. Santana said something, but it fell on deaf ears. Valentina sprinted into the center of the room, standing in the place where she knew Kit's bed should have been. There were marks on the floor, distinct grooves in the dust where someone must have recently moved the casing. She whirled, fixing her gaze on one screen, then the next. All of the monitors were off. All of the tubing and electricity were unplugged.

"No…" she breathed. "No, no, no, no…."

She ran to the nearest computer. She slammed the keys, trying to initiate some kind of boot-up sequence. The computer screen flashed, and a cursor appeared in the corner, executing the boot-up commands. A moment later, it prompted her for a username and password.

Valentina threw the keyboard, then moved to the next screen. She thumbed the power button. The screen came on with an error message, "No connection found."

She repeated this, working her way around each digital system, growing rapidly more feverish. She took off her hard hat and tossed it into the abyss below. She never heard it land, wasn't even sure that it would.

She spun back to the center of the room and threaded her fingers through her hair, inhaling deep breaths to try and induce a calm she couldn't find. It wasn't until Santana spoke that she remembered she wasn't alone.

Santana chewed her lip, eyes awkwardly shifting from Valentina to the computers. "I'm going to take a stab in the dark. You didn't find what you were looking for?"

Valentina shook her head. On the floor was a series of wires embedded into a network of conduit that lined the way to the main door. A dull blue glow lit the underside of the suspended walkway, hiding the place where Valentina imagined the core to be fixed to power the room. No wonder the surge didn't affect this room. It was a great thing that it hadn't happened. Otherwise, it might have affected Kit.

This is why you don't bring emotion into your affairs, Val. You drop the ball. Make crass decisions. Fuck it all up.

"He's gone," Valentina stated, the words hurting as they left her lips. "They've taken him somewhere..."

"Who?" Santana asked.

Valentina met her gaze, then looked away. She examined the floor, her breath beginning to steady a little from the initial discovery. "There." She pointed at the surface. "Footprints." She followed them along the walkway. "Leading out. A table on wheels, see here? That line has to be the bed."

"What bed?" Santana asked. "Val, you're going to have to give me some context. Otherwise, I can't help."

"I don't need your help," Valentina replied automatically. "I didn't pay you to help me reclaim what is mine. I paid you to lead me here. You've done your job." She reached for the door handle, the mechanism stiff and unmoving. "I'll sort your payment, just leave me to my affairs."

Santana's face hardened. "Well, if that's the way you want it to be, then fine." She drew up beside Valentina. "Get us out of here, and we'll be on our separate ways."

Valentina felt guilty for her words, but she had more pressing matters. Somewhere in this labyrinth, her brother was waiting. Somewhere...

"Do you need help with that?" Santana asked.

Valentina tugged at the handle. It remained stuck fast.

"Seriously, Val. It's only a..." Santana's words faded.

Valentina whirled, about to tell Santana where she could stick her words when she noticed that Santana wasn't there at all.

Something *thumped* beside her. She glanced down. Santana laid motionless on the floor. Her eyelids fluttered, and her chest gently rose and fell as she breathed in and out. A dart was buried deep in her neck.

"Finally," a voice remarked. Valentina turned to find a black-clad figure standing in the center of the room. "I knew I'd track you down eventually."

Valentina squared her shoulders, eyes narrowing at the figure. She recognized him instantly, his shape, his gait, his size. "Marcus. I have to say that I'm surprised to find you in my little pocket of Atlantica."

The figure chuckled and pulled on a loose swathe around his head. He unraveled his hood, slowly revealing his face. With each loop and uncoil, Valentina's face hardened, the man standing before her a far cry from her original hypothesis.

CHAPTER THIRTY-FIVE

Before

The breeze licked at the bottom of Valentina's robes.

They were midnight black, cut to her ankles, tied around the waist with a ribbon, and made of satin. Outsiders might forgive her for believing that she wore nothing at all. The material was as gentle as air, a golden pattern snaking from the left hip to her feet, wings spread in the shape of an eagle.

The establishment had redecorated the courtyard for tonight's events. The training dummies were absent, and candles illuminated the fountain. Valentina stood beside Marcus and Joseph, the three of them silent as they waited for the arrival of their master.

Marcus leaned on a crutch, occasionally wobbling, trying his best to maintain his balance. Bandages covered his body, there were bruises and lumps and scars on his face and torso, and though Valentina knew a part of her should feel guilty for the damage she'd inflicted, she found she strangely lacked remorse. A part of her was glad that he had survived the encounter on the border of the dojo, with her sensei managing to enlist the medical care needed to bring him back from the brink of death, but still…

An eye for an eye.

Beside him, Joseph remained stoic. The leanest of their cohort, Joseph looked as though a single punch could snap him in half. He had been surprisingly absent from most of Valentina's training, with only whispers of him encountered when she roamed around the hallowed halls. Now, she saw him in his full glory. She could understand the mantle he had acquired: Mantis.

The moon glimmered overhead. Koi leaped from the pond, splashing and breaking the surface.

The doors opened wide. Sensei Reyner appeared, leading a procession of their masters. While Reyner had shaped most of Valentina's education, the two women who flanked him had also played their parts, providing advice in the early hours of the morning before Valentina's training ended and she had to leave for the city. All three wore their ceremonial robes, and the moment they appeared, Valentina's heart fluttered.

They stalked slowly toward the three. Sensei Reyner stopped a short distance from the trio and waited. Valentina and the others bowed. The senseis bowed in return.

"Graduates," Sensei Reyner began. "You have undertaken a training program so advanced and so deadly that ninety percent of recruits that tread through our halls never survive to see the fruits of their labors. I am proud of every one of you, for proving your worth, for obeying commands—" his eyes lingered a little too long on Marcus "—and for emerging from the chrysalis, ready for the challenges this world throws at you."

Valentina bowed her head. Marcus and Joseph followed suit.

"With the blessing of our dojo," Sensei Reyner continued, "I wish you luck on your journeys ahead. There will be many obstacles to face along the way, but with the grace of the dojo and the flight of the eagle's wings, you will make our people proud."

Sensei Reyner motioned a hand to his left. Madame Trisk

bowed, then stepped in front. In her hands was a large rectangle of red satin. She removed the cloth cover to reveal three blades. They were long and thin, honed to a keen edge. They caught the glint of the moon, the light emphasizing an inscription near the hilt.

Madame Trisk stepped toward Joseph. "A scythe-like blade for the Mantis."

Joseph bowed low, then accepted his weapon eagerly. He took it by the hilt, then held it upright, examining its length. He gently ran a finger along the blade and blood pooled at his tip. His lips turned up, surprised at how easily the skin parted without causing him physical pain.

Madame Trisk stepped in front of Marcus. "For the Ox."

Marcus' blade was wider, and even without touching, Valentina could tell it was heavier. The inscription showed calligraphic bull horns next to the writing. Marcus glanced at Valentina, and she could instantly read what was in his mind.

Don't you fucking dare, she thought.

Finally, Madame Trask stopped before Valentina. "And, now, for the Crimson Duchess."

Valentina looked past Madame Trisk, catching Sensei Reyner's eyes. He watched her intently as she raised her blade, the lightness of the weapon hard to comprehend. It was like holding a feather or a quill, though as she stepped back and carved a couple of circles in the air, it sang to her touch. Long, shrill notes filled the air as the blade whirled, and when Valentina finished, she found Marcus glaring at her with distaste.

Yeah. Come for me, and you'll feel the wrath of my *blade.*

When Madame Trask finished, she stepped back and took her place. Madame Greene took over, handing each graduate the gift of a custom sheath for their blades. They tied their weapons around their waists, placed their hands together, then bowed low once more.

Sensei Reyner gave a satisfied nod. "You now have permission to fly, graduates. Take what we gave you from your training, and use your power out in the world for good." His gaze lingered on Marcus once more. "And please, reserve any indecent action for outside of the dojo's limits, under penalty of death."

Valentina felt Marcus' gaze turn from Sensei Reyner's to her. Her cheek burned under his intensity. She still couldn't understand how they'd given him a second chance, considering all that had happened that night. Valentina had to fight for survival, almost killing a fellow trainee in the process, and now he stood beside her, proud and true.

It's not like she hadn't asked, either. Upon hearing the news of Marcus' return to training, she had stormed into Sensei Reyner's office in the middle of the night. He wasn't there, her gaze falling upon an empty room. She had found him in the courtyard, sitting on the ledge of the fountain with his eyes closed, lost in deep meditation.

"You're letting him rejoin?" she bellowed, aware that other recruits could awake to her din and caring little. "Are you kidding me?"

Sensei Reyner's eyebrows raised before his eyes opened. "I do pray that there is no problem, Ms. Winters."

"He disobeyed a fundamental rule," Valentina remarked. "He tried to kill me *within* the boundaries of the dojo. Not only that, but it was an attack on a trainee by a trainee. It should have been an immediate dismissal."

Sensei Reyner closed his eyes, a long breath exhaling from his lips. The silence infuriated Valentina.

"Well?" she nudged when it appeared as though he wasn't going to answer.

"Your punishment will be one hundred laps around the dojo," Sensei Reyner answered.

Valentina's face turned the color of her hair. "No."

"Two hundred." Sensei Reyner kept his eyes closed.

"No." Valentina stepped closer. Her fists clenched. "I want an answer."

Sensei Reyner remained silent.

"I want an answer!" Valentina called, aware that she was shaking. "He nearly killed me. On *your* property. If you're not going to stand by your rules, what's the point in all of this? What's the point in any of it?"

"Settle down, Winters," Sensei Reyner whispered. "This shade of anger is unbecoming on a—"

Valentina reached her tipping point. Every carefree wrinkle on her sensei's face infuriated her. She imagined Marcus in the creek, the look of determination as he struck Valentina in an effort to make her breathe her last breath. Valentina lashed out a fist, her hand aiming for the sensei's face.

He caught her fist in one rapid movement, the momentum stopping as though a train had hit a mountain. His other hand met her in reply, striking her on the cheek. Before Valentina knew what was happening, he was on her, fists flying in a flurry and connecting with her side, her hips, her arms, her cheeks.

Valentina blocked one of the blows. A second struck her ear. She blocked the next one that came, her anger growing. She caught Sensei Reyner's eye, found their calm, and knew what she needed to do.

A well-placed blow knocked her head back. Valentina fell onto her ass. Sensei Reyner was unrelenting, but as he followed Valentina down, she shifted out of the way of his knee. She rolled, then picked herself up.

Sensei Reyner was on his feet.

"You've always let your emotions cloud your judgment," he stated. "That is and will always be your downfall. Look at you. Shaking. Heart rate accelerated. Mind foggy. Until you learn to calm your—"

Valentina ran at him. He side-stepped, but she followed. Her knee went into his stomach. An exhale of air spurted from his lungs. She followed with a swift elbow to the back of his neck as she swept around him. She kicked the back of his ankles and forced him to his knees as she grabbed the back of his collar to keep him somewhat upright.

A strange sound came from his mouth. She struck again, this time in the back of the head. He folded onto his hands. She straightened, walking proudly around his body until she stood in front of him. He grabbed for her ankles. She moved, then struck him once more in the back of the head.

For a moment, all was silent. She stared down at him, her breathing heavy, wondering how long it would be until he got up to fight back—if he did at all. Her jaw clenched, eyes unblinking as the storm of emotions roiled inside her.

After a pause, Sensei Reyner chuckled. His body racked with laughter as he pushed himself up to his feet. He wobbled precariously while Valentina simply watched. When he stood to his full height, his gaze bored into Valentina's with such an intensity that her breath caught. His eyes were dark. Brow furrowed. For a man who rarely showed emotion, something dark flashed behind that mask then.

He moved closer, Valentina's body tensing under his presence. "We are born and trained to be killers, Valentina. Tricksters, crafters, thieves, denizens of the night. The fact that Marcus tried to kill you is within our code and something that is not explicitly encouraged but admired. The fact you left him alive means that you failed. Marcus returns for showing the core value of what a killer is, what a mercenary can do. You…" He turned his gaze to the steps where Madame Trisk silently stood and watched. "You dishonor your sensei in front of his colleagues…" He shook his head.

Valentina tried to swallow, but her throat was dry. What had she done? Was this all some kind of perverse test that she had failed?

Sensei Reyner raised his hand. Valentina flinched. He rested his palm on her shoulder. "You are ready, my young apprentice."

Valentina saw that same expression on her sensei's face now, standing in the courtyard and adorned with her new blade. A look of pride, accomplishment, and a job well done.

And behind that, a dark glint that lingered with her long after the ceremony had passed. Brooding darkness...

CHAPTER THIRTY-SIX

...that bored deep into her, their gaze creating heat from its intensity.

Sensei Reyner smirked. His bald head caught the reflection of the lights. He had aged, though not by much. There were a few lines and creases around his eyes and mouth, but otherwise, he was the same man who had waved her and the new graduates off from his dojo.

"You seem surprised," Sensei Reyner announced. "Am I not to your satisfaction?"

Valentina's face hardened. Her fist trembled at her side. "Sensei..."

"Ah," he raised a finger. "Let me correct you straight away, Valentina, for I knew this would be a problem that we struck straight away. Sensei is no longer a correct term to use for me because I am no longer with the dojo."

"I'm sorry to hear that." Insincerity laced Valentina's every word. What the hell was he doing here? "I'm sure the dojo was sad to see you go."

Reyner laughed, the outburst unflattering, causing his features to turn sharp on his face. "No."

"No?" Valentina replied.

Reyner took a step closer. "No, Valentina. The dojo wasn't sad to see me go. Because of you, my entire life crumbled on the spin of a dime."

The dark glint returned, though now it was a full storm. His mouth turned down on either side, his nostrils flared, and the gun in his hand trembled.

Valentina frowned. "What are you talking about?"

"You!" Reyner shouted. Any composure and grace the man might once have had were gone. "You, Valentina. You were my downfall. You ended the reign of the longest-serving Master Sensei that had ever governed the dojo. Everything that came thereafter, the years of struggle, pain, hardship, searching, and discovery, it was all because of you."

Santana coughed, her eyelids fluttering.

Valentina's lip curled. "I did nothing."

"You did everything!" Reyner continued. He paced, losing himself to his memory. "You humiliated me. You defeated me on the sacred ground of my temple. You dominated me in front of a witness, and that is a shame that no sensei can recover from."

"You were fine. You were there at the graduation. You bestowed our blades. You bade us luck into the new world."

"Tradition and ceremony," he barked back. "Did you think that would last forever? The moment you left, they came for me, stripped me of my titles, and found a new Master. I was out on my ass before the sun kissed the horizon, and then all was gone. Everything I'd built my life and soul around. Gone."

Valentina felt a pang of pity in her stomach, though as Santana coughed once more, it soon diminished. "So you tracked me down, and what? What part of this makes any sense? That you would track me down to this place? Try to kill me along the way."

Reyner smiled. "Vengeance and a restoration of honor. Only in defeating those who have defeated you do you restore what was once yours. The way the alpha dominates the pack, I must once more dominate you. It's a pity. You truly are a masterpiece. One of the greatest to be born from our order. It's a shame you must die."

"If you wanted to kill me, you could have done it long ago," Valentina shot back. "Why didn't you?" She thought back to the attack on the top of the Opera house. "You wanted to play the game, didn't you? You knew that you wouldn't find pride in the silent assassination. You wanted the challenge."

Reyner smirked.

"Well, that's as it may be," Valentina replied. "I have bigger problems to deal with right now. I could take you down again as easily as I once did. I've had years of real-world experience now, and I'm confident that you still don't hold a candle. You lost once. You will lose again."

Reyner quit pacing and centered himself on the walkway. His grin was predatory as he dropped his weapons and let them clang on the floor. "Game on, graduate."

Valentina ran her fingers through her hair. She looked down at the clean grooves left from the wheel's tracks on the ground below, her mind instantly flashing to Kit. "No. Not now."

She turned to leave.

Footsteps rushed toward her.

She spun, pistol in hand, and shot.

Reyner strafed left. The bullet missed.

She shot again, deliberately missing him but wanting to try and slow him down.

He closed the gap.

Then he was on her.

The full brunt of his shoulder crashed into Valentina. She flew back, then skidded across the smooth floor. She grunted, her breath catching as she wrestled with the mass on top of her.

Reyner pinned Valentina's wrists above her head. He was strong. Somehow stronger than he had been when he was

Master of his Order. Valentina thought of her journey, honing her skills in the real world and sharpening her blade. Had Reyner set forth on the same journey, too? Had he spent all these years watching Valentina from afar, waiting for the right moment to strike?

He threw his head at Valentina, striking her in her forehead. Lights blossomed in her vision, her eyes momentarily crossing. He reared back and headbutted her again, grim satisfaction on his face.

Valentina groaned. Reyner's breath was sour. There were red cracks in the glass of his eyes. His laughter spewed droplets of saliva that landed on her cheek, offending her senses. "And here I thought this would at least be a challenge." He tutted. "Shame. After all that waiting, I could have taken you down years ago."

Valentina brought her knee up, aiming for Reyner's crotch. He shifted his hips, avoiding the blow, then laughed. Valentina smirked, then followed up with her headbutt, catching him on the bridge of his nose.

Pain exploded in her head, but it couldn't have been anything compared to his. Blood spurted from his nostrils as though there had been a capsule inside and she had burst it. He growled, throwing his head out of harm's way, and in that moment of faltered concentration, Valentina kicked again.

Her knee caught the soft flesh between his legs. It wasn't graceful, but it was necessary. His grip on her wrist loosened. She ripped her hands away and shoved him—hard. Reyner fell off Valentina, allowing her a moment to put some distance between them both.

Her head pounded. The blows had knocked something inside, and the edges of her vision were blurry. As she got to her feet, the world tilted, the walkway rocking at a sharp angle. She staggered to her left, almost falling again until she grabbed the rail for support.

Below her was darkness, a vapid void that never ended. One

tumble into the dark would be her end, this she knew without needing to look, though her dizzy mind forced her to anyway.

Reyner found his footing, fighting his own battle behind her. Valentina took large breaths and shook her head, attempting to dispel some of the fog that had descended over her.

Fog...

Valentina held the rail with one white-knuckled hand. With the other, she fished into her pocket. Her fingers rifled through the various items, looking for what she wanted—what she *needed*. Reyner drew closer, Valentina able to hear him, but unable to turn her head just yet.

Her hand clasped around her device.

She spun, jaw clenched, eyes focused. She raised the smoke bomb into the air, about to toss it between them both and cloud them in fog when she noticed it was already there.

A cloud stood between them, the gas thick and purple. The lights struggled to penetrate it, and only for a moment did Valentina see the dark figure on the other side, somehow grown larger under the illusion cast from the smoke.

The figure disappeared.

Valentina was alone, hand clasping a metal ball that she never got to set off.

She moved, knowing that every moment she stood still was a moment in which Reyner could press his advantage. She hurried to her right, heading straight for Santana. While Reyner's beef was with Valentina, there was no telling what he'd do to the woman sleeping by the entrance. Everything was a pawn in the game of war.

Something *whirred* by, a sharp something rolling through the air. Valentina had thrown enough knives to be able to identify the object that hurtled toward her. She saw it only for a moment, like a bird swooping for a dive, and she wondered whether he was intentionally aiming to miss, considering that he had only moments ago told her that he wished to reclaim his honor. Was this all a planned play? Was Reyner still toying with her?

She staggered forward, trying to remain quiet, but struggling. The blur in her eyes was lifting, though her head still throbbed. She moved faster, listening for Reyner, but all that met her was the echo of her footsteps.

She placed the bomb back in her pocket. As she did so, her fingers brushed against something cylindrical.

Another bird swooped at Valentina. She twisted out of its trajectory, the glint of the silver blade catching her eye as it passed within inches of where she'd been.

Get your shit together, Val, a voice that wasn't hers shouted from the back of her mind.

Isabella?

The voice was silent, but it had been correct.

Valentina stopped moving, stopped giving the game away. She hissed breath between her teeth and crouched low, shrinking to avoid detection.

Something dark moved on the edges of her vision, an undefined looming predator seeking its prey. Valentina slowly eased the vial from her pocket. It was half an inch in length, filled with an amber liquid that easily could be mistaken for whiskey. She thought of Dick Chambers, his grin appearing before her in the fog. She felt his touch, smelled his scent, her skin prickling at its presence.

This one's for you, Dick. She unscrewed the top of the vial, raised it in the air, then drained its contents.

For a moment, all that lingered was the strange, chemical aftertaste of the solution. The figure crept nearer, *Jaws* circling the boat and its victims. Valentina closed her eyes.

A cold wash ran through her. It happened so suddenly that she gasped as if she had dived into frigid waters to join the shark. Her skin prickled, hairs standing on end. Her eyes peeled open, pupils dilating as adrenaline coursed through her and woke her body. The fuzzy edges cleared in an instant, the headache subsiding as everything nearby fell into crystal clarity.

Oh, I'm going to pay for this later, Valentina mused. *But at least there'll be a "later."*

The shape grew larger, rushing toward the place where she had gasped. Valentina had already moved, diving into a roll and putting distance between herself and her former master. She controlled the dive, all pain gone, barely a sound made.

"You can run, but you can't hide," Reyner roared, a strange glee in his voice.

Want to bet?

Valentina knelt and removed her boots. The metal floor was cold beneath her bare feet. Each step was tentative and measured as she kept her gaze fixed on the location where she had last heard Reyner.

He was skilled. She had to give him that. She worked her way ever closer to the entrance, her heart racing rapidly as the solution—Briggan's serum—pumped through her veins. His voice echoed in her head, "Please, Valentina, remember. This is experimental. Highly untested. Use with caution..." He paused for a beat. "And record your results."

So far, so good, Doc.

Santana appeared before her. First, she was a dark mass. Then she was a person coalescing through the fog. Valentina rushed the final steps, reaching for her when Reyner rushed from the smog behind.

Valentina was ready with her sharpened senses as he approached and threw caution to the wind. She spun, leading with her elbow, and caught his cheek.

His hands were quick. He caught her sleeve as he fell off-balance. She moved with him, stumbling to keep her footing. They slammed into the metal door together, Reyner with his back to the cold surface, Valentina attempting to pin him.

He grinned, the expression jarring on a face covered with

drying and clotting blood. He spat in her face, the globule pink and thick. Valentina couldn't move fast enough, and a chunk of it entered her eye.

Reyner jabbed Valentina in the rib. Something cracked. Valentina growled and returned the favor with a jab to Reyner's neck. He coughed and spluttered. She sent another jab to his gut, but he caught her wrist and immediately twisted it to the side.

Valentina's shoulder dropped. Reyner brought his knee to her hip and sent her spiraling backward. She landed on the floor on her front, narrowly avoiding smacking her nose into the floor.

"You've still got it," Reyner crooned, wiping his nose with his sleeve. "But I've waited years for this. I know your patterns. I've seen your work. I've pictured bringing you to your knees for years, and now here we are…"

He kicked Valentina, foot connecting with her thigh.

"I can think of better ways to spend my time," Valentina replied. "Ever thought about a chess career?"

Reyner laughed, then kicked again. Valentina laughed in reply, sending a wave of confusion over Reyner's face. He reached to his side, hand grasping the hilt of the dagger as he drew closer to her. "I can't wait to slice your throat and be done with it. Maybe I'll present your head to the Order. Maybe I'll reveal you slowly from a sack, like Perseus unveiling Medusa's severed head."

"You can try," Valentina breathed, "but I feel I may beat you to it."

Reyner gave an incredulous laugh. "I've always admired that about you, Valentina. Your spirit is uncompromising. Such a shame to witness the creation that I bore into the world die under my hand. I may shed a few tears on the morrow, but for now, I'll revel in my glory."

He dropped, his knee slamming into Valentina's spine. Despite his small frame, he was dense, muscles rippling beneath his flowing robe. He forced Valentina onto her back, then straddled her. He held the knife in both hands with his eyes fixed on hers. Despite his words, there was a shimmer of remorse in his gaze. "I'm sorry that this is our end, Valentina. I'm sorry this had to happen this way."

Something shifted in the fog.

Valentina gave a resigned nod. "It's been a pleasure, master."

Reyner frowned. He shook his head, then the knife plunged, aiming for Valentina's throat.

CHAPTER THIRTY-SEVEN

Valentina turned away, teeth gritted. She twisted her neck out of the knife's reach, but she needn't have worried.

A *crack* snapped through the fog. The whip coiled around the knife's hilt. Reyner's momentum stopped as the whip tugged back. The knife pulled free from his grasp. It disappeared into the fog, and Valentina saw it in her mind's eye hurtling into the darkness.

Reyner growled, pulling his hand back as though he'd touched a hot stove. Valentina sat up sharply and punched Reyner, fist connecting with his nose again.

Reyner folded back. Valentina shifted out from under him. Reyner looked set to spring another attack when the whip *cracked* again, this time coiling around his throat.

"All this talk of my emotions," Valentina muttered. "Maybe you should have been working on yours."

His hands clutched at the whip, his fingers unable to work their way beneath the tight grip the whip held. Santana grimaced, muscles knotted as she held him steady. "Up, Val. Now."

Her words slurred, with Santana barely able to keep her focus.

Valentina had seen that look before, had induced it on many unwilling participants.

Reyner's face grew red. He sputtered, unable to draw breath. Valentina rose to her feet. "Let him go," she instructed.

Santana gave her an uncertain look, then flicked her wrist. The whip uncoiled, leaving Reyner on all fours, gasping for air.

Valentina looked down at the man, a dark shadow on her face. "You shouldn't have come."

Reyner coughed.

"All these years," Valentina stated. "All these years and you show up now. Here. In the middle of this chamber." Her eyes narrowed. "What's your part in all of this?"

Reyner smirked, the expression ugly on his blotchy face. Blood dripped steadily onto the metal walkway. "I told you, Val. I did what I needed to survive. Mercenary work is a feat of passion and a desire for coin. My shame is localized only to the Order. It does not extend into the wider world."

"Who wouldn't want a former master of the Order to fight their battles?" Santana stated, her voice weak.

"You were listening?" Valentina asked.

Santana shrugged. "Kind of. I thought I was dreaming. Turns out that whatever tranquilizer that fucker used had a strange form of lucidity in its design."

Reyner grinned. "Always leave them with enough information to warn their kind of your threat."

Valentina crouched to one knee, leveling her eyes on Reyner. "They bought you?"

"I found them," Reyner replied. "Fontana put out the call, and I answered. Though the call wasn't explicit, I knew your work. I've been watching you for some time, Val. Biding each second. Waiting. The minute that Fontana needed another hand for his work, I knew my time had come."

Valentina ran her hand through her hair. The fog was nearly

clear, and as she looked down, she spotted the tracks once more. "Where are they?"

Reyner leered.

"Where are they?" Valentina stood quickly, kicking Reyner sharply around the face.

He spat, groaned, and laughed.

Valentina shouted this time. "Where are they!"

Reyner narrowed his eyes. "They're gone, Val. They're all gone."

Valentina's breath quickened. "What do you mean they're gone?"

"You think that storming the base would get you access to your brother?" Reyner growled. "You think that it would be easy? I took pay to protect them. I took pay to keep them free from harm's reach. That's what I did. They're gone, Valentina. Long gone from any chance of you helping them." He laughed, the chuckle turning into a spluttering cough. "They're gone."

"No." Valentina's rage took over. "No!"

She kicked again, leg whipping around and gaining speed. The flat top of her foot connected with Reyner's temple and sent him sprawling on the floor. His eyes rolled back in his head. She stepped toward him, then kicked him in the gut, once, twice, three times...

Hands grabbed Valentina's arms and yanked her back. She twisted free, kicking at the son of a bitch on the ground once more, her anger and rage pouring out on him. He didn't respond. He didn't react.

"Valentina, no!" Santana declared, pulling her back once more.

Valentina leered down at the man, finally allowing the other woman to pull her away.

"Valentina, it's not worth it," Santana stated. "Don't do this. Don't turn into him."

Valentina shook her head. "Too late. He crafted me. He

molded me. He made me…" she looked at her hands, flecks of blood painting her palms, "this."

"No." Santana grabbed Valentina's shoulder and spun her around. "No, he didn't. You made yourself what you are. He may have given you your start, but you are what you did to you."

Valentina glanced over her shoulder, venom in her eyes.

Santana shook her again. "Val, you're not a bad person. You're not…him. There is good in you. I see it. It's the only reason you're here. There's something in you that needs better…that *wants* better. Don't let him take it."

Valentina saw the plea in Santana's eyes. It was a look that she hadn't seen in some time. A look that a brother would give to a brother or a sister to a sister. It was a look of compassion, of *caring*.

Valentina softened, her shoulders dropping slightly. She drew a long breath and nodded. Santana let her go. "We can find them."

Valentina nodded. "Yes. First, we have to get out of here."

Santana turned to look at the door. At that moment, Valentina landed one final kick in Reyner's stomach.

Santana frowned.

"What?" Valentina asked. "Too much?"

Kirk ran around the base, dealing his orders to the guards and chasing the trail of breadcrumbs.

The units were chaotic. The system was disorganized. When Archie had first envisioned his underground project, he hadn't given a whole lot of thought to its defense. While the guards carried weapons, and workers were being used to deal intel to their line managers, Archie hadn't foreseen an invasion so soon into its construction.

Kirk was breathless as he rounded the corner, responding to the latest information about two women acting suspiciously near the power center. He ran along the corridor, knocking workers out of his way as he closed the distance and forged ahead.

When he reached the power center's level, and he had the entrance in sight, he stopped.

Something caught his attention. The swaying beam from his flashlight caught marks on the ground. He pointed the light directly to the earthen floor and saw the thick red stains trailing from a path to his left.

He shone the light into the tunnel. His heart stopped. "No. No, no, no, no..."

He broke into a run, the flashlight throwing the tunnel into a dizzying, amorphous thing. He reached a set of stairs and ran down, two at a time until he got to the bottom and met the thick metal door.

It was closed.

Why was it closed?

Down here the stains were thickest. Blood pooled under the door, heading away and up the stairs. It was sticky beneath the soles of his shoes. He moved to the door. Someone had stuck a note on the front.

He peeled the note away and shone the flashlight.

The boss is in confinement for his safety. If you're reading this, the asset is in the east wing, floor B3, room twelve. Get Fontana out. I've got the rest covered.

Beneath the text was a crude sketch of an eagle's wing.

Kirk pocketed the note, then unlocked the door.

The door slammed open, shoving Kirk backward. He used the wall to steady himself, alarmed at the crazed maniac rushing at him. It wasn't until the man had his collar in his grip that he recognized the face of Archie Fontana.

"Sir...I..." Kirk started.

"What the fuck are you playing at?" Archie roared. "Do you have any idea how long I've been in that abysmal tomb?"

Kirk raised his hands in defense. Archie struck him in the face. He blinked stupidly. "Answer me!"

"Sir!" Kirk protested. "Sir! It wasn't me. Why would I even—"

Another blow caught his face. "Of all the negligence and defiance..."

"Sir!" This time Kirk dodged the strike. "Enough. We have to get you out of here!"

Archie growled, examining Kirk with suspicion. "What are you talking about? What the hell is going on?"

Kirk handed Archie the note. Archie took a few seconds to read it. His eyes lingered on the signature.

"Do you know who sent it, sir?" Kirk inwardly prepared to block another punch.

"Son of a bitch," Archie breathed. His eyes grew dark, and his head dropped. "We've been compromised." He roared, then lashed out, punching the wall behind Kirk's head. "How can this be? We've barely begun to get started."

"Sir?" Kirk tried to glean more information.

"No time." Archie looked wildly around as if he had lost his sense of direction. "We have to go."

"We?" Kirk questioned.

"Me, Kirk." Archie narrowed his eyes on Kirk. "You're going to get me there safely. You got that?" He turned to run, but his foot slipped on a patch of blood underfoot. "Oh, and on our way you can tell me what the fuck happened to our prisoner."

Kirk steeled himself and nodded. He ran ahead of Archie, rifle ready while thinking, *I'd love to tell you if only I knew.*

CHAPTER THIRTY-EIGHT

They bound Reyner in his robes, ensuring that he was knotted tightly to the railing. He was alive when they left, but barely. Valentina didn't so much as look back as they exited the chamber.

There was a flurry of activity in the tunnels as they exited. The commotion came from somewhere deep in the darkness to their right. Valentina recalled the floor plans and took Santana left, away from the noise and back toward the power center.

"Aren't you worried we're going to run into them again?"

"No. That whole thing about returning to the scene of the crime, it's bullshit. No one ever returns. Why would criminals go back to the place where they started it all?"

"Fair point." Santana kept pace behind Valentina, guided by the flashlights on their phones.

They ran straight past the power center, avoiding the strange utterances of the workers with their Atlanticore. Valentina couldn't believe they were still mining the stuff. They passed a couple of entrances into empty rooms before Santana slipped and fell on her ass.

"Val!" Santana called.

Valentina paused, almost slipping in another patch of something sticky. She shone the light down and saw the trail of blood. "Shit." She helped Santana up. "Where did it come from?"

They examined the trail briefly, noticing the red stains snake toward another tunnel beside them. Valentina conjured up the map in her head, but couldn't remember seeing a doorway or any other room marked there.

"Come on," she instructed as Santana attempted to get the blood off her hands and onto her shirt.

A set of stairs led to a metal door. There was nothing else around. The door was ajar.

"Fuck." Valentina sighed. The blood was at its thickest here, and as they opened the door and shone their lights inside, they spotted the shackles on the wall. Valentina stepped inside, the air thick with copper and sweat. There was a rhythmic dripping of water in the corner as droplets fell to a damp patch on the floor.

"It's a prison cell," Santana stated matter-of-factly. "They sure had their priorities right when constructing this place, didn't they? Who do you think was in here?"

Valentina didn't know for certain, but an uneasy feeling settled over her stomach. She thought of long dark locks and a cheeky grin. "Come on," she ordered, quickly exiting the prison.

"Okay?"

They followed the trail of blood, Valentina's heart beating faster with every step. They raced up the staircase, retracing their path along the tunnel, falling to a sudden stop when lights exploded ahead of them and obstructed their vision.

They held up their arms to shield their eyes from the assault. Valentina could make out maybe four sources of light, the beams intense as they spotlighted the women.

"Take another step, and it'll be your last," a male voice announced.

Valentina wished she could see them, but all she could make out was the faint outline of figures.

"Let us pass, or it'll be yours," Valentina returned.

The man laughed. He muttered a command, and a shot fired. The pain was intense, the bullet finding its bed off-center in Valentina's thigh. She growled and folded to a knee. The serum abated some of the pain, but it didn't soak up all of it.

"Last chance, Valentina Winters," the voice announced. "Stand down. Come quietly. We will spare you. You're more valuable to us alive."

"I sincerely doubt that," Valentina replied.

Someone clicked the safety off their weapon. Santana took a step beside Valentina, one arm blocking her from harm. Valentina glanced up and found Santana aiming a gun at the group. "If she's going down, I'm going down with her."

Another shot fired. Santana clutched her arm as the bullet ripped through the skin. Her pistol clattered to the ground.

The man laughed again. "Final. Warning."

Valentina bowed her head. Her jacket flowed over her knee, the contents within irritating the wound. She slipped her hand discreetly inside.

"Fine," she stated, breathless. "Fine. You've made your point. We'll come quietly."

"First time for everything," Santana muttered.

Valentina couldn't help but chuckle.

Two of the figures broke free. As they drew closer, they blocked the light and revealed themselves. They were two women, one with a harshly drawn back ponytail, the other with hair cropped at the shoulder. They aimed their rifles at Valentina as they approached, fingers ready on the triggers.

"Up," one commanded.

Valentina struggled to rise. "You know you shot my leg, right?"

One woman looked at the other. She nodded. Ponytail offered an arm under Valentina's shoulder.

As Valentina rose, she whispered, "Sorry. It's nothing personal." She cradled the orb in her hand, then tossed it at the figures with the flashlights.

Sparks erupted like fireworks trapped inside the chamber. The crackling was intense, distracting the group from their focus. They jumped back, shouting in alarm, allowing Valentina the chance to shove Ponytail against the wall. She grabbed her head and threw it against the earth. The woman grunted and slid down.

Santana took the cue and snapped her whip. A red-hot line appeared on the woman's hand. She lowered the gun and Santana ran. She shoved past the woman, whacking her to the side.

They charged at the group, distracted and flapping their arms at the explosions before them. Valentina lowered her head as she ran, weaving around the group, her leg faltering with every other step. Still, she pushed through, taking a right turn and clearing space between them as the fireworks faded.

"No!" the male voice roared. "Get them! Get them!"

Gunfire erupted. Dirt flew around them. Clouds of dust kicked into the air. Valentina threw the orb over her shoulder, not bothering to turn. She triggered a second explosion, and the walls crumbled. Rubble caved in, the ceiling collapsed, and as the tunnel filled with dust and debris, the sounds of their attackers were muffled and muted.

They ran until they were a clear distance from danger. When they finally slowed, they turned their flashlights to the blockade, just to check that it finished the job.

"Risky maneuver," Santana stated.

Valentina nodded. "Sometimes it's necessary."

Santana narrowed her eyes. She looked between the blockade and Valentina. "Never a dull moment with you, is there?"

Valentina smirked. She glanced down and found more blood on the floor, this time sparse and thinly painted. "Come on. We have work to do."

They jogged through the tunnel, following the trail of blood.

Compared to the rest of the tubes they'd traveled down, this one was straight, with only a few doors opening off either side. One of the rooms appeared to be in progress with tiles stacked nearby and plasterboards that would finally make the hole feel like a room, but that wasn't where their attention went. The rumble of an engine sounded from a short distance along the tunnel.

They exchanged a look, then broke into a sprint. A light appeared ahead, and Valentina couldn't help but think of all the stories of patients on the operating table talking about their bright light appearing as they bordered on death. Was this to be hers now? Was this to be Kit's? Bradley's?

She broke ahead of Santana, the adrenaline coursing through her and giving her the advantage. She broke out of the constricting tunnel into a chamber very similar to the one she had left Reyner in, only this one had a large cut-out in the ceiling, wide enough to dock a flying saucer. The brisk, chill air was refreshing although it took her breath away. The night was subsiding, and shades of purple and pink hung in the sky.

The engine thrummed. A vehicle that looked like an oversized drone lifted off the floor as four sets of propellers drove it into the air. Valentina's eyes grew wide as she spotted Archie's face in the window, looking down at her with a mixture of anger and relief.

"Son of a bitch," Valentina growled. She reached for her pistol, her hand finding nothing but air. She glanced down. When had her pistol fallen free of its holster?

Santana appeared beside her.

"Shoot them down!" Valentina shouted.

Archie stared at her, unblinking, hatred in his eyes. Only when Valentina shouted at Santana did his eyes shift to the girl standing beside her, momentarily flashing with wonder.

"Now!" Valentina commanded.

Santana glanced at her hip. She grimaced as the scrape on her arm reminded her of what had happened in the tunnel. They were weaponless and helpless as the giant drone lifted into the air. Valentina searched frantically, her eyes finding the strange blue glow at the back of the craft. A bearded man with glasses sat nearby, defiantly avoiding her gaze.

"No!" Valentina bellowed. "No!"

She dipped her hand in her pocket, gambling with whatever she could find. She pulled out a handful of orbs and triggered them. Electricity sparked, fog erupted, lights flashed, something crackled, but the drone was too high. Santana was beside her, calling and shouting words that Valentina couldn't hear.

Meanwhile, all Valentina could think of was Archie's head exploding from the fury of the bullets she didn't carry.

The craft reached the opening. The blades accelerated. The drone faded from sight, disappearing over the tops of the trees as it emerged into the world…

…and was gone.

The hum of the engines faded soon after. Valentina stood there, breathless, processing it all. He was gone. Archie and Kit were gone. Santana stood beside her in respectful silence, no words able to pacify the woman standing beside her. Hot emotion rose in Valentina's chest, but she swallowed it. To cry would mean to admit defeat.

"Val…" Santana muttered at last, soft and quiet. "We need to get out of here."

Valentina finally turned to her. "Right." Her voice was flat and devoid of emotion. "Let's go."

Valentina turned to go back the way they had come, but Santana stopped her. "Over there. Look." Santana pointed at the gleaming black SUV on the far side of the chamber. Nearby was a tunnel with a makeshift road passing through it.

But Valentina didn't see any of that. Her gaze stayed fixed on the tunnel they had run through moments before. A man stood in the entrance, clinging to the walls with every ounce of strength he had left. He was ashen white, his front covered in blood. One hand clutched the wound as his legs wobbled.

"Bella?" Bradley breathed, his words almost lost as he buckled to his knees. He smiled, a weak gesture, then folded onto his front, face smacking the dirt beneath him.

Archie kept his eyes peeled on the break in the land beneath him as the drone soared off farther into the jungle.

It had been a narrow escape and one that filled his gut with anger and frustration. He had kept his chief staffer, with Friedrich riding in the back, monitoring their modern miracle and keeping the only leverage he had ever had over Valentina. Soon he would find a new angle, a way to bring the raging renegade under control, but for now...

His mind replayed the moment. He saw Valentina, red-faced and furious, without weapons as they made their escape. But the girl who had been standing next to her. That girl...

The gold chain flashed around her neck, a curious pendant glinting in the light cast by the dawning sun. It could be nothing, but it could be everything. Why else would a mysterious adventurer be aiding Valentina Winters in her quest to reclaim her brother?

Archie rested his head against the seat as the propellers hummed above him. The pilot was smooth, and the vehicle lulled him into a transitive state. He closed his eyes and remembered Kirk, thought of the sextant and its missing component. As sleep took over his mind, his dreams filled with glowing blue rocks and golden items...

...and the possibility of a thousand riches.

EPILOGUE

One week later

The week had been a blur. Isabella trundled up the stairs to her apartment. The same weight rested on her shoulders, and the dark cloud that had followed her all week still loomed over her.

Her hands still smelled of sanitizer from the hospital. Bradley was stable now and had recently moved out of the critical care ward and into extended recovery. His organs were holding. His heart rate was regular. They'd removed the bullet that had lodged between his lower ribs and sewn the wound shut. In a few weeks, he would be able to head home where his doctors expected him to make a full recovery.

But where was home now?

Isabella had spoken with Valentina and settled on an agreement to move locations once again. It was a shame. Isabella had grown fond of the apartment, but her complicated history with Valentina meant that this wasn't unusual. Never before had she stayed in one location so long, but now the time had once again come.

"You promised..." Isabella muttered. "You promised it'd be over soon."

She made the final set of stairs and entered the hallway on the seventeenth floor of a new-build of apartments on the west side of town. The view from a large glass window showed the sun setting across the river, a large bridge allowing traffic to cross over the body of water. Skyscrapers towered all around, and the fog obscured a good deal of what could have been a beautiful vista.

Isabella sighed.

Turning the key in her door, she looked back at the apartments she had hired on this same floor. One of them could soon be Bradley's if he wanted to move in. She felt a heavy sense of responsibility for him now and wanted to find a way for him to forgive her. He said he had, but that didn't stop the guilt.

Isabella walked inside her dark apartment. Curtains covered the window, and the smell of last night's takeout lingered in the air. There were a few telltale signs that Valentina had begun work on her new secret spaces, but Isabella ignored them, her intention only to head over to the couch, slump down, drain a glass of wine, and watch *The Price is Right* for the sixth consecutive night in a row.

Someone was sitting on her couch.

"Isabella," the woman greeted with a nod.

Isabella drew a long breath. "Who the hell are you?"

The woman was small, with a neat crop of dark hair that fell to her shoulders. She wore a luxurious robe of red and gold and uncrossed her legs as she patted the couch beside her to indicate Isabella should join her.

When Isabella showed no sign of obeying, the woman chewed her lip. She looked up at Isabella with graceful confidence. "I'm sorry for the intrusion, but I'm afraid I have some incredibly relevant news that would benefit you in finding your brother."

Isabella's cheeks warmed. "I don't know what you're talking about."

"No?" the woman replied coolly. "Then I suggest that you

invite Valentina here to join the conversation. The three of us have a lot to discuss."

Thank you for not only reading this story but these author notes as well!

Out of our four protagonists who make up this set of stories (John Chambers, Valentina Winters, Terra Kris, and Santana Sokolov) Valentina Winters is by far the most complex.

Noir detective straightforward character? *Check.*

Aggressive straightforward police character? *Check.*

Straightforward Indiana Jones / Tomb Raider character? *Check.*

Multi-personality, not-sure-what-country she comes from librarian / assassin…

Hold up a second.

I believe that humans have separate sides, people they could have been had things been just a little different for them. A good person might have been bad. A bad person might have become a saint.

Or at least made it to "good person."

It was this concept that led to Valentina Winters. As an aside, she owes her name to the Milady de Winter character in *The*

Three Musketeers by Alexandre Dumas. I always liked that name and felt it would work well for our character.

You never know exactly what she is up to.

Have a great week or weekend and I look forward to chatting again in our next series about Terra Kris!

Until next time!

Ad Aeternitatem,

Michael Anderle

BOOKS BY MICHAEL ANDERLE

Sign up for the LMBPN email list to be notified of new releases and special deals!

https://lmbpn.com/email/

For a complete list of books by Michael Anderle, please visit:

www.lmbpn.com/ma-books/